Praise for Eileen Watkins and her Cat Groomer mysteries!

The Bengal Identity

"A first-rate sequel to *The Persian Always Meows Twice*. It doesn't take a cat lover to fall in love with this perfectly crafted cozy series."
—*Publishers Weekly* (starred review)

"The story is well-paced, and readers will enjoy the way the mystery plays out. Another good tale by Watkins!"
—*RT Book Reviews*

The Persian Always Meows Twice

"A fantastic thriller that is sure to make your pulse race, *The Persian Always Meows Twice* is an awesome mystery debut from Eileen Watkins."
—*Modern Cat*

"Cassie McGlone is a great character with spunk, strength, and a great group of people surrounding her. The story is interesting and will keep readers guessing all the way to the surprise ending."
—*RT Book Reviews*

"The purr-fect mystery to curl up with for a lovely cozy read, preferably with a cup of tea, cuddly cat optional but recommended."
—**Leslie Meier**, author of *Silver Anniversary Murder*

"[A] delightful first novel and series opener."
—*Publishers Weekly*

"*The Persian Always Meows Twice* is a delightful debut mystery. It's smart, well-plotted, and features a cast of characters—both human and feline—that I want to see more of. This book will be catnip for cat lovers."
—**Laurien Berenson**, author of *Ruff Justice*

Books by Eileen Watkins

THE PERSIAN ALWAYS MEOWS TWICE

THE BENGAL IDENTITY

FERAL ATTRACTION

Published by Kensington Publishing Corporation

Feral
Attraction

EILEEN WATKINS

KENSINGTON BOOKS
www.kensingtonbooks.com

KENSINGTON BOOKS are published by

Kensington Publishing Corp.
119 West 40th Street
New York, NY 10018

All Kensington titles, imprints, and distributed lines are available at special quantity discounts for bulk purchases for sales promotion, premiums, fundraising, and educational or institutional use.

Special book excerpts or customized printings can also be created to fit specific needs. For details, write or phone the office of the Kensington Sales Manager: Kensington Publishing Corp., 119 West 40th Street, New York, NY 10018. Attn. Sales Department. Phone: 1-800-221-2647.

Kensington and the K logo Reg. U.S. Pat. & TM Off.

ISBN-13: 978-1-4967-1060-4
ISBN-10: 1-4967-1060-6
First Kensington Trade Paperback Printing: October 2018

eISBN-13: 978-1-4967-1061-1
eISBN-10: 1-4967-1061-4
First Kensington Electronic Edition: October 2018

10 9 8 7 6 5 4 3 2 1

Printed in the United States of America

For Mia, who needed a new "mom" at the same time that I needed a new feline companion, and happily moved with me to a new house!
And for Dave, who brought the two of us together.

Acknowledgments

As usual, I'm indebted to the members of my weekly critique group, which I reluctantly left behind when I moved several counties away, and particularly to Joanne Weck, who stepped in as my beta reader for this book. Much gratitude, again, to my fellow members of Sisters in Crime Central Jersey; my agent, Evan Marshall; and my editor, John Scognamiglio.

And a special thanks to Anne-Marie Cottone, my own equivalent of Cassie's best friend, Dawn Tischler. Though we've never shared any adventures *quite* as harrowing as theirs, Anne's experiences while trying to provide food and shelter for a single feral cat in her community inspired me to research and write this story.

Chapter 1

"Please, Cassie! I know it's a big favor to ask, but maybe you can get through to these people. After all, it's a matter of life and death!"

My friend Dawn sometimes overdramatized things, but technically I supposed she was right. I probably owed her a favor, anyway. We'd come to each other's rescue so often over the past year, it was easy to lose count.

"They might just throw me out of the meeting," I warned her, while refilling our coffee mugs and bringing them back to the front sales counter of my shop. "At least your mother lives at The Reserve. I have no business being there at all."

"You'll be there as my invited guest, and . . . and professional consultant." Alighting on one of the secondhand wooden stools behind the counter, my tall, auburn-haired, rather Bohemian friend fanned her hands in supplication. "Face it, my only argument will be that if my mother wasn't away on vacation, she'd be part of this protest. Even though I took in one stray—that I love to death—I'm no expert on feral cats. But as the owner of Cassie's Comfy Cats, you've got real cat cred."

I'd never thought of it that way before—maybe I could

turn "real cat cred" into some kind of advertising slogan. Have it stenciled on the front window under the name of my shop? Or maybe across the front of my hot-pink sales counter?

I still wondered just how welcome Dawn and I would be at this meeting tonight. From what she'd already told me about The Reserve at Chadwick, most of the homeowners were older. Dawn and I, being only in our late twenties, might stand out as nonresidents interfering in the community's private business.

"Remind me, again, what the issue will be tonight. You're trying to persuade the condo board to try a trap-neuter-return program?"

"They did try it once. My friend Sabrina worked with a local rescue group—people from FOCA, you know them, right? Anyway, they caught a few of the cats, not all of them. Some residents say that just proves the approach doesn't work. We need to persuade them to try at least once more." Dawn sighed. "Sabrina's a terrific advocate, but she can be a little . . . forceful, and the other residents are starting to tune her out. That's why we need you!"

My sixtyish assistant, Sarah Wilcox, emerged through the doorway that led back to the cat playroom. She preferred to look professional for the job—unlike me, in my jeans and T-shirt— and usually dressed in a self-chosen uniform of a patterned tunic with solid-colored pants. Today her outfit followed a dark green theme that complemented her rich, chestnut complexion.

Now she tried tactfully to catch my eye. This let me put off making any commitment to attend the evening's meeting, at least for a minute longer. "Yes, Sarah?"

"Want me to put the Van away before I go?" she asked.

Dawn brightened. "What's happening with that? Did you finally find somebody to convert that old thing?"

I paused in confusion for an instant, then realized she

thought I was referring to the aged, matte-black vehicle that had been parked for about two months in my rear lot. It formerly belonged to a local rock 'n' roll impresario who had relished its sinister appearance. I'd gotten it at a bargain price, in the hopes of turning it, someday, into a mobile grooming studio.

With a laugh, I told Dawn, "Oh, no, she means a cat. A Turkish Van. Semi-longhair white with red points, very pretty." When I turned back to Sarah, she was grinning over the mix-up. "Yes, Taffy can go back in her condo. Gee, is it closing time already?"

"Time flies when you're having fun." She brushed one hand over her nose and mouth. "Fur, too."

I laughed again. "In this business, it sure does."

Sarah disappeared through the doorway in the screen that separated the front of the shop from the playroom. Equipped with assorted tunnels, perches, trees, and a complex network of wall shelves, that central space allowed our boarders to get some safe exercise. Farther back lay our well-equipped grooming studio and another large room fitted out with a dozen cat condos—each the size of a broom closet—to accommodate our boarders. All of our services catered to felines only.

"As for the actual van with wheels," I told Dawn, "that project is stalled. So far the only quote I've gotten has been way beyond my budget."

"Too bad. I like the idea of you being able to take your grooming services on the road." She took another swallow of her coffee and returned to her main objective. "So, will you come with me tonight?"

I'd had a long, tiring day and was looking forward to a quiet evening at home. My store dated from the turn of the century, so that second-floor apartment was far from luxurious. It consisted of a living room, a dining room or second bedroom, and a single bathroom and kitchen last renovated in the 1950s. Because I had three cats of my own, the seating pieces were pet-proofed with cotton slipcovers and fleece throws, the area rugs an indoor/outdoor material that cleaned up easily. The framed artworks included some of my own from my college years and a surrealistic print, of a woman looking in a mirror and seeing herself as a leopard, from a downtown gallery. Bookcases held volumes on human psychology, cat breeds and behavior, and favorite mystery novels.

The place wouldn't end up in a design magazine anytime soon, but to me it was a cozy haven after a long day on my feet. Right now, I looked forward to lounging on the sofa while I flirted on the phone with Mark, the local veterinarian I'd been dating for about eight months. His days were even busier than mine, though, so we both probably would be too tired for more than a quick chat. Afterward, I'd maybe catch a new detective show on TV that was getting a lot of buzz, then have an early lights-out.

I definitely hadn't figured on driving out on this damp, chilly November night, over dark country roads, to listen to a bunch of strangers debate an issue that was pretty much none of my business.

Still, Dawn had made a good case. For what it was worth, I guessed that I could add my voice to those who wanted a humane solution to The Reserve's feral cat problem. There were, indeed, feline lives at stake.

With a sigh, I ran a hand through my shoulder-length brown hair, limp after the full day I'd spent prettying up other people's pets. "I'll have to pull myself together a little . . . put on some decent clothes . . ."

"Fantastic! Thank you so much." My friend clapped her long, graceful hands. "I'll drive us. It's kind of hard to find your way around, because the roads curve and, of course, most of the buildings look alike. Fortunately, it's not an awfully big community—only about fifty units and maybe seventy or so residents."

"I'll finally get to meet the legendary Sabrina." I took both of our empty mugs to the small coffee stand behind the counter; I'd wash them up later in the grooming studio sink. "You said you connected with her when you were in college? But isn't she your mom's age?"

"Older, probably around seventy now. And that was about twelve years ago. I took a self-defense class Sabrina taught on campus. She had such a great attitude, so tough but so funny, that we went on exchanging e-mails and meeting for lunch every now and then. I'd tell her about starting my health food store and she'd keep me up to date on all her protests and causes." With a bemused smile, Dawn added, "How she ended up living at The Reserve, I'm really not sure. Kind of like throwing a lit firecracker into a haystack."

Dawn said she'd stop back for me in an hour, and by the time she'd left, my attitude toward the meeting had changed. If this gutsy older lady was ready to mix it up with her neighbors at some stodgy suburban enclave, I wanted to be on her side.

"They're taking over our community! They're vicious, and who knows what diseases they're carrying?"

"They do all kinds of disgusting things right outside my front door. My grandkids visit me, and I don't want them exposed to that."

"Our walking group used to love strolling down the trails with our binoculars, looking for new birds. Now we keep coming across dead bodies."

"I don't see that they're hurting anyone. They have a right to live, too."

"This is a nice, upscale neighborhood. They don't belong here."

I squirmed on my stiff metal chair. When I'd agreed to accompany Dawn to this meeting, I hadn't expected a mêlée—especially given the ages and conservative bent of the residents. Although The Reserve at Chadwick wasn't technically an active-adult community, most of the forty or so people jammed into the conference room looked past middle age. Dawn and I probably did stand out, not only because we weren't residents but because we were actually under thirty.

It was a prosperous, sedate crowd dressed in comfy corduroy and practical pullovers; I even spotted one turtleneck patterned with tiny autumn leaves. They hardly looked like a bunch of rowdy protestors, but something sure had set them on fire with rebellion tonight.

I asked Dawn in a whisper, "Are these meetings always so . . . lively?"

She shook her head. "According to Mom, most of the time very few people attend and the agenda is pretty boring. But like I warned you, this issue has everyone riled up."

The condo board members, seated behind a long table at the front of the room, also looked unnerved by the strident complaints. Poster-board placards on the tabletop identified them as Lauren Kamper, the board president; Alma Gunner, vice president; Joan Pennisi, secretary; and Dan Greenburg, treasurer. Also present at the table was Sam Nolan, the resident manager.

Lauren leaned into her microphone and tried to regain control of the gathering. "Folks, we can't have everyone speaking at once. Yes, Ted?"

A strongly built man with a shaved head stood up at his seat. "Some group came here last month to fix this problem.

They were supposed to catch all these stray cats and take 'em away. What happened with that?"

A woman a few seats to his left, with short gray hair and a shrill voice, replied. "They only caught a few, and a week later they brought them all back! What the heck good does that do?"

Nolan, tall and lean with salt-and-pepper hair, thumbed through some paperwork on the table in front of him. "Okay, let's review. Two months ago, we contacted the county Humane Society about the issue. They said they don't have the resources to deal with every feral-cat problem in the area, and referred us to FOCA, Friends of Chadwick Animals. A FOCA committee, called Fine Feral Friends, came here in October and set traps. They reported afterward that they were able to capture, neuter, and vaccinate ten of the cats."

"And they did it for free," added Dan, the thin, nearly chinless treasurer.

Joan, the prim-looking secretary, suggested, "We can call them to come again. . . ."

"Forget that!" shouted a pudgy man in a rust-colored sweater. "Ten cats? There's at least two dozen, and they're breedin' all the time. We need to get rid of 'em, permanently." He swept his finger across his throat.

Dawn shot me a pleading look. "Cassie, can you explain to them? About trap-neuter-return?"

At this point, I would sooner have stuck my head into a hornet's nest than provoke this crowd. But to speak up for the animals was, after all, the reason I'd agreed to come along this evening. Gathering my courage, I raised my hand until Lauren pointed at me.

"And you are?" she asked, sounding wary.

I stood up. "Cassie McGlone. I own Cassie's Comfy Cats, a grooming and boarding business in downtown Chadwick. I'm here tonight at the request of my friend Dawn Tischler"—I glanced down at her—"whose mother, Gwen, is a resident here at The Reserve. She's off on a three-week vacation in Morocco right now."

Joan, a brunette in a ruffle-necked blouse and ladylike oval glasses, bent her head over her electronic notepad, probably to jot down my credentials. I was prepared to add that I also had a certification in animal behavior, just in case someone asked. No one did.

Lauren wore her highlighted blond hair skinned back in a low ponytail, which emphasized her good cheekbones; her aqua, V-necked sweater subtly flattered her trim figure. She seemed impatient now with my recital of my bona fides. "And your interest in this matter, Ms. McGlone?"

"Dawn asked me here to explain the reasons behind the trap, neuter, and return approach. See, if you just remove the wild cats, others will come to take their place."

"Why would they do that?" Lauren asked, in a mildly baffled tone.

"This land obviously used to be forest, and you're still surrounded by woods. There are probably a lot more wild cats out there who don't come any nearer right now, because there's already an established colony."

Joan tilted her head and nodded, as if the explanation made sense to her. Sam also seemed to be paying close attention.

Encouraged, I pressed my case further. "That's why it's better to leave the existing cats there, but neuter and vaccinate them so they can't reproduce or spread any diseases to pets or people. They also won't get into as many noisy fights with one another, so they'll cause less disturbance."

"Trouble is," Ted interrupted, "people keep feeding them. It says in our bylaws that you're not supposed to feed wildlife. And that's what these cats are!"

"Even that doesn't stop them from killing the birds," complained Alma Gunner.

At the back of the room, a woman's strong contralto rang out. "May I say something?"

Sam responded with a tight smile. "Might as well, Ms. Ward. After all, you're a big reason why our community's in this situation."

When I saw who had spoken, I yielded the floor and took my seat. I had not met Sabrina Ward yet, but Dawn admired her tremendously, and I knew the woman had a long history of feminist and animal activism. Now that Sabrina lived at The Reserve, she'd become the staunchest champion of the feral cat colony.

She rose to her full, diminutive height with the help of a cane. A dark knit cap barely tamed her long, wavy hair, dyed a burgundy shade and threaded with gray. She wore a purple paisley shawl as a muffler and a faded denim jacket over a loose, flowered, thrift-shop dress. As if she needed glasses, Sabrina squinted in the direction of the board members' table. Even so, she somehow radiated steely will and determination.

"It's true what you say, Ted. Residents who feed the cats close to their homes aren't helping the problem. That's why the FFF people and I have set up feeding stations farther out in the woods. Once the ferals get used to eating there, and nowhere else, they'll be less likely to hang around the town houses."

"Those feeding stations are dangerous, too," protested a rosy-faced man with a blond comb-over.

"Why is that, Bert?" asked Lauren.

He stood. "They're too near the community trails. I was walking my dog Jojo the other day, and he got into some of the cat food that was left out. I stopped him before he ate very much, but an hour later he was so sick I had to rush him to the vet." With a catch in his voice, the man added, "They've still got him there, trying to figure out what's wrong with him."

"She probably put a hex on him!" The lady with the short gray hair stabbed a finger in Sabrina's direction. "She's a witch."

Dawn shifted irritably in the seat next to me. "Oh, God, some of these people! How does Mom stand to live around them day in and day out?"

A better question, I thought, might be how Sabrina fit into this community. Not only would her appearance and attitudes make her conspicuous, but if she dressed from thrift shops and couldn't afford eyeglasses, how did she even buy a condo here?

Meanwhile, Sabrina ignored the accusation and regarded Bert gravely. "Mr. Chamberlain, I'm very sorry about your dog. But I doubt it was just the stale cat food that made him so sick. More likely, someone in this community poisoned the food in hopes of harming the cats, and Jojo was an accidental victim."

This caused a stir through the gathering, and I heard mutters of, "Now she thinks we're poisoners!" and "Getting paranoid. . . ."

Lauren took command of the microphone again and ordered the group to settle down. "Ms. Ward, I doubt anyone would do a thing like that. But even if someone did, it just goes to show that matters have escalated to a dangerous level. Ted is right, our bylaws do prohibit feeding wild animals. We've made an exception in this case, because you and the FFF convinced us that you had a plan to reduce the colony. But as Heidi said, so far it hasn't been very successful."

I couldn't resist jumping into the fray again. "It takes time to get a whole colony under control. After a few cats get caught, the rest catch on and avoid the traps. You have to keep trying until you get them all."

Alma, a round but pretty woman with pink cheeks and gray curls, batted a hand at this idea. "This is a nice community. We have beautiful buildings and landscaping, and we all pay plenty to live here. I don't see why we should have to put up with cat traps cluttering the grounds."

Sabrina's jutting jaw made her look fierce as an Easter Island statue, and her rich voice rang out in anger. "You can't put up with a little temporary inconvenience to save more than twenty lives? Because that's what we're talking about. These are innocent creatures that aren't doing us any real harm. They may not be pets, but they're living the way nature intended. We need to find a way to coexist with them, not haul them off to be euthanized just because they interfere with our scenic views."

Next to me, Dawn applauded. I joined in with more restraint, and so did a few other residents. The board members remained impassive, though, as did most of the folks seated in the rows of metal chairs.

"Thank you, Ms. Ward," Lauren said evenly. "Your concerns will be taken into consideration."

Off to my left, the man in the rust-brown pullover muttered, "Not doing any real harm, aren't they? What about our damned property values?" With a scowl, he added, "Crazy old bat. Somebody oughta euthanize *her*."

Chapter 2

Even after the board meeting had adjourned, a few residents gathered around Sabrina and continued to harass her. She seemed unruffled, with a dry quip to deflect every accusation. But the board members wanted to lock up the room, and Sabrina clearly wanted to leave, too.

"I think the rescuer needs rescuing," Dawn whispered to me, and she and I intervened.

Of course, no one welcomed us that warmly, either. When Ted saw us approaching, he demanded, "Who invited you ladies to this meeting, anyway? Neither of you lives here."

"My mother has been a resident for five years, ever since The Reserve was built," Dawn announced, to him and anybody else ready to challenge her. "I'm keeping an eye on her condo while she's on vacation, and she asked me to attend this meeting in her place."

Sabrina swung toward me, a trace of humor in her squint. "And you attended as an expert witness, isn't that right?"

"Guess you could say that, though I didn't expect it to be a trial!"

Joan Pennisi politely intervened. "So, Ted, let's not be rude.

We don't want these young ladies to think we're a bunch of old grouches or animal haters." After he'd stalked away in a huff, she added quietly, "I apologize for Mike Lawler, too. He's one of those cranks who has to complain about everything, I'm afraid."

Dawn explained to me that Mike was the hothead in the brown sweater. Then she formally introduced me and Joan to Sabrina, and the four of us made casual chitchat for a minute about why Dawn's mother had chosen Morocco for her vacation. After Joan excused herself to catch up with the other board members, Sabrina commented, "She has her faults, but she's always been good at diplomacy. I'm afraid that's never been my strong suit."

I smiled. "Dawn's told me so much about you. I guess you made quite an impression on her when you taught the women's self-defense course at her college."

"Wow. That would have been, what, ten years ago?" Sabrina glanced at my friend for corroboration. "Mostly, I just narrated. Someone more limber did the actual moves."

"You demonstrated at least one yourself," Dawn reminded her. " 'Stomp and scream'—stomp on the attacker's foot and yell your head off. You didn't really stomp the guy's foot, of course, but you really nailed the scream."

Sabrina laughed at the memory. "That much, I guess I was up to, ten years ago. Now, instead of stomping, I'd have to use this." She wiggled her cane.

As we left the meeting room and started down the carpeted, tastefully beige main hallway of the clubhouse, she asked me, "You work with cats for a living?"

"Full-time." I handed her my hot-pink business card.

She read this by holding it a few inches from the tip of her long nose, and mouthed the words to herself. "Cassie's Comfy Cats."

Dawn told her, "Cassie also helped the county SPCA this past summer, when they raided an illegal breeding operation. It was even in the papers."

"Hmm, I think I did read about that." Sabrina dropped my card into her hippie-style, fringed shoulder bag. "Nasty business. If you helped shut those guys down, Cassie, good for you."

"FOCA was involved, too," I told her. "Friends of Chadwick Animals. FFF is an offshoot of that group, aren't they?"

She nodded. "The feral cat issue has gotten so big in this area, they formed a committee to deal just with that."

We strolled past a double doorway that I guessed led to the community's indoor pool; closed and dark for the evening, it still gave off a whiff of chlorine. Farther on, in a smaller activity space, I spotted several women clustered intently around a card table. The lights remained on above the front concierge desk, which had its own alcove, but no one seemed to be staffing it at the moment.

I supposed the special meeting about the feral cat issue had been the highlight of the evening. When we reached the glass-walled main exit, some of the attendees still gathered on the sidewalk outside. A few scowled at our approach, and the stocky man in the rust pullover muttered something to Sabrina under his breath. Apparently her hearing was better than her vision, because she smiled as she passed and told him sweetly, "And the same to you, Mike." Otherwise, the fact that Dawn and I flanked her seemed to ward off any more hostile remarks.

The automatic doors shut behind us, and an early November breeze knifed through my short leather jacket. Dawn tucked her long hair inside the collar of her calf-length wool coat, which was striped like a Peruvian blanket. The coat reminded me of the wall hangings created by her mother, Gwen, a professional fiber artist. Dawn had pursued a different line of work, but did show some of the same weaving skill by braiding her rusty hair in a variety of ways, using the front part to restrain the wild waves in back. Now, as Sabrina wrapped her paisley shawl more tightly around the loose skin of her neck and strode ahead of us with rhythmic taps of her cane, it suddenly seemed less odd to me that the two women had stayed in touch over the years. Along with their similar concern for social issues, Dawn resembled—in style, at least—a younger, taller, healthier, and chic-er version of Sabrina.

Now Sabrina suggested, "Well, Cassie, as long as you're here at The Reserve, want to take a tour?"

"Of . . . the community?" I already knew it consisted of about fifty units, most of them two-story, semidetached town houses set along twining, intersecting drives. From what I'd seen at sunset, when Dawn and I had arrived, the architecture was typical of any upscale planned community these days—trying for colonial, but with prominent garages and odd extra wings that would have baffled our founding fathers.

Sabrina made a cynical face, hinting that she also found no special charm in The Reserve, and pointed instead to the woods beyond. "Naw, of our rescue station."

"Of that? Yeah, sure."

The three of us trekked down a long path edged with miniature lanterns while I formed a clearer idea of the community's layout. It centered on a grassy oval plaza with a fountain—not functioning right now due to the cold—and some Victorian-looking benches. Obviously, a large swath of woods had been cleared when The Reserve had gone up five years earlier, and all of the townhomes backed up onto what remained of the wild area. This had to be the planner's intention, to give the residents picturesque "country" views. I'd noticed that too often, in such cases, homeowners were upset to find that the wooded settings came with actual wildlife—deer that nibbled on the carefully designed landscaping, and small predators that stalked the local birds or even pets that ventured outdoors.

We followed a manicured walking and jogging trail, designed for the residents to take their exercise without running into any poison ivy or trip hazards. Maybe thirty yards down, Sabrina detoured into the woods. In a small clearing, barely visible from the path, we came upon three twenty-five-gallon gray rubber storage bins turned on their sides and partially draped in black plastic sheeting. She pulled aside the cover of one to show me and Dawn a sturdy plastic dog dish filled with fresh water and a gravity food dispenser, which released dry cat kibble into a dish as needed.

"So far the water isn't freezing, but we'll have to find some way to protect it once the weather gets colder," Sabrina commented, half to herself. "I fill the dishes once a day, usually in the evening when there's nobody around to notice and complain. The FFF kids check them at least once a week, too." Turning to me, she added, "You can see, we've tried to make the feeder stations as inconspicuous as possible. We put them well away from the walking path, but people still call them eyesores."

While she was speaking, three cats silently appeared out of the woods, from different directions—a skinny gray, a fairly healthy and young-looking tortoiseshell, and a scruffy, wiry black. The short coat on the last cat appeared dry and thin in spots, but he still sported the full jowls of an unneutered male.

I suspected the trio had been drawn by the sound of Sabrina's voice. *No witchcraft in that—they just know who their friends are.*

Dawn chuckled and said, "These guys look like they're hoping for a late snack."

"There's enough food left, if they need it. See those two females?" The little woman pointed to the gray and the tortoiseshell. "Their ears are notched. That means the FFF kids already trapped, vaccinated, and spayed them, so they won't be spreading any diseases or breeding. Now, Omen, here"—she nodded toward the black male—"they haven't caught him yet. He's too damned smart. But at least if we fix all his girlfriends, he can't make any more babies."

The tomcat sprang lightly onto a boulder just a couple of yards from Sabrina. His luminous, chartreuse eyes regarded her calmly, as an equal. Meanwhile, I reached a hand toward the tortoiseshell, and she approached within a few inches, but never close enough to touch.

"These two girls seem friendly enough," Dawn said. "They couldn't be trapped and adopted out as pets?"

The older woman shook her head. "Not likely. Even if you could get one into your house, she'd probably yowl constantly to get out, scratch at your doors, and cause all kinds of mischief."

"And after that happens," I explained, "the poor thing gets hauled away to a shelter, anyhow, and probably euthanized."

Sabrina nodded. "A cat that's lived wild all its life is better left that way."

We trekked back to the walking trail, stepping carefully through the brush and around rocks and fallen branches. Once we had retreated to a safe distance—from their point of view— the three cats converged on the feeding station. Sabrina lingered a bit to watch them.

"Usually I hang out here for a while," she said, "to see how many show up, and which ones. If a cat's missing for a few nights in a row, and I know it was old or sick, I figure it must have died. If it was younger and friendly, I prefer to think someone else started putting out food for it."

"My mother was feeding a couple," Dawn said, "until the board told her not to."

"Well, as I said at the meeting, they were correct," Sabrina admitted. "This colony can probably survive okay, at least in warm weather, on what prey they catch in the woods. Gwen, your mom, meant well. But when she and some of the other residents started feeding the cats on their own patios, that's when the ferals moved closer to the community. A few busybodies reported it, and we got into this whole 'feeding wildlife' debate. I had to explain that our community created the situation, and now we had to solve it the right way. By trap-neuter-return, and by providing food and shelter for the animals that remain. Especially in the winter."

"You provide shelter, too?" I asked.

"We will." The stark planes of Sabrina's face softened with the hint of a smile. "FFF has come up with two kinds of shelters. They can line one of those black storage bins with insulation and cut a flap for an entrance. A jumbo-sized Styrofoam cooler works, too, and it's cheaper. Unfortunately, even though we can get by with just a few feeding stations, we'll need a fair number of the shelters—at least half a dozen."

I could only imagine how the HOA board would react to that many white Styrofoam coolers scattered throughout the woods along their walking trail.

Dawn voiced a similar concern. "Your birdwatchers are going to love that."

Sabrina snorted. "They get so cranked up about coming across a dead sparrow now and then. Wait 'til winter, when they start finding cats that have starved or frozen stiff. Then let them explain to their grandkids why they wouldn't let us put out food or shelters."

The heat of her anger seemed to steam through the chilly night air. I asked her, "If the people here are so out of tune with your values and give you such a hard time, why did you move to The Reserve in the first place?"

The older woman gave us a sly wink. "My brother-in-law

got me a deal—you might say he made me an offer I couldn't refuse." Sabrina glanced back toward the woods. "And now that I'm here, I can't just walk away. Who knows what might happen if I did?"

Dawn and I escorted Sabrina back to the door of her own condo—just in case. Then we drove back to downtown Chadwick in Dawn's Jeep, which she'd recently purchased as pre-owned. She'd been charmed by its distinctive gecko-green hue, which she thought might go well with her eco-friendly business. When she'd boasted to me about its low mileage, I'd joked that its first owner could stand looking at that color for only so long.

On our way home, I marveled aloud at Sabrina's determination. "It's great that she's trying so hard to save the cats, but I don't know how she can stand to live in such a conservative community, where people are calling her a witch and threatening her. Even I might throw in the towel and decide it's just not worth it."

Her eyes on the dark country road ahead, Dawn lifted her strong chin just a little. "Not Sabrina. She's marched for women's rights, civil rights . . . She's even spent a night or two in jail for leading protests. When she's serious about a cause, she doesn't quit. She'll see it through to the bitter end."

As we turned onto the main drag of Chadwick, a light snow had begun to fall. It was almost nine, and most of the retail businesses had closed by now, though dimmed lighting still showed off displays in the front windows of the funky jewelry store, Jaded; the art gallery, Eye of the Beholder; and Towne Antiques. I liked that even the newer, trendier merchants had mainly kept the turn-of-the century façades for their shops, in some cases even enhancing them with extended porches and eye-catching paint jobs.

I realized that I could appreciate the quaint charm of our downtown better this winter. Last year around this time, I'd been frantically rehabbing the shop, juggling paperwork for a business loan and a new lease, and then moving from my old apartment in somewhat more urban Morristown. The fact that I'd been doing all this while trying to stay off the radar of my abusive ex-boyfriend, so he wouldn't track me down at my new location, had only made things more stressful. This fall, thank goodness, I could breathe a little easier.

I had shut off my cell phone while we were in the woods, to avoid spooking the cats. In the passenger seat now, I checked it and found one message. It was from Harry Bock, who'd boarded his Sphynx cat at my shop for a week and had picked her up the previous day. Everything had seemed fine then, so why would he be calling me tonight at almost nine p.m.?

"Ms. McGlone, I'm sure you're not open at this hour, but we need to talk first thing tomorrow. My cat Looli has come down with a hideous skin rash, and I hold you responsible!"

Chapter 3

The hairless, ivory-white cat crouched on my sales counter wearing a pink feline sweatshirt—kind of like a baby's onesie, without the legs. Poor Looli did look miserable. It might have been just from the indignity of wearing clothing, though I did spot one red pimple on top of her head.

Her owner, Harry Bock, had been waiting outside my front door with the carrier when I'd opened at nine a.m., in a greater state of distress than Looli. Bock, who gave a highly strung impression to begin with, stood only a couple of inches taller than my five-foot-six and had coloring almost as pale as his cat's. With help from Sarah, he wrestled Looli out of the stretch garment.

"Explain to me," he demanded, "how this could have happened twenty-four hours after I picked her up from your shop, unless it was caused by something you did to her."

When the Sphynx, whose Egyptian name meant "pearl," had left my shop, her downy hide had resembled that gem, warm white with a soft luster. Now an ugly rash had spread over most of her wrinkled little body, from her nape to the base of her tapered tail. One sore near her neck looked especially raw, and I could see why. As soon as Bock let go of her, she frantically scratched that spot with her long hind leg.

I shuddered in sympathy, remembering one summer at camp when I was eleven and had naïvely blundered into a poison sumac bush.

Meanwhile, Sarah clucked her tongue and murmured, "Poor thing!"

I slipped on some thin latex grooming gloves and examined the rash more closely, but without real medical training, I couldn't tell very much. "Have you taken her to a vet?"

Bock ran an agitated hand over his thinning blond hair. "My vet couldn't give me an appointment until this afternoon. In the meantime, you need to figure out what you did to cause this, so he can treat it. I know you bathed her, so it must be a reaction to the soap, or—"

"We use only mild, hypoallergenic soap. We need to, because we get a variety of breeds and even cats with medical conditions, so some are more sensitive than others. Sarah, would you show Mr. Bock our shampoo and conditioner?"

As my assistant went to our rear grooming studio for the products, Bock continued to brainstorm possible causes. "Then she must have been exposed to another cat with this condition."

"I wouldn't have accepted any cat for boarding who had a rash like this. Besides, you've seen our cat condos. Each animal has its own enclosure, and I turn them out in the play area individually. The only time I let two out together is if they come from the same household. So no other cat could have bitten Looli or scratched her or even rubbed up against her."

"Maybe a flea from an infected cat . . ."

"We don't take cats with obvious fleas, and we spray our shop regularly. Whether this might be an allergic reaction to a flea bite, I can't say for sure. That's why you need to see a vet, get a blood test and a skin scraping—"

"Why should I go to all of that trouble and expense? This has to be something you caused. It happened right after she came back from your shop."

Sarah returned with the shampoo and conditioner bottles, her dark eyes worried behind wire-rimmed glasses. She took her job of assisting me very seriously, something I truly appreciated. With no prior experience, but a love of animals and a game attitude, Sarah had learned cat grooming on the job and had gotten very proficient over the last few months. Her prior experience as a high school math teacher meant she also handled our cash register with far more skill and confidence than I did.

Bock took the bottles from her and scrutinized the ingredients, which supposedly were all natural. He asked me about a couple of plant-derived things that I had to admit I knew little about.

I thought of Dawn and told him, "I do have a friend who's more up on botanicals. She owns the health food store down the street, Nature's Way. Want me to call her?"

Bock creased his nose. "Aaah, your *friend* will probably just back you up."

Though the man had reason to be upset, he was getting on my nerves. Still, I tried to stay calm and professional. "And it's true that Looli might have an allergy even to some natural product."

Sarah suggested to Bock, "If she's never reacted to the soap you use at home, maybe we should've just let you bring us some when you left her here, the way you did with her food. We can do that next time."

"Like there'll be a next time!" he sneered.

I wasn't sure I ever wanted his business again, either. "The good news is, if it was an allergic reaction to some substance here, it should clear up now that she's home with you. Let me know if that happens. And please let me know what the vet says, too."

With my help, Bock stuffed the reluctant Looli back into her pink onesie and then into her carrier. I never like to see animals in clothing, but I guessed a Sphynx needed some protection from cold weather. Not to mention from the embarrassment of a full-body case of acne.

Bock spoke through clenched teeth, as if struggling to control his emotions. "Looli competes in shows as a Purebred Altered. She's had three Winner ribbons so far and only needs three more for the Premier title. I have her entered in a regional show next Saturday, but I can't imagine this rash is going to clear up that soon. It might even leave scars that will ruin her chances forever! If I can prove you're responsible, Ms. McGlone, you'll be hearing from my lawyer."

On that note, he stormed out of my shop with cat and carrier and slammed the glass door behind him.

Sarah faced me, her complexion ashier than normal. "Does he mean it? Could he really sue you?"

I tried to brush it off. "He's just upset right now. I'm sure it won't come to that."

"We do have people sign a release when they bring their cats in for grooming. It covers us for certain things, right? Like, if we have to cut out a tough mat, and there's a chance of nicking the cat's skin . . ."

I nodded. Unfortunately, the release said nothing about the cat developing a mysterious rash that didn't show up until she'd left the shop. I opened my laptop on the sales counter and spent a few minutes researching. The websites I found said cats also could break out from allergies to certain foods. But as my customers often do, Bock had left us some of the same food he'd been giving Looli at home, a premium brand.

While I mulled over these things, Sarah had a thought that seemed to cheer her up. "Well, at least if he does try to sue, your mom should be able to get us a good lawyer."

I smiled at the grim joke. My mother worked full-time as a paralegal with the Morristown firm of McCabe, Preston, and Rueda, which did have a stable of high-powered attorneys. Whether I could afford them, or get a break in fees from one of them, might be another story.

There was nothing more we could do at the moment, so we went about our daily routine. We let a Burmese boarder out for a break in the playroom, then methodically scooped out litter boxes and cleaned up any other messes the animals might have made in their condos. Meanwhile, we couldn't resist brainstorming on our most pressing problem.

"Maybe after Bock brought Looli home, he let her run loose through a patch of poison ivy," I suggested, mostly in sarcasm.

"His precious show cat? I doubt that." Sarah sniffed. "I didn't realize they even had classes for altered cats."

"It's fairly new, I think, and they're different from the classes for household pets. The cats still have to be purebred and top quality. I would imagine when Looli's at her best, she does make quite an impression with that milky white coloring."

"Such a shame." Sarah shook her head. "On a cat with regular fur, the rash would hardly show. On her, though, it really does look awful."

"I know. Sphynxes have a problem with the oil their own skin produces, to begin with, because there's no fur to absorb it. That's why Bock wanted her bathed while she was here." I sighed. "Well, let's just hope his veterinarian can figure out what's causing the rash and clear it up quickly."

Sarah finished tidying the last condo and dusted her gloved hands on her apron. "Bet our Dr. Coccia could get to the bottom of it. You should've suggested that Bock take the cat to him."

"It crossed my mind." I glanced at my cell phone calendar to see what other duties I had on my agenda for the day. "But if Bock wouldn't trust Dawn's word about the shampoo ingredients because she's my friend, I'm sure he wouldn't trust a diagnosis from a vet I'm dating. Still, I'll ask Mark when I see him tonight."

"You two finally found enough time in your hectic schedules to get together?"

I smiled at Sarah's not-so-funny ribbing. Like me, Mark sometimes found himself a victim of his own career success. After growing up in Philadelphia and getting his DVM degree at the University of Pennsylvania, he'd worked for a while in a larger practice in South Jersey. Eventually, though, he'd felt the urge to have a clinic of his own. He'd found an older, more seasoned vet who was willing to partner with him, Dr. Margaret Reed, and they'd looked around for an area that seemed underserved in terms of veterinary clinics, which led them to Chadwick. Their market research had paid off—after only two years, they had almost more patients than they could handle. Mark was making good money and building up a stellar reputation but put in long hours. Even when not besieged with emergency cases, he normally worked, like me, five and a half days a week.

I told Sarah, "Yes, wonder of wonders, we're both free tonight. We're going to a movie at the Paragon." The early-twentieth-century downtown theater had recently been restored to show classic films, and I'd been eager to have a look inside. "They're doing Hitchcock films all this week, and tonight it's *Vertigo*. Neither of us has ever seen it, but it's supposed to be great."

"Seriously, you never saw that? Not even on any of the old-movie channels?"

I shrugged. "Always missed it somehow."

"I'm surprised, knowing how you love a mystery," Sarah teased. "Anyway, you should have fun. Let me know what the theater's like inside. I've gotta get in there myself one of these days."

We went back to work, grooming Simon—a Cymric, or longhaired Manx, who had been brought in earlier that day. He was a new customer with a few stubborn mats in his thick double coat, but with the help of some spray-on conditioner, a blunt-nosed scissors, and a lot of patience, I got them out. Sarah held him steady, and fortunately Simon had a sweet temperament and seemed used to the routine.

While we worked, my assistant asked me how things had gone during the big meeting up at The Reserve.

"Oh, boy." I blew out a breath. "Those folks have issues that go beyond a few feral cats." I explained about the attempts by Sabrina Ward and the FFF to deal with The Reserve's problem and the small but stubborn group of residents who ridiculed their efforts. "Now that the weather's getting cold, Sabrina wants to put out shelters in the woods near the feeding station."

My assistant rolled her eyes. "How's that going to go over?"

"Not well, I'm afraid. But Sabrina's stubborn, too. And apparently she's got some kind of 'in' with management, so the board can't just boot her out, thank goodness. Maybe if FFF does one more round of trapping and neutering, they might be able to take care of the whole colony and things will quiet down."

"Well, at least that's not anything you have to worry about," Sarah reminded me.

"You're right, it isn't," I agreed.

But I knew I'd worry, anyway.

Chapter 4

For my date, I went through the usual mad scramble at five p.m. to shower off the *arôme de chat* and fluff some life back into my own brown fur. A smidgen of peachy blush livened up my pale complexion, and some plum shadow brightened up my brown eyes. Winding up with a light spray of cologne, I felt revitalized.

There was some consolation in knowing Mark would be going through a similar rushed routine, after putting in a long day himself at the veterinary clinic—though he wouldn't have to choose from among quite so many casual-but-cute fashion options. And it didn't seem fair that he could look spectacular even with his dark hair mussed, a trace of stubble over his strong chin, and a few lines of fatigue around his sapphire-blue eyes, while I felt obliged to gild the lily with mascara and lipstick.

Of course, I did this mostly to meet my own unrealistic standards, since Mark probably would tell me I didn't need makeup. I guess I still couldn't quite take my good luck for granted—that the tall, dark, and handsome veterinarian I'd been eyeballing ever since I moved to Chadwick also turned out to be attracted to me. I remained well aware that, no matter how contented Mark seemed with our relationship, plenty of other women still viewed him as catnip, so I had to stay on my toes.

Because the movie was the splurge part of this date, we just grabbed a quick dinner at Slice of Heaven, the town's newest and best pizza parlor. Another business that obviously hoped to take advantage of Chadwick's growing popularity among weekend tourists and young professionals, the restaurant had adopted a cool, modern décor. Subway tile on the walls and industrial pendant lights helped set the ambience, and the tomato-red tabletops with their bentwood chairs all offered a view of the central, fiery brick oven. Nearby, a chalkboard wall announced the day's specials, which always had imaginative names and ingredients and usually featured at least one gluten-free option.

As Mark and I entered on this cold night, with a tang of snow in the air, the restaurant enveloped us in welcome warmth. We both inhaled the mouthwatering, overlapping scents of tomatoes, peppers, sausage, garlic, oregano, pesto, and various cheeses.

Mark closed his eyes in bliss. "Ah, just smell that!"

I savored it, too. "They ought to pipe that aroma out into the street. Not that they're hurting for customers."

Tonight we both agreed on a vegetable pizza, which included eggplant, zucchini, mushrooms, and olives, among the more usual ingredients. The restaurant was dry, and since both of us tended to be tired on weeknights, we hadn't bothered to bring any wine and stuck to caffeinated cola.

We made pleasant small talk until poor, unsuspecting Mark asked me how my day had gone. You'd think after almost eight months of dating me, he'd have learned this was a risky thing to do. After I had burdened him with my tale of woe, he tried to advise me on the case of my dissatisfied customer, Harry Bock.

"If this guy doesn't get a decent explanation from his vet, sure, send him to me. You don't have to let on that you and I have a relationship," Mark said. "A rash like that does sound like some kind of allergy, especially if the cat isn't sick otherwise, but it could be caused by almost anything. Something she touched, ate, or even breathed."

"So it might be hard to pin down, eh?" Though Mark's company and the yummy pizza had lifted my spirits somewhat, I still couldn't forget Bock's parting threat. "Even if it starts to clear up now, that will just convince the guy that I caused it somehow and made his cat miss out on this important show. Do you really think he'd sue me?"

Mark raised a skeptical eyebrow. "I don't think he'd find any lawyer to take the case, with no proof of the cause. People say they'll sue vets, too, but mostly when they're emotionally wrecked over a pet that didn't make it. They hardly ever follow through."

Since he'd done a good job so far of reassuring me about the Sphynx's ailment, I also asked for Mark's take on the controversy at The Reserve. To my surprise, he already had heard something about it, because his partner at the clinic, Dr. Reed, was treating the dog that was poisoned.

"He came in with ulcers," Mark told me, "and she has to get that situation under control before she can release him back to his owner."

"What kind of poison would cause ulcers?" I asked.

"Probably an over-the-counter NSAID painkiller. There are some types formulated especially for animals, but the human kinds are really bad for them, especially in a high concentration. From what the owner told Maggie, the dog was on one of those long, retractable leashes and came across a paper plate with what the guy figured was cat food. Before the owner could pull the dog away, he'd scarfed it all down. Later that day, the dog vomited and acted weak and listless. Fortunately, he's a collie mix, so the stuff had less effect on him than it might've had on a smaller breed. When the guy brought him in, at first he just thought the food had gone bad."

I considered this. "It was wet food, on a paper plate?"

Mark nodded. "Someone must have crushed pills, or opened up a couple of capsules, and mixed in the medicine."

"Sounds very thought-out. We saw Sabrina's feeding station last night. She uses dry kibble enclosed in a feeder. I was wondering how someone would be able to tamper with it. But I guess the poisoner didn't bother—he or she provided the food, too."

Mark frowned. "That's really twisted. Sabrina had better tread lightly if she's dealing with people like that."

"She won't, though. You should have heard her telling off everyone at the board meeting. Dawn says Sabrina's been advocating for causes all her life and doesn't scare easily."

"Huh. If she saw this poor dog, stuck in a cage with an IV drip, she might have second thoughts. And you and Dawn should, too, before you get mixed up any deeper in this business."

I raised my hands. "I'm not mixed up in it. I just explained the TNR concept to the residents and urged them to give it a chance. That will be the extent of my involvement."

Mark nodded in approval and used the checkered napkin to pat some tomato sauce from the corner of his mouth. "Then let's change the subject, and talk about humans eating things that are actually good for them. Got any plans for Thanksgiving?"

"Gee. I haven't given it too much thought, but I guess I'll be spending it with my mom. Why?"

"Well, I'll be heading to Philly to see my folks, and I was wondering if you'd like to come with me."

That caught me off guard, and my emotions slipped and slid as if they'd hit a patch of black ice. It was a compliment, I realized, for him to even ask me to meet his family. He'd met my mother, but she lived only forty-five minutes away and stopped by the shop now and then. Philadelphia was two hours from us, and since Mark had two brothers and a sister who had stayed closer to home, he mostly visited them rather than vice versa.

On the other hand, because it was kind of a big deal—traveling that far, for a major holiday celebration—the idea made me anxious. Would his family start to see me as not just the latest of several women Mark had dated over the past couple of years, but as *the* girlfriend? It was one thing to feel warmly toward a particular guy, another to fit in with his family. And if I didn't, would that be a deal breaker?

Beyond that, I had family commitments of my own.

"That's so great of you to ask," I told him. "I'd just be concerned about leaving Mom alone. She's got no other family nearby, and I've told you how she is since Dad died. On holidays, especially, she gets blue and misses him."

I understood this, because I often missed Dad, too. His playful personality always had made the holidays more fun, and whenever Mom would get obsessive about some detail, he knew just how to calm her down—something I'd never quite gotten the hang of. But even though Dad's career as a periodontist hadn't been especially stressful, he'd suffered from a congenital heart problem that he'd monitored all his life, and it eventually had caught up with him. The timing had been very unlucky—he'd been alone in his office after hours. He'd dialed 911, but by the time an ambulance arrived, he had passed. At least back then, I'd been living closer to Mom, so we could support each other.

At my explanation, Mark dropped his gaze to the tabletop and nodded. I could almost hear him thinking, *Your dad's been gone three years, though. She could let you off the leash for one holiday!* But he would never say that to me.

He looked so disheartened that I added, "I'll sound her out about it, okay? Maybe she wouldn't mind too much."

This time he met my eyes with a more cheerful nod, as if this sounded reasonable. It also gave me some time to think about whether I was ready to make such a trip, and an "out" if I decided I wasn't.

It had begun to snow lightly as we walked to the Paragon. I'd followed the newspaper stories about its restoration, so I knew it dated back to 1939 but had stopped showing first-run movies in the 1990s. For a couple of decades it had housed meetings of various community groups and live performances by a dance school, until a local-history buff with deep pockets had given it a new lease on life. He'd cleaned up the brown brick exterior with its art deco stepped-limestone trim and re-stored the vertical marquee that proclaimed PARAGON in gold-and-green neon letters. That color scheme continued in the dark green framework and brass handles of the lobby doors and the diamond pattern of the carpet inside.

Along with the expected popcorn, the lobby refreshment stand also specialized in nostalgic candies such as Goobers, Good & Plenty, and Swedish Fish. For our evening's dessert, Mark and I shared a box of Crows, a type of licorice gumdrop I hadn't seen in many years.

We settled in to watch the 1958 movie, wryly noticing that most other people in the theater were old enough to have seen it the first time around. I reflected on the differences in moviemaking back then—how long the credits rolled before the action got going, and how Hitchcock built suspense with many slow, quiet passages that probably would make audiences impatient today.

Though I got caught up in the story and could feel that Mark did, too, from time to time my thoughts strayed back to his Thanksgiving invitation. Was I making a big deal over nothing? Hard to tell without knowing his family. Were they a casual, modern crowd, happy to welcome his latest squeeze to the table without any further expectations? Or were they an old-fashioned bunch who would read a lot into my presence and start asking whether Mark and I were serious? Or even, when was the wedding, and how soon could we give them grandchildren?

Mark and I hadn't even discussed those questions yet. I sure didn't want to do it for the first time in front of his parents, siblings, and who-knew-how-many other relatives!

I felt a little tremor and almost chalked it up to my nerves, then realized I'd put my phone on vibrate and had tucked my bag right next to my hip. Subtly, I pulled it out and checked the screen. Just Dawn. I hadn't mentioned to her that I'd be going out. If she wanted to talk more about the feral cat problems at The Reserve, it could wait until morning.

The movie wound up a little after ten, and on our way out of the theater, Mark and I had a brief chat with the skinny blond usher, Dave, who looked like a kid even to our eyes. He turned out to be a communications student at the County College of Morris and a member of the Student Film Association; he picked up extra bucks working a few evenings at the theater. Though Mark and I had enjoyed *Vertigo*, we did have some questions for Dave about the twisty plot and rather downbeat ending. He proved very knowledgeable and offered some insights we probably never would have thought of.

"Hitchcock himself was obsessed with a certain type of

cool, unattainable blond woman," he explained. "The character of Madeleine is probably the best example of this, and of
course, Jimmy Stewart's character, Scottie, becomes tragically
obsessed with her. The movie's use of steep stairs, bridges, and
the hills of San Francisco all kind of play on Scottie's fear of
heights, too."

After this chat, Mark and I both felt better informed about
the film. By the time we stepped outside, the snow was falling
more steadily, and a couple of inches coated the sidewalk. I was
glad I'd worn low-heeled boots, even though they wouldn't
have gotten me through a real blizzard.

"I gotta say, though," Mark joked as we walked back to his
RAV4, "that guy Scottie sure didn't have much luck with
women."

I smiled at this understatement. "Serves him right for ig-
noring the nice girl-next-door type, who was always there for
him, and chasing after the frosty blond goddess."

"Never much cared for frosty blond goddesses, myself." He
opened the passenger-side door for me. "Though she did
make me wonder why *you* never wear little white gloves when
we go out on a date."

Climbing into the car, I held up my hands in their cozy
green knit gloves. "This is the closest I come, until you start
wearing a tie and a fedora."

Mark laughed. "Well, maybe the next time we take in one
of these vintage movies, we should both dress the part. Crap,
it's really coming down, isn't it?" He slid in behind the wheel,
cranked the ignition, and turned up the windshield wipers to
top speed.

I wanted to suggest that he spend the night at my place,
but . . . would that open the door to more conversation about
my going to Philly with him for Thanksgiving? Or to an even
bigger conversation about where our relationship was going?

If I said I was pretty content right now with things as they were, would I find out that Mark wasn't? Would I risk blowing things with the smartest, kindest, most simpatico—and, okay, the hottest—guy I'd ever known?

To stall, I pulled out my phone and pretended to notice the message for the first time. "Dawn called me. I didn't tell her I was going out."

I tapped play and heard a hoarse version of my friend's voice, as if she'd been sobbing. "Cassie, I'm sorry to call you so late, but I had to talk to somebody. . . . Sabrina's dead! I went over to The Reserve tonight and found her in the woods. The cops think she was st-strangled!"

Chapter 5

Stunned, I shared this news with Mark.

"Man, that's awful!" he said. "Is Dawn okay? Is she safe?"

"I guess, though she didn't say."

As he drove carefully down Center Street, which was growing slick by now, I called my friend back. Dawn was quick to assure me that, after spending a couple of hours at The Reserve talking to the police, she was home now in the apartment over her shop.

"You poor thing!" I sympathized. "That must have been a terrible shock. What on earth happened?"

"I don't really know, but . . . after I closed up the shop for the night, I went over to Mom's condo to get her mail and water her plants. On the way back to my car, I saw it was snowing pretty steadily and decided to just do a quick check of the cat feeding station. I had a little flashlight with me. Still, it was dark out there, and at first I thought somebody had dumped a pile of clothes in the woods. Then I realized it was S-Sabrina, lying on the ground. I tried to revive her, but she was already dead . . . cold. The snow had started to drift over her b-body."

"So you called the cops?"

"Yes, of course. Even Detective Bonelli came out."

"She did?" Angela Bonelli usually didn't get involved unless there was some suspicion of a serious crime.

"Sabrina was wearing a long scarf that apparently got tangled in some branches. Bonelli thought maybe she tripped and fell in the dark and the scarf strangled her."

I tried to picture this. Sounded a bit unlikely to me, but I supposed it was possible.

By now, Mark had picked up on the gravity of my tone. He glanced over and asked, "Dawn's all right?"

I muffled the phone against my chest. "Yeah, but she's really upset. I think maybe I should stop at her place."

"No problem. I'll drop you there."

Meanwhile, I kept Dawn on the line. "We're on our way to your shop right now, okay?"

"Who was that, Mark? Were you two on a date? I didn't mean to wreck your evening, calling you about something like this."

"Please, don't worry about it. After all, I know how scary it can be to stumble across a dead body."

A graveyard chuckle on the line. "Oh, my God, that's right. You actually do." We both were thinking of an incident the previous spring, when I'd found one of my best customers deceased in his own home.

Out of the corner of my eye, I saw Mark wag his head and try to hide a grim smile, as if to say, *Some conversation!*

We pulled up in front of Nature's Way, and Dawn let us in the front door. She hugged me, her tight squeeze filled with grief. To lighten the mood a little, I glanced around and asked, "No Tigger, trying to dash out into the street?" Her year-old kitten had been a stray, and it took months of clicker training to—mostly—cure him of that habit.

"I just fed him," she said of the brown tabby. "Poor little guy was starving by the time I finally got home."

Mark also hugged Dawn. "I'm so sorry. Cassie tells me you knew this lady a long time."

"We only saw each other now and then, but Sabrina was one of a kind. Most people are only focused on their own interests, y'know? But she was always fighting for the underdog, putting herself at risk for others." Dawn's lower lip trembled and another tear rolled down her cheek.

"You shouldn't be alone tonight," I told her. "Have you called Keith?"

"I left him a message, but he's staying in New York this week, at some corporate thing. An advertising company hired him to do cartoons for their new holiday campaign. It's big bucks, but he'll be under the gun all this month."

Sounded like a windfall for her boyfriend, a freelance commercial artist, but Dawn could have used his comforting presence right now. "Want to come over to my place?"

She hesitated and glanced from me to Mark. "Oh, no . . . I'll be fine. Bad enough that I interrupted your date!"

"That's okay, really," Mark assured her. "I have to work tomorrow, anyway. And Cassie's right, you shouldn't be alone after a shock like this."

"You're sure you don't mind?" I asked him, wondering if I'd made the offer a little too quickly.

"I'm sure. Dawn, pack up whatever you need, and I'll drop you at Cassie's." He glanced out the front window of her store. "Then I should probably get on back to my own place before the roads get worse."

About half an hour later, Dawn and I sat at the 1950s yellow laminate table in the minuscule kitchen of my apartment, over my shop. I had offered her some herbal tea because she usually followed such a healthful routine. She surprised me by asking for a lite beer instead. I figured she needed it, though I stuck to cocoa.

My own three cats—sleek, black Cole, orange tabby Mango, and patchwork calico Matisse—had, of course, nagged me for more food when I'd come home, even though I'd given them dinner before I'd left the house at six o'clock. Now Matisse sat on my lap, while Cole sprawled on the kitchen rug and Mango in the living room doorway, as if they were all curious to hear what had kept me out so late.

Popping the cap off her beer, Dawn told me, "I still feel lousy about screwing up your evening with Mark. I know it's not easy for the two of you to find time to get together. Hell, we all work long hours and even Saturdays. . . ."

"Don't give it another thought. He might not have stayed over, anyway, with the bad weather. He has to be at the clinic bright and early tomorrow, and he'd still have needed a change of clothes."

"He should keep some at your place." She sent me a sly look before taking a swig from the amber bottle.

I thought of the decision about Thanksgiving that I was all too happy to postpone a bit longer, and changed the subject. "I'm sorry you have to go through this with so little support. Keith and your mom both being away . . ."

Dawn's face fell again. "Just as well my mom isn't here. When Sabrina first moved to The Reserve, about three years ago, I introduced the two of them, and they hit it off right away. You know how artsy Mom is—she's a weaver, she's spent time in art colonies, and she's very, very liberal—so she sometimes feels out of step with the rest of the condo community, too. In a lot of ways, she and Sabrina spoke the same language."

I hadn't spent much time with Gwen Tischler, partly because she always seemed to be on the move. I'd visited her condo only once, with Dawn, and admired the way Gwen had individualized it with her own woven throws and wall hangings. She'd just taken up Indian cooking at that time, and served us a dinner to rival anything at a good ethnic restaurant.

I always had the sense that she played by no one else's rules except her own. Dawn once confided in me that her parents had never officially married, only taken vows in some neopagan handfasting ceremony at an art colony in Asheville, North Carolina. They'd chosen to raise their daughter in a New Jersey suburb for the quality of the schools. But eventually her father, Joel, had gotten tired of such a conventional existence. A musician who played a couple of electronic instruments, and had made some successful New Age ambient-music recordings, he got most of his work on the West Coast and finally had moved to California. Joel, Gwen, and Dawn all remained on good terms, though, and traveled to see each other from time to time.

"Are you going to tell your mom what happened to Sabrina?" I asked.

"I guess I should, though I hate to spoil her trip. I should prepare her before she gets back, but she's going to be in Morocco for a while, touring a few cities and villages. So I have a couple of weeks yet."

"There's no way to soft-pedal it, really," I admitted. "Not as if Sabrina just passed in her sleep, or something."

Leaning on the kitchen table, my friend buried one hand in her thick, wavy hair. "She didn't deserve to die like that. Alone, in the dark, in the snow. Like some old bag lady."

The pain in my friend's voice wrenched my heart. "Bonelli actually thought she'd strangled on her scarf?" I knew the police detective was pretty sharp and didn't usually jump to conclusions about the cause of a death.

Dawn's amber-brown eyes blazed as they met mine. "It looked that way, but I think it was *made* to look that way. The end of the scarf was wrapped around a low branch a couple of times. How does that happen by accident?"

"The wind?" I suggested, weakly.

She brushed away that theory with a sweep of her hand. "Cassie, you heard those residents at the board meeting talk about Sabrina. A few of them absolutely hated her. Hell, Mike Lawler even said somebody ought to 'euthanize' her!"

"Now, Dawn." I began to wonder if she should have stuck to herbal tea, after all. "That doesn't mean . . ."

"Somebody did try to poison the cats. That's a fact. I think maybe one of those folks got riled up after the meeting and decided the only way to get rid of the ferals was to get rid of Sabrina."

It might be a stretch, but I'd learned over the past year that sometimes murderous conflicts could simmer beneath the surface of our seemingly peaceful and picturesque little town. "I sincerely hope that didn't happen. If it did, though, Angela Bonelli will get to the bottom of it. She's very good at her job."

"Maybe. A couple of times, she's gotten some major help from you."

Wary of the direction our chat had taken, I hurried to say, "Thanks, but I have enough problems on my plate right now." Briefly, I explained about the customer whose cat had come down with a mystery rash and who had threatened to take me to court. "Tomorrow, after we've both rested, maybe you can look at the ingredients in my organic shampoo for anything that might have caused a reaction."

"I'm not really trained as an herbalist," Dawn said, "but I'll give it a shot."

"I'll take all the help I can get," I told her. "Anyway, you can see why I don't want to meddle in Detective Bonelli's investigation. If Mr. Bock decides to sue me, I could have my hands full proving my own innocence."

"Amazing, isn't it, how low some people can sink?" Dawn gazed out my kitchen window to where a nearby streetlight illuminated the falling snow, but her focus had turned inward. "Do you know, when I found Sabrina's body, that black cat was sitting on a rock just a couple of yards away? The one she called Omen. He ran off right after I came. It was like he'd been standing guard over her."

The next morning, Dawn returned to her own shop and apartment, though not before having a look at the organic shampoo I used on my customers and saying all the ingredients looked harmless to her. When Sarah arrived for work, I filled her in on what had happened with Sabrina Ward.

"That's terrible," my assistant said. "They think it was just a freak accident?"

"Bonelli told Dawn that there will be an autopsy. But the woman was around seventy, had bad eyesight, used a cane, and went tramping out into those woods at night by herself. There are plenty of rocks and tree roots she could have tripped over, plus it was snowing last night, which probably made things slippery."

"So it's not hard to imagine that she fell," Sarah concluded. "The weird part is that her scarf got wound around a tree branch."

"Yeah, that does sound strange. I'd love to ask Bonelli about it, but I doubt that she'd tell me anything. Not this early in the investigation."

I saw the light blinking on my shop phone and played the one message. Bock was asking me to call him as soon as I could. He sounded a little calmer than when he'd last been in

my shop, but not necessarily more cheerful. I braced myself
with a cup of coffee, then dialed.

"You wanted to know what the vet said about Looli's skin
condition," he began. "He also thought it was an allergy, but
couldn't say to what. It had to be something she came into
contact with, something she breathed, or something she ate.
Since I supplied you with her food, the last one doesn't seem
likely. And if it was something in the air at your place, she'd be
over it by now. But the rash is actually spreading and getting
worse!"

To my way of thinking, this alone should have acquitted
me. "It's gotten worse since you brought the cat home, but
you still think it was caused by something we did here at my
shop?"

After a pause, Bock admitted, "I don't know what to think.
This vet did a skin scraping and didn't find any germs or para-
sites causing the condition. Now he wants to do some kind of
inter . . . intradermal test?" Bock sounded as if he had read
that from a note. "It's a bunch of injections of different aller-
gens. But it's damned expensive."

Luckily, I've developed a tactful voice to use with customers. "Well, I'm sure you paid a lot for your cat and you
spend money taking her to shows. You need to be willing to
invest in her health, too."

Over the line, he snorted. "You sound like my ex-wife.
Except she'd say I *wasted* money on a fancy cat and on taking
her to shows." Then a sigh. "That's part of the problem—
since the divorce, I've had to watch expenses. But I'll be
damned if I'll give up Looli. She's a better companion than
my ex ever was."

My cranky customer was exposing a whole different side
of himself now. I'd thought of him as status-conscious, prissy,
and a little paranoid, but maybe he was just a lonely guy who'd

become a little too obsessed with his pet. If I could help him, I might clear myself in the process.

"Would you be open to getting a second opinion?" I suggested. "From another vet, at no charge?"

"Well . . . sure. But would anyone do that?"

"We have one here in town who's really good. I'll see if I can arrange it, okay?"

"All right." Bock's tone sounded cautious. "Thank you."

When I got off the phone, Sarah was smiling in my direction. "Gonna send him to Mark?"

"Why not? He may tell Bock all the same things, but he also might come up with an angle the other vet didn't think of. Honestly, if his cat's skin is getting worse now instead of better, it *can't* be due to anything she was exposed to here. But I don't think Bock will be happy until he has a definite answer."

I called Mark's cell, rather than the clinic number. He didn't answer, which often was the case in the middle of a workday. Since he already knew about the situation with Bock, I just left a message asking if he'd look at Looli as a favor to me.

Sarah and I went back to our routine then, turning one restless boarder loose in the playroom and grooming the Turkish Van, whose owner was picking her up that afternoon. We both enjoyed Taffy's personality because, at only three years old, she was full of energy. Her medium-length coat—mostly white, with rusty patches on her head and a matching tail—was easy to groom, but we still used a loose harness to keep her from scrambling off the grooming table. She even tried to chase drifting clumps of her own hair!

We were just finishing up with Taffy when I heard the front door open and close. The shop's budget surveillance system showed me the visitor was Dawn, even before she called out, "Hello-o! Any humans in the house?"

"C'mon back," I invited her. "That is, if you don't mind flying fur."

When we groom longhairs, the stuff does end up all over the place, which is why Sarah and I wear aprons and sometimes even head scarves. We had put Taffy back into her condo but were still spitting silky wisps out of our mouths as Dawn joined us.

"Hi again, Sarah!" she greeted my assistant. "This job hasn't driven you crazy yet?"

"Are you kidding? Never a dull moment around here." Sarah's expression sobered as she added, "I heard about your friend. That's so awful! Do they know yet what happened to her?"

"They think they do. That's why I came by to talk to Cassie." She sank onto a scarred old wooden chair that I kept next to the steel grooming table. "I called Bonelli today for an update."

I could imagine the police detective loved that, especially since Dawn wasn't even related to the deceased. "And she actually gave you one?"

"She did. They haven't got the complete autopsy results yet, but the ME has revised the cause of death. Now he says Sabrina died of a heart attack."

Probably a better way to go, I thought, than strangled by her own scarf. "Well, I guess that's not too surprising, given her age and—"

"Cassie, it's wrong. She was murdered, I know she was. You have to help me prove it!"

Chapter 6

I saw my assistant's look of alarm and decided not to subject her to Dawn's meltdown. "Sarah, would you go staff the front counter, in case anyone drops by?"

She quickly took my meaning and left me alone with my distraught friend.

The grooming studio was fairly separated from the rest of the shop, a good safeguard in case any of our feline customers became really agitated, broke away from us, and jumped off the table. It hadn't happened so far, but there was always that chance. Because the building used to serve as a hair salon for humans, this space came with a scarred but serviceable checked linoleum floor and a sink deep enough to bathe the cats who needed it. On the wall nearest the table, I'd hung a big piece of corkboard, painted the same hot pink as my sales counter, and used hooks to hang a wide array of grooming tools. Some got more use than others, but eventually they all came into play.

After a minute, Dawn got enough control to keep her voice low. "It's just too much of a coincidence," she insisted, "coming a day after the meeting. Poisoning the cats back-fired—that just made Bert's dog sick. So the next step was to attack Sabrina herself. And she was such an easy target, wasn't she? Everyone knew she went out to that spot alone every night after dinner. At this time of year, it would be dark, and she couldn't see that well, anyway. Someone could easily have crept up behind her."

I'd been prepared to soothe Dawn's fears and say she was imagining things, but she did have a point. "Easy to make it look like an accident, too."

"You see? Maybe I could have accepted that it was natural causes if it weren't for the scarf. It was one of those Indian-import styles, long and pretty thick, almost a muffler. Maybe a light, gauzy scarf could blow and get tangled by accident, but not one like that."

"Unless Sabrina wrapped it around the branch herself," I thought aloud. "Maybe to give her something to hang onto?"

Dawn creased her straight nose. "She wouldn't have left it around her neck!"

"Still, it's possible that she was trying to do something tricky to keep her balance. It didn't work out, she slipped and fell, and the shock was too much for her heart."

"Possible, but I still don't believe it. If Sabrina needed help to keep her footing, why wouldn't she have used her cane? She had it with her—Bonelli said it was found underneath her body." My friend's anguished eyes locked on my own. "Cassie, can you do just one thing for me?"

I leaned back against the edge of the grooming table for support. "I may regret asking this, but . . . what?"

"You've got an 'in' with Bonelli. I know she may not tell you much until they've closed the case, but you can still give *her* information. Explain to her what it was like at the board meeting. She thinks I'm exaggerating because Sabrina was my friend and I'm upset over her death. You're more objective, so maybe she'll listen to you."

It wasn't much to ask, and I did think the circumstances were hinky enough to warrant more investigation. "Okay. I can't promise anything, but I'll talk to her."

"Soon?"

I could have reminded Dawn that I also had a business to run, and other problems to deal with, but I understood her urgency. The more time went by, the greater the chance that evidence could be destroyed, people could concoct alibis, and tracks could be covered. I'm sure she sensed this, even though she didn't read and watch as many crime stories as I did.

"I'll go to the station this afternoon."

"Thank you. Thank you so much." After another hug, she headed back to her own shop. "I put an OUT TO LUNCH sign on the door—pretty lame, for someone who sells food!" Passing Sarah at the counter, she added, "I need to do what you did, Cassie, and hire an assistant."

"Or train Tigger to work the cash register," I suggested. "Try to relax, okay? We'll get to the bottom of this."

Once Dawn had left, I heard Sarah tut-tutting next to me. "She dragged you into that mess. I just knew she would."

"Now, be fair. Dawn doesn't usually get me embroiled in murder investigations. Up until now, I've managed to do that all by myself." I heard the jazzy tones of "Stray Cat Strut" from my phone and checked the ID. "This is Mark. Maybe he can at least help me solve the mystery of the scabby Sphynx."

"Hi, what's up?" he asked.

"I'm sure you're busy, so I won't keep you long," I began. "Anyway, this is work-related."

"So I gathered. You want help with your cranky customer?"

"Mr. Bock seems to be losing confidence in his usual veterinarian. You said last night that you'd be willing to give him a second opinion. Can I tell him to call you?"

"Sure, we'll fit him in. I'm actually pretty curious about this mystery rash—just as long as it isn't some new plague that's going to spread to all my other patients." Mark must have heard my startled hiss, because he reassured me, "Kidding. At least, I'm almost positive that I am."

"Thanks, babe. I owe you one."

"Hmm . . . you already do, don't you?"

He probably meant because of our interrupted date. "And that's one debt I won't mind paying off," I purred.

"Really?" His tone also went husky and intimate. "Talk to your mother yet?"

Oops, I walked straight into that one. *Dirty pool, Mark!*

"I will," I promised. "Haven't had the chance, between Bock and Dawn . . . She's convinced her friend Sabrina was murdered."

Mark groaned. "Don't tell me. She wants you to investigate."

"She just asked me to talk to Bonelli, which shouldn't do any harm. I don't plan to get any more involved than that."

"You shouldn't," he said. "And speaking of plans, remember that Thanksgiving is only two weeks away."

"I'll talk to Mom soon, I promise. And thanks again for making time to see Bock."

Letting Mark get back to work, I warned myself that I wouldn't be able to dodge the holiday question much longer. But I could put it off until I made good on two other promises. I phoned Bock, got his voice mail, and left a message with Mark's name and the clinic's number. Then I called Angela Bonelli and asked if I could stop by and give her some information about Sabrina Ward's death.

For someone not actually on the Chadwick police force, I'd spent a fair amount of time over the past few months down at the station, usually sitting in Detective Bonelli's glass-walled office. Her furnishings were modest and mostly old-school: a Formica-topped, L-shaped computer desk; a black, multiline phone with an actual cord; a framed vacation photo of her husband, Lou, with their two preteen boys. On a metal table against one wall stood a burgundy Keurig coffeemaker, usually brewing something aromatic.

It was all low-key but well-organized, as was her appearance. Bonelli's work wardrobe ran to pantsuits in neutral shades combined with pastel shirts or high-necked sweaters and low-heeled pumps. She wore her dark hair in a practical, chin-length bob and sometimes fell behind schedule in touching up the gray roots. I'd never seen anything but the same pair of small silver hoops on her earlobes. When she took the time to apply makeup, it was basic shadow, blush, and lip gloss; her nails generally went unpolished. She used half glasses only for reading fine print, and they looked like the kind you could pick up in a drugstore. This was not a woman who'd accept nonsense from anybody, though at times she could appreciate the absurdity of some of the cases that came across her desk.

I occupied the straight and rock-hard visitor's chair that seemed designed to discourage civilians from wasting too much of her time. But at least Bonelli was willing to share with me a few of the details her team had discovered that might suggest whether Sabrina had met with foul play.

"We went through her condo and found vials with two types of blood pressure medication," she told me. "Both were from more than a year ago and still had pills in them. From the information on the labels, we called her doctor, and he confirmed that Sabrina hadn't come to see him in a while."

"That doesn't prove—" I began.

"The ME found a seventy-five-percent blockage in her

coronary artery. Now, if that condo meeting the night before was as heated as you and Dawn say, it's possible the stress built up for Sabrina and brought on her heart attack. But that's what killed her, not her fellow residents."

"What about her scarf? Dawn said the end of it was wound around one of the low branches in an odd way."

"The ME wondered about that, too. She had some neck abrasions that looked as if she might have found herself caught, fallen, and struggled, but the force wouldn't have been enough to strangle her."

"Could *that* have triggered her heart attack?"

"It might have. Still an accident." Bonelli shrugged. "None of it really is surprising. She insisted on going out into those woods at night, even in the snow. She had hip problems and used a cane. She had cataracts, and the only glasses she had were such an old prescription that she seldom even wore them. The woman just didn't take very good care of herself."

I remembered the thrift-shop clothes and obviously home-dyed hair. "Maybe she didn't have the money."

Bonelli responded with a small, sour smile. "Whatever problems she may have had, poverty wasn't one of them. Sabrina married well—the Wards are an old, wealthy family in this area. As Philip's widow, she had an inheritance to last a lifetime. Plus, she'd gotten a bargain on her condo. Her brother-in-law, Victor Ward, is a vice president of To Market, the advertising firm that represents Gladstone Development. That's the chain that created The Reserve and three other communities like it in New Jersey. Apparently Gladstone is gearing up now to move into Pennsylvania."

Bonelli was interrupted by a call, and while she discussed the outcome of another case with Doug Hardy, the police chief, I could tell she was trying to be circumspect. I sensed that I was taking her attention away from more important matters. But if this turned out to be a murder, what could be more important?

I slumped back in my chair, a bit thrown by this new information. The other residents at The Reserve had seemed to feel that Sabrina didn't fit in, so I'd assumed she was poor and living there on someone's charity. That if something happened to her, no one would miss her. Apparently, though, that wasn't the case.

Once Bonelli hung up the phone and turned her attention back to me, I told her, "Okay, I can see that you and your guys aren't blowing this off. You've really looked into Sabrina's health and her background. But still, you weren't at that board meeting. Some of the other Reserve residents said vicious things about her. Did you question that Mike Lawler guy, the one who said—"

"We did. He denied making any threats against Ms. Ward, and claimed that at the time of her death he was visiting his son in Delaware. The son confirmed this."

I wondered if that really qualified as an airtight alibi, but I didn't want to argue with Bonelli. "All I'm saying is that, with some of these residents, their anger seemed to go beyond just the cat issue. I think they felt Sabrina was an embarrassment, that she didn't belong there. And somebody *did* try to poison the cats, and ended up making a resident's dog very sick."

The detective acknowledged this with a nod. "Along with the autopsy, we're doing a toxicology screen, of course, but I don't expect it to turn up anything. The ME saw no sign that Sabrina was poisoned."

"I'm not saying she was, just that people were starting to play rough. Isn't it possible that one of them waited for her to come around for the evening feeding and pushed her or struggled with her? Wouldn't that leave some evidence?"

"We did a routine check for other hair and fibers, even skin cells. But if the other person wore winter clothes and gloves, he or she wouldn't have left many traces. And unfortunately, there weren't any footprints at the scene . . . not even Sabrina's. The ground around her, and even her body, had a dusting of fresh snow."

"Y'see? It *is* possible. Someone might even have left her there hoping the snow would cover his tracks. There's a resident manager, Sam Nolan, who was at the meeting. Does he live on the property?"

"He does, and his condo is fairly close to the woods, so we talked to him," Bonelli said. "His alibi for that night is pretty shaky. He said he went to the movies, alone, but didn't keep the ticket stub."

At the meeting, Nolan hadn't seemed all that worked up about the cat issue, but maybe he'd been smart enough not to show it. Or maybe somebody had paid him off to get rid of her.

I noticed Bonelli stealing a glance at the wall clock and once again sensed that I was keeping her from more urgent matters. Still, I thought of another angle that could be important. "Exactly how wealthy was Sabrina? If she has a will, who's in line to inherit?"

Bonelli shot me a patient look. "Of course, we're checking into all of that. We'll have the answers before we release her body for burial."

I dialed back my intensity. "Sorry. I know you and your department are good at what you do. It's just that Dawn's really upset. She idealized Sabrina, I think. Saw her as living a life dedicated to standing up for the underdog. Now she could be in need of someone to stand up for her."

The detective's dark brows drew together. "That's admirable, but I'd suggest you and Dawn both steer clear of this situation. If someone did kill this woman, we'll find him . . . or her. If not, though, you shouldn't be meddling in The Reserve's community business. In the past, Cassie, you've investigated situations related to cats that were boarded at your shop, and I understand that. But this case involves wild animals. They're not worth your being arrested, or worse."

I pretended to agree, but on the way out of the police station, I countered her argument in my head. *Except that, like Sabrina, the ferals have no one else to stand up for them.*

Back at the shop, I found Sarah at the front counter chatting with Gary Lukasha of YourWay Van Conversions. The FOCA crowd had put me on to Gary, who, with his modest height, tats, and ginger hair and beard, resembled a biker leprechaun. He explained that he'd had another stop in the area and decided to drop by to give me an estimate on the semi-derelict vehicle in my parking lot.

The two of us strolled back to assess the hulking van, which was commercial-sized and covered in dull black primer paint. At least the former owner had gotten it back into reliable, drivable condition before selling it to me.

After scrutinizing the van inside and out, Gary told me, "It's got good bones for what you want. Strong enough to support a generator, a water tank, hydraulic grooming table, and other heavy add-ons. Mainly, we'll need to install those things, raise the roof so you can stand inside, and give you ventilation, storage cabinets, and lighting."

I'd done some online research myself and agreed with all of this. "The interior would have to be easy to keep clean."

"Sure," he said. "For something like pet grooming, we'd use molded fiberglass. With insulation underneath, so you can work year-round. And of course, we'll repaint the exterior, with the name of your business and any other information you want."

The idea of such a makeover sounded exciting but also stirred fresh worries about whether I could afford it all. We went back into the shop to discuss specifics, and Gary said he'd write up an estimate and drop it off the next day.

Speaking of vans, an hour later Taffy's owner came by to pick her up. Then Sarah and I got to work on another boarder, a striking charcoal-gray Persian with round, orange eyes. She had a complicated purebred name, but for everyday just went by Spooky, and she could have been a walking Halloween decoration. For the most part she was easy to groom, though touchy about her paws—as many of my customers are—and impatient when I had to tease out any stubborn knots.

At least I didn't see many cats anymore who were declawed. I'd even heard that some vets absolutely refuse to do the procedure these days. Word has gotten around that declawing is cruel, probably leaves the cat with chronically sore paws, and even makes them more likely to become biters, once their first line of defense has been taken away from them.

While working on Spooky, I reflected again on my problems with Harry Bock. Whether by coincidence or ESP, Sarah quipped, optimistically, that we hadn't heard any more complaints from him in a whole twenty-four hours. I didn't even have a chance to answer her before my shop phone rang, provoking ominous chuckles from both of us. Judging by what little I could hear from the grooming studio, though, the message being left sounded like a woman's voice.

I wondered if it might be my mother. *You really have to call her, Cassie, and ask about going to Philly for Thanksgiving. It's only fair, since Mark is supposedly giving Bock a free consultation as a favor to you.* But why did I feel so reluctant?

"Sarah, I need some real-world advice from a mother of grown kids and a retired high school teacher," I said.

She worked baby powder into Spooky's dark coat to give it extra pouffiness. "I presume that means me?"

"You do fit the profile. Mark has asked me to come to Philly with him for Thanksgiving to meet his family, and it scares the crap out of me. I told him I didn't want to leave Mom on her own for the holiday, which is true. But mainly, I guess I feel as if it's a big step toward something serious."

My assistant pursed her lips in thought. "I can see why you'd feel that way. It's a little like going with your boyfriend to a family wedding."

"Exactly! He comes from a fairly big Italian clan. What if they pounce on us, asking stuff like, 'Did you two set a date?' Or worse, what if they don't like me? When we first started seeing each other, Mark had just gotten out of a really serious relationship. What if they act like, 'She's okay, but she's no Diane'?"

Sarah laughed loud enough to startle the Persian. "I can't imagine that. Didn't you tell me his last girlfriend cheated on him and then lied about it? They probably spit on the ground at the mention of her name!"

That made me smile. "I guess you're right. I don't know why I'm so skittish. I really do love Mark, and it's not like we're kids. But still, I'm not ready for the marriage pressure."

We finished Spooky, petted her for being a (mostly) good girl, and put her back into her condo.

"Well," Sarah said, "people don't get married these days as young as they used to. You've just started your business here, and you're doing pretty well. You have your apartment upstairs for space and privacy when you want it. Even if you do love Mark, maybe you're not ready just yet to give up your independence."

Her insight made me feel literally enlightened—as if a weight had been lifted. I wasn't necessarily neurotic, gun-shy from my last, oppressive relationship, or divided in my feelings for Mark. I was just happy with my life right now and with our relationship as it was. "That's really it, Sarah. Thank you for cutting through the murk! I guess the trouble is that I don't expect other people to understand or believe that explanation. I'm most afraid that Mark might not."

"Guess that's something you two need to talk about. If you're both on the same page, it won't matter so much what his family thinks."

"You're right, of course." I dusted gray fur from my apron. "That reminds me, I'd better check that phone message."

I heard an unfamiliar female voice that quavered a little with age. "Hello, Miss McGlone? My name is Edie Seibert. I live up at The Reserve, and I heard you speak at the board meeting the other night. I have a problem with my cat, and I hope you can help me." The woman left her phone number.

With a break in my day's schedule, I called Edie back.

"I read on your website that you're an expert in cat behavior," she began.

"I studied that in school, yes."

"I have a six-year-old tabby, Sonny, who's driving me crazy. He's always been a house cat and never gave me a problem before. But lately he's piddling outside his box, mostly in my family room. It's so embarrassing, because when my family or friends come to visit, that's where we sit to watch TV. The worst part is, I have a balance problem—they call it a vestibular disorder—and use a walker, so I can't do a whole lot of the cleaning up myself. Lately I've had the housekeeper come twice a week, and I'm sure she's also getting disgusted with the job."

"Sonny is fixed, I hope?"

"Oh, yes. He was a rescue, so they did that when he was a kitten."

I asked if the cat had seen a vet lately. She assured me that he had, and got a clean bill of health. Meanwhile, from my visit to Gwen's condo, I recalled how the typical town houses were designed, which suggested a possible explanation. "Do you have one of those family rooms that's mostly windows? With sliders opening onto a patio?"

"Yes, exactly. Sonny loves to sit there on his cat tree and look out at the woods. But wouldn't you know, that's right where he usually misbehaves. In this community, we're not allowed to let our pets roam, but . . . do you think he wants to go outside?"

"In a way. How close are you to the woods?"

She started to follow my train of thought. "Not awfully, but my patio does face in that direction. And the lady next door used to feed some of the feral cats, so they still come around. Could that be upsetting Sonny?"

"It could be, yes."

As we talked for a few more minutes, I could tell that Edie was an animal lover and didn't want to cause more trouble for the ferals, but she also couldn't go on living with Sonny's new habit. "Is there anything you can recommend?"

"Probably, but I'd need to have a look at your family room and the area just outside. Want me to drop by?"

"Oh, could you? I hate to impose, but I'd gladly pay. . . ."

"It's no imposition. I'd like to help you folks get along with the ferals, too, as far as it's possible. What time would be good for you?"

We made an appointment for later that evening. By the time I hung up, I realized it was already quarter to five.

Sarah, doing a final sweep of the studio, paused over her broom. "Sounds like the Cat Lady's work is never done."

I answered with a rueful smile. "Your son, Jay, once told me, when I was giving free cat advice at the street fair, that I should charge for the service. If I start having to make house calls, I might just do that."

"Where do you have to go?" When I told her, her eyebrows rose above the rims of her wire glasses. "Tell me you won't go poking around into that woman's death."

"Don't worry. Unlike Sabrina, I'm not brave enough to go traipsing into those woods alone. Not even to feed a bunch of hungry cats."

On the other hand, this might be a good chance to ask a sympathetic resident a few discreet questions. . . .

Chapter 7

Anyone could have detected the problem as soon as they stepped into Edie Seibert's living room. In spite of her housekeeper's best efforts, a faint *eau de* cat box perfumed the air even as far as the front door.

Edie greeted me at the door with a smile and kept one hand on her walker while the other clasped mine. "Thank you so much for coming." Probably in her late sixties, with white-blond hair that waved softly around her face, she wore a velour track suit in a deep rose color. It might not be the height of fashion, but at least the hue flattered her delicate pink skin tone and big blue eyes.

I heard a light thump, probably Sonny jumping down from his cat tree, and then the honey-colored tabby trotted up to join us. He rubbed lightly against my legs and let me scratch his fluffy cheek. "Seems like a sweet little guy," I said.

"He *is*." I heard dismay in Edie's voice. "That's why I can't believe he's suddenly acting like this. Why would he be upset about a few stray cats outside? They can't get in to hurt him."

"Sonny might not be so sure about that. Let's go have a look."

The three of us strolled through her living/dining area, traditionally furnished in burgundy and beige tones with an Oriental rug, a plump sofa, a pair of matching chairs, and formal window treatments. From what I could see, one tall sisal scratching post in here had been enough to distract Sonny from abusing the upholstered pieces.

We continued straight out to the family room, which was outfitted with more casual and sturdy furniture. I noticed right away that, except for one wall with a flat-screen TV above a low cabinet, all the others featured deep windows. They'd been dressed with pleated shades that could be lowered, I guessed, if the sun's glare got too intense. Vertical blinds partially hid the siding glass door to the outside, but Edie had left them open about a foot so Sonny could see out from the various levels of his cat tree.

The odor came through strongly here, and traces of stains showed along the edge of the carpet and even on the walls below the windows. They might be so entrenched by now that only a strong enzyme cleaner, specially formulated for pet mistakes, would remove them.

Meanwhile, Sonny hopped onto a middle shelf of his cat tree and peered into the dusk outside. After a second he pricked his ears and his slim, striped tail began to switch back and forth.

I pointed this out to Edie. "See that? Right now he's reacting to something out there. Is it okay if I close the blinds?"

She nodded, and I pulled them shut to block the cat's view. Sonny jumped down from the perch and sniffed along the bottom.

"Cats are very territorial," I explained. "It upsets them to be able to see or smell an unfamiliar animal around their home. The problem might be worse if it's a feral male that hasn't been fixed. He sprays outside to mark your patio as his territory, and

Sonny feels compelled to do the same thing inside to reclaim his turf."

"I see!" Edie sounded genuinely intrigued by this explanation. "But how do I deal with it?"

"Where are Sonny's actual litter boxes?" I asked.

"He just has one, in the laundry room."

I asked her permission to get the box and moved it out to the family room, right next to the patio door. "This should be the quickest and easiest fix. He's going to pee here anyway, so at least get him to use his box. It wouldn't be a bad idea to buy one or two more and put them along the other wall."

Edie wrinkled her nose but admitted, "I do have another, smaller one that he used when he was a kitten. I guess I could move them both in here, but . . ."

"I know. In the long run, you and your guests don't want to socialize or watch TV surrounded by litter boxes. And you shouldn't have to. But the rest of the solution is a little more complicated."

I explained that she could get a motion-sensitive system that would chase away any stray cat who ventured too close to the house. "Some spray water, but I wouldn't recommend that for the winter—you could end up with ice on your sidewalk and patio. There's another type, a canister that shoots a blast of air. You can get a couple and hide them close to the patio doors. They won't hurt the feral cats, just scare them. But after that happens once or twice, they'll avoid your house. And I predict Sonny will relax and go back to behaving like a gentleman."

"Sounds wonderful, but where would I get something like that? And how much do they cost?"

I explained that large pet supply stores usually stocked them and the prices were reasonable. "If you want, I can pick up a couple for you."

"Really? I feel like that's a lot to ask. And I'm sure I'd have to pay you for your trouble."

I knew she wouldn't want to be treated as a charity case. "Reimburse me for the cost of the items, and if you want, pay for my gas for running to the mall. How's that?"

Edie seemed satisfied with this arrangement, and we agreed upon a list of things I would pick up for her at the highway PetMart. As we returned to her living room, she turned somber. "I suppose you heard about what happened to Mrs. Ward, the woman who was feeding and taking care of those outdoor cats. So tragic! I can't imagine why she was stumbling around in those woods after dark. That would be dangerous for anyone."

I shrugged. "You saw at the meeting how hostile some of the residents were toward her. I guess Sabrina didn't want to draw too much attention to what she was doing."

Edie accompanied me to her front door with the aid of her walker, and I asked if she found it at all hard to navigate the two-story condo.

"Well, I moved here before I developed my balance problem," she said. "My daughter, who lives in New York, keeps telling me I should go into an apartment or a ranch house, something with just one level. But moving's a lot of trouble, and I like this community. Besides, I can climb the stairs fine with my walker." She demonstrated by folding the appliance to be more compact and using it almost as a cane, along with the banister, to help her climb a few steps.

I smiled. "Looks like you've got it all worked out—that's great! Anyway, nice meeting you, and have a good evening."

"You, too, Cassie," she said.

Back outside, I was about to unlock my car when I saw movement down the walking path, at the edge of the woods. I remembered Sarah's warning and didn't plan to go charging blindly out there, but I did cross the parking lot for a better look. A dark SUV had parked at the curb, and two figures with flashlights, in hooded down jackets, were unloading bags from the vehicle's hatch. At first I worried that I'd stumbled across another attempt at poisoning the ferals, and ducked behind some bushes to watch. The figures moved too quickly and nimbly, I thought, to be any of the older residents of The Reserve that I'd seen at the meeting. Then one pushed down her hood to reveal a shaggy cap of pale blond hair, and when she half-turned, I recognized Becky Newmeyer from FOCA, whom I'd met during a rescue effort that summer.

Still quietly, I stepped out to say hello to her. "I guess you're the only ones feeding the cats now?"

She dropped her gaze sadly. "We are, now that Sabrina's gone. I still can't believe it—she was such a force of nature."

"I just met her briefly, a couple of nights ago, but I sensed the same thing."

Becky's companion, a slim young man I recognized as Chris Eberhardt, emerged from the woods, and I nodded in his direction. Both of them, I knew, were college students and fit their volunteer work into their spare time.

"I can see that you two are being careful," I said. "Do you think the community will let FFF keep coming here?"

"It's anybody's guess," Chris told me. "Sabrina was a resident, and she also had money and connections. She arranged for the security guard, Lee, to let us in. But now, if the community decides to ban us, he could just stop us at the gate."

"Then the cats won't eat this winter, except for whatever prey they can catch themselves," I concluded.

Becky sniffed. "It could be worse than that. They could call animal control to round up all the ferals and destroy them. There are some residents pushing for that to be done."

"Well, some others are on our side," Chris reminded her.

"We just have to hope those people are willing to stand up and be counted."

"It takes more," Becky insisted. "You have to rally people. You have to call in favors, put on pressure, make noise. Sabrina was good at all that." Her tone turned bitter. "Though, in the end, where did it get her?"

She didn't sound as if she were referring to Sabrina's heart attack. "What do you mean, Becky?"

The girl's expression made her look tired beyond her years. "You figure it out." Then she tossed an empty cat food sack into the hatch of the SUV, hitched herself into the passenger seat, and she and Chris drove away.

That night I was trying to work up the nerve to finally phone my mother when she called me instead. I told her about my cranky customer Bock—leaving out his threat to sue me—and about the death of Dawn's friend Sabrina, omitting the possibility that she could have been murdered. Mom can handle bad news as long as it doesn't seem to pose any immediate threat to me.

Eventually we came around to the subject of Thanksgiving, with Mom announcing plans to purchase a twelve-pound turkey and experiment a bit with the stuffing and side dishes. "You're probably getting tired of the same old thing we've always done," she said, with a happy lilt, "so I've been searching around online for some new ideas."

I hated to interrupt her, but I figured sooner would be better than later. "Actually, I'm in kind of an awkward spot. The other night, Mark invited me to spend Thanksgiving in Philadelphia with him and his family. I told him I always go to your place so you don't have to spend the holiday alone. He gets that, but he still seemed disappointed. So I promised I'd at least talk to you about it."

For a few seconds, I heard nothing on the phone and figured Mom was as taken by surprise as I had been. I suppose in the old days there would have been etiquette books to cover things like this. *How should courting couples decide whose family to visit for the holidays?* Or would the question not even have come up until they'd been dating at least a year?

Finally, a sad little laugh from my mother. "Kind of pathetic, isn't it? That at your age you should have to worry about holding my hand on every holiday so I don't get blue?"

"No, Mom, not at all. It's a special situation. Dad's only been gone three years, and we don't have any other relatives close by." My father's people all lived in the Midwest, and though my mother still had some cousins in upstate New York, due to various nonsensical grudges that went back decades, we'd become estranged from them. "I can understand why you wouldn't want to be alone when other people are celebrating together."

"But I can't stand in the way of your happiness, either. I know how much you like Mark, and if he asked you to meet his family, he must care a lot for you, too."

I decided to be honest and told her, with a chuckle, "Actually, it threw me a little that he wanted me to meet them over Thanksgiving dinner. No pressure, right?"

"I'm sure they'll love you, Cassie. Who wouldn't?"

Gee, that was bordering on mushy talk for my mom. Now I really felt torn. "But you were making all those plans to cook. . . ."

"I can do that another time. If you won't be coming, I'll just get something easy for myself."

I tried to think of a compromise. "Maybe you and I can do Thanksgiving a day late, on Friday?"

"There's an idea!" Then her enthusiasm flagged. "But

they're predicting a bad snowstorm that Friday. It's supposed to come right up the East Coast. A lot of people at work have said that wherever they're going for the holiday, they plan to stay put there until the weekend, or until they dig themselves out."

"Wow, I didn't hear about that." Mom tended to follow the Weather Channel a lot more religiously than I did, maybe because she still commuted to a job. No way did I want to risk being stranded a couple of hours away from my apartment and my shop for that long. Even though I had few boarders at the moment—probably because of the looming holiday—I still had my own three cats to think of. Their automatic feeder only held so much dry food.

"How about this," I brainstormed out loud. "Maybe I can drive down to Philly on my own—follow Mark, if I'm able to. I can meet his family and have an early dinner there. Then I'll come back to your place and we can eat supper at the usual time. Even if I have to stay at your condo overnight, with the snowstorm, it shouldn't be too hard for me to get to my shop the next day."

"Gee, Cassie, that sounds like an awful lot of driving for you. Especially if the weather's bad."

I used my phone to quickly check the forecast. "Like you said, Friday's supposed to be the worst day, starting in the morning. So I should be okay driving on Thursday." For the moment, I ignored Mark's reminder that Thanksgiving getaway traffic was notoriously bad. "I'll see how Mark feels about the plan, but it could work for everybody."

"Thanks, dear. I really would like to spend the holiday with you, if I can."

After hanging up, I calculated the number of miles I'd have to cover to pull off this scheme. But it would make Mom happy and also limit my exposure to Mark's family, just in case things in Philly got uncomfortable. For that, I could put up with a few highway hassles.

Anyone who thinks family holidays are supposed to be relaxing, though, must live in a dream world!

Chapter 8

"When you told me the name of that woman who died in the woods, I thought I'd heard it somewhere before." Sarah set her big, saddle-brown satchel of a purse on the sales counter and pulled out the latest copy of the *Chadwick Courier*, folded open to the obituary page. "This brought it all back to me. She helped expose the Merrywood Suites scandal, about six years ago."

I took the paper from her. I had read Sabrina's obit online over my breakfast that morning, but hadn't paid particular attention to any of the various causes she'd championed over the years. "Oh, yeah? I vaguely remember hearing about that at the time. That used to be a pretty fancy hotel chain, right?"

Sarah nodded, a fierce spark in her eye that I'd rarely seen before. "My cousin Yolanda worked as a hostess in the restaurant at their Morristown hotel. She was pretty and had to dress up for the job, so she got hit on all the time. The crude comments she could put up with, but a few times things also got physical. She complained to the management but was told to play nice and not to be rude to the customers."

"Swell." I could easily imagine this no-win situation; every woman probably encounters something like it at least once or twice in her life.

"Turns out, it was even worse for the housekeeping maids. They got harassed not only by the guests but by their supervisor. Almost all of them were either black or Latina, worked for low pay, and couldn't afford to quit or get fired."

"That's terrible," I said. "How did Sabrina get involved?"

"Somehow she heard about it—maybe one of the women approached her. They wanted to file a class action suit, but even together, they couldn't afford a good lawyer. Sabrina had money, so she hired one for them, a heavy hitter. Then she reached out to all the women who had made complaints, including my cousin, and persuaded them to meet with the lawyer and tell their stories."

From her bag, Sarah fished a second newspaper clipping, slightly yellowed and with bits of tape still clinging to the edges. "I had this tucked away in a family scrapbook because it was a great thing for Yolanda at the time."

The six-year-old article described the success of the class action, and the discovery that Merrywood's "culture of sexual harassment and discrimination" ran through its entire chain of seven luxury hotels in New Jersey and New York State. It mentioned Sabrina's name only briefly, but a group photo showed her smiling broadly along with several of the women involved in the suit.

"Terrific!" I said. "I already respected her for defending the ferals, but now I really understand why Dawn thought so highly of her. Dawn never mentioned this case to me, though. I wonder if she knows about it."

"If they've been friends for so many years, she probably does."

Sarah started to tuck the clipping back into her purse, but when I asked, she let me photocopy it first. Instinct told me that if Sabrina's death had been foul play, the information in the article just might come in handy.

The two of us got to work then. A couple of customers were picking up boarders that afternoon. Both cats were short-hairs, but we gave them quick groomings anyway so they'd look their best for their owners. Around eleven I took a coffee break and, with almost clairvoyant timing, Mark called me.

"I saw your pal Harry Bock." With a sad chuckle, he added, "Boy, that cat of his caught a rough break, didn't she? She looks like a kid with measles."

"I know. Bet she'd give anything right now for a nice, normal fur coat. So, what do you think?"

"Well, I've got a theory that might make everyone happier, if I'm right. I think it's a food allergy."

"But Bock brought us the same food she was eating at home, and we gave her nothing except that the whole time she was here."

"I know, but he told me he'd just started her on that food a week before, and allergies can take a little while to show up. He said Looli is a picky eater and this was the first food she really liked. But I don't think it likes her."

"Wouldn't she have some digestive issues, though, if that was the case?"

"You'd think so, but that's more typical of a food intolerance. A food *allergy* is more likely to cause itching or a rash."

"So, what's the solution? He already balked when the other doctor wanted to do an expensive series of allergy tests."

"That may not be necessary. I recommended an elimination diet and gave him a list of foods that are the least likely to cause problems. There's enough variety that even Looli should like some of them. If that works and the rash goes away, she'll feel better, Bock will be satisfied, and you'll be off the hook."

"You're a genius!" I told him, warmly. "Thanks so much."

"My pleasure. I like coming up with solutions that make everybody happy."

"Speaking of such things . . ." It seemed the perfect time to bring up my plan for the impending holiday. "What time does your family usually eat Thanksgiving dinner?"

I heard the upbeat shift in his tone. "Usually in the afternoon, around three or four. Of course, everybody tends to get hungry again later on, and we pick at the leftovers."

"That's perfect. Here's my plan." I explained why I thought it would make sense for me to share the early meal with him and his family, then drive back and have a later version with my mother, especially because of the forecasted snowstorm. "I'd really like to spend more time with you, but besides not wanting Mom to be all alone, I can't risk being stranded away from my shop for too long. I've still got four cats boarding over the holiday to take care of."

"I do see your point," he said, but the note of disappointment crept back in. "Going to look a little strange, though, if we drive down separately."

"I know, but I certainly don't want to cut your visit short, and this is the best solution I can think of. Besides," I added lightly, "if I don't stay overnight, at least we'll avoid any awkward issues about where I'll sleep."

Mark paused for a second, then came back with a half-serious quip of his own. "If I didn't know better, Cassie, I'd think you were trying to avoid spending too much time with my family."

I forced a laugh. "Of course not. Why would I do that? I've never even met them."

"Exactly. They don't bite, I promise." That comment apparently reminded Mark of his patients. "Look, right now I'd better get back to work. I'm not against your idea, but we'll talk again before Thanksgiving, okay?"

"Absolutely."

When he signed off, I blew out a breath. At least I'd given myself an escape clause, if I needed one.

I put the phone away to see Dawn chatting with Sarah at the front counter. Joining them, I asked my friend, "Who's minding your store?"

"Tigger, of course—he's really getting good with the cash register! Seriously, it's slow today, so I figured I could close for a few minutes."

I spotted the newspaper clipping on the counter between her and my assistant. "Sarah showed me that story this morning. Did you know Sabrina was involved in that suit?"

"I remember her mentioning it in passing," Dawn said. "But I was so young then, I don't think I realized what a big deal it was. And Sarah telling me about her cousin makes it so much more real to me."

"I know Yolanda will always feel grateful to Sabrina," Sarah said. "She'd been feeling trapped, beaten down. But when they won in court, it gave her back her confidence. She went on to get a good job in a respectable hotel, and she's reservations manager there today."

"Sounds like Sabrina left a worthy legacy," I said.

"That's what I came to talk to you about," Dawn said, with an intent look. "They've scheduled her funeral for tomorrow. It's way down in South Jersey, though—she asked for a green burial, at a natural site with just a pine casket, and only a few places do that. So of course that means the autopsy's completed, and the police probably don't expect to find out anything suspicious about her death."

I wasn't so sure. "When I talked to Bonelli, she said they'd keep checking out Sabrina's contacts. The other residents, her relatives . . . especially anyone who might stand to inherit money in her will."

"Anybody expecting that will probably get a rude surprise. She once said something to me, offhandedly, about leaving her money to a couple of favorite charities. She supported them in her life, and I suspect she planned to keep doing it after she died."

I considered this. As Dawn said, it would be consistent with the woman's character. Meanwhile, Sarah asked me if she should turn out Heckle and Jeckle—two "magpie" brothers who boarded with us often—into the playroom. I gave her the go-ahead.

After my assistant had left us via the door in the screen, Dawn resumed her analysis of what she believed was Sabrina's murder. "I heard that her brother-in-law, Victor, is named as her executor. He plans to come by her condo later this week and clean it out. That means anything that might show she was murdered, and by whom, will disappear."

"That's rough, Dawn, but there's nothing you can do about it."

"Oh, no?" She reached into her shoulder bag and pulled out a braided leather key chain with two standard-sized brass keys. "Since my mother was the only one at The Reserve that Sabrina trusted, she gave Mom spare emergency keys to her place. I think bringing her killer to justice qualifies as an emergency, don't you?"

"I don't know about that. If she's dead, and the police are investigating, I don't think you can just go in there. . . ."

"They never did put up police tape at her town house. And Victor Ward may be her executor, but that doesn't mean the place is his. I'm going there tonight, before he can destroy any evidence." Dawn thrust the keys back into her purse with a determined air. "It's not like I'm going to steal anything. Just look for clues. Things like that newspaper clipping, maybe. See if she had any protests planned that someone wanted to stop. I've been thinking just in terms of her neighbors, Cassie. But the *Courier* ran a story last month about the feral cat problems at The Reserve and mentioned Sabrina's name. Anyone from her past could have seen that and figured out where to find her . . . and how to kill her."

Sarah returned from the playroom in time to hear the end of this argument. "I hate to stir up trouble," she said, "but Dawn's right about that."

"You don't need to come along," my friend assured me. "I can get away with it, because I have a legit reason for coming to the community—watching my mother's place while she's away."

I sighed. "Actually, I have business there, too. I promised Edie Seibert that I'd install a couple of cat repellent devices outside near her patio. If you can stop off at PetMart on the way, I'll come with you."

Chapter 9

It took me just a few minutes to place two motion-sensing devices near Edie Seibert's patio. I used short bungee cords to attach one can to her lattice privacy screen and to hide another within the lower branches of a dormant azalea bush just outside her sliding doors. They faced inward, so any animal approaching her doors would be startled by a blast of air. I figured the trick should be particularly effective with cats, who react strongly to any kind of hissing or spitting noise.

Edie thanked me for my trouble and reimbursed me for the cost of the products. She also said Sonny was doing less damage now that he had two litter pans around the perimeter of the family room, and was staying a bit calmer since she had started closing the slider blinds at night. We both expressed hope that the new air blasters would keep the ferals at bay and solve her problem once and for all.

"Y'know," she said, "after we talked last time about that Ward woman having a heart attack in the woods, I remembered something. I often sit in the family room at night, watching TV with the lights low so I can see the screen better. That evening, when I was watching the ten o'clock news, I thought I heard some kind of commotion outside in the distance. At first I thought it was coming from the program—they were showing footage of cops breaking up an angry political rally—but then I heard a woman's scream. It wasn't until the next day, when I found out about Sabrina, that I wondered if it was her! Maybe when she felt herself falling, she screamed for help?" Edie glanced down at her walker. "Of course, I couldn't have done much to save her myself. But if I'd thought someone was in trouble out in the woods, I'd have called security. So I feel bad about that."

"Did you mention that to the police when they were here?" I asked.

Edie looked embarrassed. "None of them questioned me. Even if they had, at the time I might not have remembered. It just came back to me the other night when I was sitting alone out in the family room. Do you think I should tell someone?"

"I can mention it to Detective Bonelli, if you're okay with that."

She gave a single, brisk nod. "I'd like to know if anyone else in the community heard anything."

Leaving Edie's place, I reflected that the noise probably had come from her TV, after all. A person being choked by her scarf probably wouldn't have wind enough to scream. In fact, she probably also wouldn't have been able to scream if she were suffering a heart attack.

But maybe if she'd seen someone about to attack her . . . ?

After that, I strolled a few doors down to Sabrina's condo, where I found Dawn already sleuthing away.

Both Edie's and Sabrina's homes had been built within the last five years, with similar layouts and materials. Yet the atmospheres inside were worlds apart. Edie's home epitomized con-

ventional good taste, and though she had mobility issues, she
paid a housekeeper to visit twice a week and keep it in perfect
order.

Sabrina Ward's condo would have taxed the skills of any
housekeeper. And although it showed signs of having been ti-
died up since her death, the air held onto a faintly stale smell.

She'd obviously furnished the place with secondhand pieces
chosen for utility rather than style. The living room's boxy orange tweed sofa wore several Indian-print shawls as throws,
possibly to hide threadbare spots. A low Mediterranean-style
chest supported the squarish, old-school TV. Two oversized
floor pillows in fake animal prints—one leopard and one
zebra—supplied extra seating, along with an orange molded-
plastic chair that might have wandered away from some school
cafeteria. At least the small dining table matched the buffet,
both with a rough-hewn, Mexican look. Twin bookshelves—
the collapsible kind college students use in their dorms—were
stuffed to bursting with volumes on inspirational, ecological,
and political topics.

"Funny," I said to Dawn. "Sabrina lived alone, but it looks
like she was always ready to accommodate a crowd."

"She probably was. I came here a couple of times when she
was meeting with the FFF people. Wouldn't surprise me if she
used it as a home base for her other causes, too."

The walls throughout the living-dining area displayed eco-
nomically framed artworks and various knickknacks on float-
ing shelves, all with either a souvenir or a handmade look.
Sabrina also had framed a small poster of the famous Calvin
Coolidge quote that begins, "Nothing in this world can take
the place of persistence."

The one item that looked expensive, and as if its display involved some real thought, was an art nouveau silver frame
about six inches high that stood in the center of the buffet. It

held a slightly faded color photo of a fit, handsome, blond man, maybe in his thirties, in warm-weather hiking clothes. His white grin stood out against his deep tan as he leaned against the massive trunk of a tropical tree.

Dawn noticed me peering at the photo. "That was Phil. Her husband."

"No kidding." I swallowed my surprise that someone as . . . well, plain as Sabrina had snared such a good-looking partner. From what everyone said, she'd also lured him away from a life of wealth and comfort.

"He died pretty young," Dawn told me. "Awful story. He picked up some weird brain parasite while they were in South America, when he went swimming in a river. Didn't see a doctor until they came back to the States, and by then he was too far gone. Guess he was the love of Sabrina's life. They'd never had any children, and she never remarried."

"Was Phil into causes, too?"

"Big time, according to her. They met at the end of their college years, at a peace rally, I think—it would've been toward the end of the Vietnam era. Guess they hit it off right away. Phil told her he was impressed by how much she knew about the issues and how passionate she was." Dawn smiled ruefully. "Of course, I think Sabrina also might have been a bit cuter back then. A free-spirited, hippie girl of the sixties."

I glanced around again. "She may have lost Phil, but it doesn't seem like she ever lost any of that passion."

"You haven't seen the half of it yet. Check out the family room . . . or, in her case, the command center."

Transformed by Sabrina, that modest space did resemble base camp for an underfunded third world revolution. Matchstick blinds, half lowered, would have modified the sunroom effect by day and gave us privacy now after dark. The rear windows were blocked the rest of the way by three office surplus file cabinets with more books and pamphlets stacked on top. A desk with peeling wood veneer held an old-fashioned desktop PC and a wire in-basket that overflowed with papers.

Dawn stood facing a freestanding bulletin board, and I joined her. It displayed many tacked-on notices, including the latest *Courier* article about the feral problem at The Reserve and the memo about the special meeting. Nearby, the only solid half wall almost disappeared beneath a cascade of strident posters, overlapping in spots, that demanded justice and equal rights for women, minorities, immigrants, and animals.

"The police saw all of this?" I asked my friend. "They must've also checked her storage unit for bomb-making materials!"

"All I know is, they searched and confiscated as much as they felt they needed to. This was never an actual crime scene, anyway. I give Bonelli credit for checking out Sabrina's home at all." She pulled out her phone. "Cassie, I'm going to take pictures of anything I think might be relevant. Maybe you can make some notes?"

"No problem." I plucked up a small spiral pad and a pen from the cluttered desktop, not sure what I was looking for. Like a forensic photographer, Dawn roamed around snapping shots of the bulletin board notices and the top layer of documents that littered Sabrina's desk.

I tried the file cabinets, too. None were locked. Sabrina had neatly labeled the folders inside, though the titles meant little to me. Each tab included something like a proper name of a person or location paired with some indication of the subject matter, such as "investigation," "complaint," or "abuse."

Only when I got further back in the alphabet did I come across a familiar reference: "Merrywood Harassment." I pulled out the file and flipped through it quickly. It contained copies of legal briefs, an official statement on the settlement of the class action in favor of the hotel workers, and personal thank-you letters some of them had sent to Sabrina afterward.

I advised Dawn, "When you're done over there, you might want to photograph this material."

She crossed to where I stood and leafed through the folder, too. "Hell, yeah! See if you can find any more stuff like this. Cases where she really stuck it to some bad guys."

I walked my fingers through the rest of the files and found two or three more that might fit that description, including a disreputable pet breeder called Wags 'n' Hugs and a small town with an untreated toxic waste site. I jotted some notes, then let Dawn take pictures of the paperwork.

"You didn't find her will in those cabinets, by any chance?" she asked me.

"Nope, nothing that personal. Maybe the police already found it and took it as evidence. After all, if someone did kill Sabrina, the most likely suspect would be someone who stood to inherit from her."

We toiled for over an hour before we both grew tired, more mentally than physically. My friend finally planted her hands on her hips and declared, "There's just *so* much here. I can almost forgive the cops for not going through her stuff too intensively. How on earth do you sort out what's important from what's not?"

"If Sabrina had been a major public figure, maybe they'd have been more thorough," I suggested. "And if they seriously believed she was murdered."

"That's the damn trouble. Too many people didn't take her seriously."

Remembering the successful Merrywood case, and others like it that I'd come across in her files, I wagered that at least a few people over the years had learned to take Sabrina very seriously.

"Think it's worth searching upstairs?" Dawn asked. "From what Bonelli told me, the cops went through her bedroom and bathroom looking for medications that related to her health problems. I'd feel kind of creepy poking around those private areas, but you never—"

A tall silhouette strode swiftly past the shaded family room windows, following the paved walkway. A second later, we heard the muffled sound of a key turning in the front lock.

Dawn's eyes met mine. We both muttered the same sibilant four-letter word.

"Who else has a key?" I asked.

She shrugged. "Dunno. At least I parked my car in front of Mom's place."

But we'd left a lamp on in the living room. Unless Sabrina had been in the habit of keeping one on a timer—which didn't seem likely—that would give us away.

The front door shut and steps echoed from the entry hall.

"What do we do?" I asked. "Hide?" Not much chance of that, though, with the condo's open floor plan.

Too late, anyway. A man's voice called out in accusation, "Hello! Is somebody here?"

Dawn whispered, "Let me handle this." Straightening to her full five foot nine, enhanced tonight by her stack-heeled boots, she marched back toward the dining room. I practically tiptoed in her wake.

Even my friend's extra height did not put her on an equal footing with the man who waited in Sabrina's living room. He stood over six feet, and his well-cut silver hair and dark tweed overcoat gave him a prosperous, executive air.

When he scowled at Dawn, she headed off his ire with a sweet smile. "You must be Sabrina's brother-in-law. Victor, isn't it?" She held out her slim hand.

He took it, but with obvious reservations. "And who are *you*, young lady?"

"We haven't met. I'm Dawn Tischler. My mother and I were good friends of Sabrina. And this is Cassie McGlone." When she glanced back over her shoulder at me, I dared to step forward.

"You two live here at The Reserve?" Ward asked, still guarded.

"My mom does. Gwen Tischler?" Dawn gave her standard explanation about watching the condo in her mother's absence.

"That still doesn't explain why you're here, in my late sister-in-law's home, at almost nine o'clock at night. How the hell did you even get in?"

Dawn socialized with enough neo-hippies and New Agers to be able to act ditzy when it served her purposes. Now she grimaced in classic Diane Keaton style—*I'm so-o-o stupid!*—and fluttered one hand next to her temple. "I'm sorry, I can only imagine what you must think! Y'see, Sabrina gave my mom a spare key to use in case of an emergency, and I figured this counted. I was just worried about the poor kitties. I know Sabrina would want someone to take care of them."

Bewildered, Victor shook his head. "She didn't have any pets."

"No, but she was trying to provide for the feral cats in the community. I'm honoring her memory by taking up where she left off. Cassie and I"—she glanced at me again—"were checking to see if she left any food or other supplies here in the house."

We had come from the direction of the family room, not the kitchen, and I worried that Victor might have noticed that. So I jumped in. "We also thought maybe she'd kept some records about the cats in her office. Which ones have been fixed and vaccinated so far, that kind of thing."

He fixed me with a sharp look. "And what's your involvement in all this?"

I explained about my business, and that it sometimes included dealing with animals that had behavior problems. "Earlier tonight I was helping Ms. Seibert, around the corner, set up devices to keep the ferals off her patio."

"I don't know or care anything about those damned cats," he snapped. "Sabrina made nothing but trouble for both of us, carrying on about them the way she did. I regret that I ever arranged for her to move here. I should have known she wouldn't fit in."

Still playing the innocent, Dawn persisted. "But she was trying to help the residents here solve the problem, and I'm sure many of them appreciated it. My mother certainly did."

Victor only harrumphed at this and made Dawn hand over the spare key. "I can't stop you from dropping by your mother's place, or your friend from doing errands for other residents. But I'd better not hear about either of you hanging around *this* unit again. I'm Sabrina's executor, and no one comes in here without my permission. Is that clear?"

"Of course." Dawn ducked her head contritely. "Very sorry for the confusion."

Victor stepped past us into the dining area and scanned it, as if making sure we hadn't removed anything valuable. He must have realized, though, the futility of his effort. First, how could anyone tell if something was missing from all that clutter? And second, Sabrina didn't seem to own anything valuable. Except maybe that silver picture frame.

Then it struck me, only because I was looking for it, that her brother-in-law did bear a distinct resemblance to the young blond man leaning against the tree. It took me a minute to notice, because Victor certainly lacked the adventurous, life-loving attitude that Sabrina had captured in her photo of Phil.

"God," he muttered, "it'll take at least a week to clear out all of this stuff. At this point, it'll probably have to wait until after Thanksgiving. And most will have to go in a Dumpster."

Dawn's eyebrows shot up. "Maybe I could take some things off your hands. The files in her office . . . records of all the things she's accomplished . . . They should be preserved. If you're just going to throw them away—"

"*I'll* deal with my sister-in-law's estate, thank you very much." Still in his coat, Victor angled his body sharply toward the front door, showing us out. As we passed him, he muttered, "As for the cat nonsense, now that Sabrina's passed, I'm sure it will disappear, too. The community will probably round up those strays and get rid of them, as they should have done a long time ago."

Chapter 10

In the spirit of her role model, Sabrina, Dawn does not respond well to threats. Neither do I, for that matter. But at the moment, I was most afraid that my friend might do something rash.

"That man is *not* going to destroy her legacy," Dawn vowed, behind the wheel on our drive home. "I may not legally be able to keep him from disposing of her files, but I'm going to do whatever I can to protect that feral colony."

"Do I need to point out that you never even liked cats much before little Tigger wandered into your life?"

"Well, he—and you—have converted me. But I'm also determined to find out if there's any possibility that Sabrina was murdered."

"The medical examiner said she died of a heart attack," I reminded Dawn.

"That scarf also had been pulled pretty tight around her neck. Maybe someone tried to strangle her, but didn't need to finish the job because she died of fright."

"And you rib me about reading too many mystery novels!" But it was time to come clean with another piece of evidence.

"I didn't want to tell you this—I thought it would just make you feel worse—and that there probably was nothing to it. . . ." I related what Edie had said about having heard distant sounds of a struggle, followed by a scream, the night Sabrina had died.

Dawn shot me a sideways, wide-eyed glance. "Oh, my God, that's it. That must be how it happened. We have to find out if anyone else heard it, people in that part of the complex!"

Ordinarily I might have questioned her use of "we," but I was starting to buy into her theory. Plus, I did not like the idea of Dawn taking on this quest alone. "Bonelli and her guys already questioned some of the residents, but I'll tell her that Edie heard something suspicious. They should be the ones to follow up."

"You've told me yourself, in the past, that people are on their guard when they know they're talking to a cop. They might open up more to one of us."

That could be true, but I still thought we needed to give law enforcement the first crack. "Please do *not* go poking around asking questions, or go out to that feeding station at night by yourself. I know you're younger, healthier, and have faster reflexes than Sabrina, but we don't know who or what we're dealing with. Somebody still could get the drop on you out in those woods. Or even in an empty condo at night."

It surprised me when my friend didn't even argue. "I guess I can coordinate with the FFF people and partner up with one of them every time I tend to the station or the shelters. But going to The Reserve during the day and asking questions shouldn't be too risky."

"Even so, tread carefully. Maybe I can help you with that. Two of us can talk to twice as many people, right?"

That drew a wide smile. "I was hoping you'd offer, Cassie. After all, you've got some experience at this. Even a record of success!"

"Well, records were made to be broken. But I'd like you at least to feel satisfied that Sabrina died of purely natural causes." I mulled a second. "How about the Saturday after Thanksgiving? We'll both be free in the afternoon, and probably a lot of visitors will still be coming and going at The Reserve."

Dawn's face lit up. "Yes! That should be a great time for us to blend in. We'll visit some of the common areas and strike up conversations. Oh, Cassie, thank you for helping me. You're the best friend!"

"Want to make it up to me?" I asked, with a skewed smile. "You're staying in town for the holiday, right?"

"Believe it or not, Keith will be back home through the weekend, and I'm making dinner for just the two of us."

"At your place?" I knew Dawn's boyfriend had a loft in the next town, in a trendy converted warehouse near some long-abandoned railroad tracks. One reason Dawn often gave for their never moving in together, even after three years, was that her apartment above the shop wouldn't provide Keith with enough room or light for his drafting studio.

"Yes, my place," she acknowledged, cautiously. "Why do you ask?"

"Then can you also look in on my cats, plus my four boarders, on Thursday? It seems I have not one, but two commitments for Thanksgiving."

The next morning, I called Bonelli at the police station. She wasn't at her desk, which at least meant she wouldn't have a chance to tell me to stop playing detective. In my message, I told her what Edie Seibert had experienced the night Sabrina died. I suggested someone might want to question other Reserve residents whose family rooms faced that stretch of woods, in case they also had heard disturbing noises.

Sarah and I tended to our customers' cats as usual, but during coffee and lunch breaks, I read over the notes I'd taken while browsing through Sabrina's files. Some of her other successes, all in nearby counties, included shutting down a cruel puppy mill and exposing a local fast-food franchise for failing to pay overtime and for stealing workers' tips. In both cases, she organized picket lines, printed and circulated flyers, and encouraged the workers to speak out against the abuses. In the puppy-mill case, Sabrina even went undercover herself as a prospective customer. I could easily imagine that the owners took her for a harmless, dotty animal lover who'd be a soft touch. No doubt they were stunned, months later, when she testified against them eloquently in court.

The more I read about Sabrina's activities, the more I wished I'd had more than just one conversation with her before her life had come to such a mysterious end.

I suggested to Mark, on the phone, that I get cannoli from the local bakery to bring to his mother's house for Thanksgiving. He laughed and said, "Oh, boy. What's the old expression, 'coals to Newcastle'?"

"Don't tell me—your mom makes the world's best cannoli."

"Well, no, I don't think she's ever actually made it from scratch. But there will be a *lot* of food. Trust me, none of us will go hungry." Instead, he suggested I pick up a particular red dinner wine that he knew was a Coccia family favorite.

"What's the latest head count?" I asked him. "Who are you expecting?"

"My sister, Tricia, and her husband, Gil, will be coming with their son, Frankie, who's two. My brother Art lives with Mom these days, so he's sure to be there; whether he'll invite a girlfriend is anybody's guess. I'd think he was gay if he didn't salivate over cartoons of buxom female superheroes. Then there's my other brother, Ben, and his wife, Nancy, who have no kids there so far, to Mom's great regret. And we usually get a couple of drop-ins from the neighborhood. My dad might even show up, if he's in the holiday spirit."

"Does he still live in town?" I asked.

"Yeah, and he's on staff at Temple U Hospital. He tends to get hung up on holidays, though. Either by work or by his new fiancée, as he likes to call her."

Mark's sarcasm surprised me. Though he didn't talk a lot about his family, up to now he'd said mostly positive things about his father, Frank Coccia, an orthopedic surgeon.

"I thought you and he were close when you were growing up," I said, trying to be tactful. "You said he inspired you to doctor stray animals, when you were a kid, and also taught you how to cook." Someone sure had, because Mark could slice, dice, and sauté rings around me.

"Things were better between us in those days. Later on, I guess the pressure got to him, or he had a midlife crisis. . . . Who knows? He and Mom started to fight a lot more, and he spent less and less time at home. It was almost a relief when they finally stopped trying to stay together for our sakes and got divorced." Mark appeared to shake off these painful reminiscences. "I'm just saying that, if Dad doesn't show, none of us will be that surprised."

I was left hoping that the holiday wouldn't revive more unpleasant memories for Mark than pleasant ones, and also that I wouldn't be stepping into the middle of too much Coccia family drama.

On Thursday morning, I did a final, hypervigilant check of my apartment and my shop. I set automatic feeders to give at least two more meals to all of the cats, and Dawn had promised to stop by late in the day to check on things. If anything unexpected happened—I got stuck overnight in Philadelphia and/or Dawn had some kind of emergency—Sarah had agreed to serve as backup. As I set the shop alarm and finally locked up, Mark noted that, aside from my purse and the wine in its red foil gift bag, I was traveling pretty light.

"Should you have a change of clothes?" he asked. "What if we get snowed in down there?"

That brought me up short. I'd put some thought into my holiday ensemble, a teal green cowl-necked sweater over skinny black pants and boots; I thought it struck the right note between casual and festive. Much as I liked it, though, I wasn't sure I wanted to be stuck in it for two days straight. Well, too late to worry about that now.

"Guess I'll just have to borrow something of yours," I teased. Privately, I vowed that I *would* make it back to Jersey, somehow, to have a late Thanksgiving dinner with Mom.

In the parking lot behind my shop, we stopped by my car and went over the directions, printed out from my computer. "As you can see," Mark said, "it's pretty straightforward until you get close to the city, then there are a lot of twists and turns. And it's ninety miles—more than two hours—on a few different highways. I'll try to drive slowly enough for you to follow me, but I can't promise we won't get separated."

"No problem. Got the directions and GPS." I let him watch while I programmed the address into my car's device.

His nod was still skeptical. "Still, phone me or my mom if you get lost. Even GPS can throw you a curve sometimes."

"I'll be fine." I kissed him, temporarily, goodbye. "See you there."

He went to his RAV4, parked at the curb. Royal blue, at least it should be easy to follow, even in traffic. I pulled out of my driveway and, when he headed off, fell in behind him.

After we hit Route 206 South, I relaxed and turned on

NPR for a while. I only half-listened to an interview with the producer of a controversial new documentary, though, because I was mentally reviewing what little I knew about Mark's family. His mother's name was Donna, and she worked as an administrative assistant for an insurance office in the city. Eldest brother Ben was considered the big success in the family, pulling down major bucks as a business systems consultant, which meant he advised various companies on their computer networks, etcetera; Ben's wife, Nancy, also had some kind of serious corporate career. Artie stood at the other end of the spectrum as the family screwup, unable to stick with one job or one woman for very long, and possibly with a touch of ADHD.

Tricia and Gil ranked in the more normal range of achievements—she was an assistant store manager at a Bath & Body Works and he was an HVAC contractor. They lived just outside Philly in Drexel Hill, which Mark described as an affordable, family-friendly neighborhood.

Oh, and he'd mentioned that his mother had a dog named Daisy, an elderly beagle. Maybe I should have brought some Milk-Bones for her? Though Mark might not approve—he'd also commented that his mother overfed Daisy.

As he had predicted, traffic was pretty heavy. By taking 206, a slower, local road, we ironically hoped to avoid the backups on the major highways. A few white flakes already had started drifting down; the radio threatened that a major snowstorm would descend later and continue into the following day. Mark's words came back to me—what if I did get stranded overnight? Well, I'd just have to make the best of it. Mom certainly would understand. As for sleeping arrangements, I'd bunk wherever caused the least hassle. I'd wear the same clothes two days in a row, call Dawn and ask her to watch the shop and the cats on Friday, also. We'd all survive.

I wondered again why I hadn't had the courage to just explain to Mark why I was anxious about this visit, the way I had
to Sarah. Tell him that I loved him but, for now, I also liked
having my independence. The thing was, I couldn't accuse *him*
of pushing for us to get married, because he'd never even
brought up the topic so far. So was it awkward for me to be
the first to mention it?

Face it, I was a bundle of neuroses.

Finally, Mark and I both merged onto I-95, aka the New
Jersey Turnpike, and crossed over the toll bridge at Trenton
into Pennsylvania. As expected, once we got closer to Philly, a
couple of other, more aggressive drivers slipped between us.
Luckily, we had arranged to park in a public garage near his
mother's neighborhood, and after one wrong turn that took
some time for me to correct, I caught up with him there. By
the time we'd taken our tickets and started out on foot, snow
already had begun to coat the sidewalks.

Mark had told me his mom lived in the same brick row
house where he'd spent his teen years, but it still startled me to
see how urban the neighborhood was. I could understand now
why he'd insisted we pay for a garage, because the residential
street allowed parking on only one side, and with holiday visitors, the curb already was jammed with cars.

"It's funny to think of you growing up as a city boy," I told
him, "because you've always been so involved with animals."

"When I was really small, we did live farther out in the
suburbs and had more pets. But even after we moved here, I
was always taking in strays and fixing them up," he recalled.
"Now you understand, though, why I set up my practice in
Chadwick. I'd rather live around trees and grass and have a little elbow room."

From across the street, the brick row house and its neighbors looked well kept up, with clean white limestone trim and

crisp black shutters and doors. Mark paused to take stock of the vehicles parked along the street. "Let's see . . . I spot a Mercedes, so Ben must already be here. The beat-up red PT Cruiser belongs to Artie."

We crossed the street. Just as we mounted the stone stoop, we heard from inside the sharp yelp of a dog and the delighted shriek of a small child.

Mark turned to me with a mock frown. "That's Frankie Junior, so I guess Tricia and Gil made it, too."

He pressed the bell.

"Somebody get the door!" a woman's voice hollered from beyond. Then she added, with a playful lilt, "That's probably Mark and his new girlllllfriend!"

I swallowed hard. *No pressure.*

Chapter 11

The door was opened by a tall, slim man a few years older than Mark, with the same coloring but a trimmed beard and mustache. Even before he introduced himself I knew he must be Ben, the successful brother. He wore pressed corduroy slacks and a spruce green pullover that looked like cashmere. He smiled, shook our hands, and accepted the foil bag, crushed by now into an obvious wine bottle shape, from me.

Meanwhile, Ben looked embarrassed and whispered to us, "Some welcome, right? I told Mom, 'They can probably hear you out on the stoop.'"

Mark wagged his head in a way that asked, *What're ya gonna do?* I just laughed it off. But I was glad for the diversion created by Daisy, Mrs. Coccia's geriatric beagle, who waddled up to greet us.

While Mark and I entered and stooped to pet the dog, a round-faced young woman with big, dark eyes also welcomed us. Her highlighted hair was gathered into a topknot by a red scrunchie that matched her long, fluffy sweater. "Oops, I guess Daisy knows the animal people when she sees 'em." She thrust a hand toward me. "Hi, Cassie, I'm Tricia."

Another sibling accounted for. Her handshake felt slightly sticky, and the probable reason, her two-year-old, toddled up behind her. Blonder than his mother, he wore a sweatshirt patterned with orange football helmets, navy sweatpants, and only socks on his feet, probably because he'd shucked his rubber snow boots at the door.

"And this is Frankie," Tricia told me. "Say hi to Uncle Mark and his friend Cassie."

But the gleam of mischief in Frankie's eyes told me that neither of us interested him much. He had only one objective at the moment, and made a dive for Daisy. She dodged between our legs to escape.

We moved on to the living room, which was long and narrow, typical of an older row house. Two more young men sat at opposite ends of a gray sectional facing a wide-screen TV on a low cabinet. A football game was in progress on the screen, but only one of the men, who looked himself like a slightly out-of-condition ex-quarterback, was watching it. When we entered, he tore himself away from the action, jumped up, and introduced himself as Gil, Tricia's husband. Then he deftly blocked another linebacker charge by Frankie and tickled the boy to break his trajectory.

The other guy on the sectional—a younger, plainer version of Mark, with longer hair and a scruffier beard than Ben— waited to finish reading something on his cell phone before he set it aside. He rose briefly to greet Mark with a manly hug. "Bro, happy Thanksgiving!"

When we were introduced, Artie shook my hand and looked me over with a detached interest. He had dressed for the occasion in jeans and a black sweatshirt printed with images of a wolf's head, crossed swords, and the ominous message, *Winter Is Coming.* When I dared to ask, he told me it was a *Game of Thrones* reference. Guess that's what I get for having ignored both the books and the TV series. As soon as Artie could manage it, he flopped back down on the sectional and picked up his smartphone again.

"Welcome, welcome." Donna Coccia bustled out of the kitchen. Her short, dark hair looked tousled from her labors at the stove, but her good bone structure and lively eyes conveyed a youthful spirit. She wore glasses with plum-colored frames and silver snowflake earrings. Across her slightly chunky midriff stretched an apron bearing a red, white, and green flag and the philosophical statement, *The trouble with eating Italian food is that 3 days later you're hungry again.*

Well, Mark had given me fair warning.

She asked me, "Were you able to follow him all that way? Or did he speed off and let you fend for yourself?"

"Would I do that?" Mark objected.

"I didn't lose him until we got into the city and some cars cut between us," I admitted. "But we connected again at the parking garage."

"Ugh, that garage charges a fortune, especially overnight." Her eyes widened. "But that's right, Mark said you can't stay over?"

I explained about my mother's situation, and Donna Coccia sympathized.

"I'm sure it's very hard for her," she said. "It was even tough for me for a couple of years after the divorce. At least I had a few grown kids, though, not just one. Come in, sit down."

Taking a seat in the middle of the sectional, I could see through almost to the rear of the row house. Past a dining table and chairs scaled to the narrow space, I glimpsed what looked like a very well-equipped kitchen.

"Your house is larger than it seems from the outside, Mrs. Coccia," I said.

"Please, call me Donna. Thanks, honey. We renovated last

year. Took out all the old walls, made it open concept. Too bad we didn't think of that back when the kids were growing up, but we probably couldn't have afforded it then."

Over the next few minutes, their general conversation helped me fill in the background Mark had given me. Artie currently worked part-time as a stocking associate at the Trader Joe's across town and had recently moved back home with their mother. On the other hand, Gil, with his contracting skills, had renovated the downstairs for her, while Ben had footed the bill for that project.

When Donna excused herself to check on something in the kitchen, Tricia went along with her. Mark noticed the absence of Ben's spouse and asked him, "Didn't Nancy come?"

"She's getting over the flu, but she insisted I come for a few hours, anyway. She's not so sick anymore that she needed me to stay with her, but she didn't want to spread the germ around to you guys. Especially not with Frankie here."

"No, that wouldn't be a good idea," Mark agreed.

As he took a seat next to Gil and asked casually how the Giants were doing, I felt an unspoken pressure to join the women in the kitchen. I'm a capable but unenthusiastic cook, so if someone hands me something to mince or braise, I'm always a little out of my element. But I figured I could at least offer to help.

Donna's renovated kitchen had a Tuscan flair, with light cherry cabinets, a backsplash of mixed earth-toned tiles, and a mammoth refrigerator. Scrumptious odors emanated from both the upper and lower ovens, and pots steamed or simmered on four of the five burners on her stainless-steel range. If Ben had footed the bill for this reno, his consulting business must be doing pretty darned well.

Tricia lifted the bottle of wine that Mark and I had brought from its gift bag. "Oh, Cassie, that's funny—you got the same Chianti as we did. Mark must have told you it's Mom's favorite."

"That's okay." Stirring some gravy, Donna glanced back over her shoulder. "We'll need it. We've got seven people . . . not counting Frankie."

"Well, at least one of the adults won't be drinking," Tricia said.

I thought she might be referring to me—I knew I'd need a clear head for the long ride home—but she laid a hand on her angora-covered midriff, and her mother nodded.

"That's right, how could I forget?" Donna told me, as if I could miss the hints, "Trish has another one on the way."

"Congratulations!" I said.

"Thanks." With a sheepish smile, Tricia added, "It's a little soon after Frankie, but we'll make it work."

"Of course you will," said her mother. "Children are always a blessing. *You* might as well give me grandchildren. Ben and Nancy keep putting it off because they're so busy with their careers, but if they wait too long, it won't be so easy. As for Artie—*phfft!*" She threw a glance toward the living room. "No girl with any sense will look at him twice until he gets his life together."

"Well, he's the baby of the family," said Tricia, probably echoing an excuse they'd used for Artie all his life.

"He is that." Abruptly, Donna pivoted toward me, and I feared that she might demand to know my intentions toward her son. "Cassie, the table's all set, but would you bring out the big salad bowl? And tell them to turn off that stupid game, 'cause dinner's ready."

Those two chores, I could handle. As for the second, I didn't feel comfortable bossing around someone else's family, so I made it clear the words were Donna's, not mine. As the men filed into the dining area, she also told Artie, "Put that away! No phones at the table, especially not on Thanksgiving."

With that in mind, we all sat down. When Donna brought out a large baking dish of lasagna, I wondered what had happened to the turkey she'd kept checking in the lower oven. I noticed that she and Tricia took only small portions from the dish, so I did the same. Sure enough, the lasagna turned out to be just an appetizer, and while the guys and maybe the pregnant sister could afford the calories, I definitely could not. After that came all the usual Thanksgiving staples—the bird, stuffing, mashed potatoes, garlicky green beans, glazed carrots, and two kinds of cranberry sauce—"Because only Ben likes it chunky," Tricia explained.

She asked me about my business, and several of the others also seemed intrigued. I explained, as I often do, that cats need to be groomed differently than dogs. In fact, because cats also can be more temperamental, many pet groomers actually refuse to handle them.

"Cats also don't do very well at boarding facilities that also take dogs," I added. "The barking and even the smell of dogs can make them nervous, so they can come home to their owners in worse shape than they went in. At my place, they don't have to deal with any of that. And I also have room to let them out for exercise."

"I never would've imagined how much there is to consider," Tricia said. "So your business really fills a special need, doesn't it?"

I smiled. "That was the plan. I'm winding up my first year, and so far things are going pretty well."

When the Chianti was poured I took only half a glass, which I figured I could counteract with a cup of coffee before I hit the road.

"Save room for dessert," Donna said. "We have mince pie and cannoli."

Mark laughed. "Mom, you won't be satisfied until we all look like Daisy."

"What's the matter with Daisy? She's a cutie pie."

"She is, but she's also about twenty pounds overweight. If someone brought a dog like that into my clinic, I'd read them the riot act."

"Huh. If you're that tough on your patients, it's a wonder they ever come back."

Tricia sat on my right, and I overheard her whisper to her mother, "Is Dad supposed to drop over later?"

Donna's answer included a verbal shrug. "Who knows? He'll probably call to say he's tied up at the hospital, whether he is or not. I don't think Angela, the new *fiancée*, likes him coming over here too often."

"Nothing changes, eh?"

"Except these days, at least we know better than to count on him."

Halfway through the meal, Frankie refused to eat any more and began to fuss. Gil left the table briefly to give his son a set of magnetic building blocks and encourage him to play in the carpeted living room. Returning to the rest of us, Gil joked, "That oughta hold him for at least ten minutes."

Ben offered more wine around, but I declined, saying that I'd promised to drive home and have a second, late supper with my mother.

"Cassie's father passed away last year," Donna filled in, and I didn't correct her. "She's afraid her mom will get depressed if she's alone on Thanksgiving."

"Oh, well, of course," Ben said. "A shame you have to leave early, though."

"Hope you don't have too bad a drive back," said Gil. "It's really starting to come down out there."

"Where do you live, again?" Tricia asked me.

"Chadwick, like Mark. But my mother's in Morristown."

Murmurs of concern went around the table. Everyone knew northwest Jersey got colder weather—which usually meant heavier snowstorms—than Philadelphia.

Donna had just offered a last round of turkey and fixings when I caught a flash of movement in the corner of my eye, followed by an indignant yelp from the living room. Mark's lips tightened and he popped up from his seat, followed by Gil. Daisy trotted up to them, then stopped to paw at her face.

"Frankie, what did you do to the dog?" his father demanded.

Mark knelt beside the beagle and checked her over. "He threw one of the blocks at her. He got her in the head, I think, but she doesn't seem to be really hurt."

I went to stoop next to them. There was no sign of an injury, but Daisy raised her big, sad eyes to us. *I was just being friendly, and this is the thanks I get?* The gray hairs in her muzzle reminded me that she was too old for such rough treatment.

Gil proceeded to lecture his toddler on treating the "nice doggie" more gently, and I hoped the message would sink in. Still at the table, Tricia sighed, put a hand on her waist, and joked to her family, "I hope the next one's a girl."

"That's no guarantee," Donna warned her.

"Oh, c'mon. You know I didn't cause you half as much trouble, growing up, as my brothers did."

"You had your moments," Donna said. "And the worries are different with a girl."

Meanwhile, standing close to the front window, I could see that Gil had been right. The lazy white snowflakes of the earlier afternoon had morphed into speedy pellets that meant business. And I still had to tramp back to the parking garage to get my car.

I'd better make my excuses and get moving soon.

I almost regretted that. Though the afternoon had been tense at times, at least no one had gone out of their way to make me uncomfortable. Generally, I liked Mark's family.

Before he and I could return to the table, the doorbell rang.

Mark looked up in surprise. "Huh. Maybe Dad made it, after all."

Gil answered the door and did not appear to recognize the young blond woman standing on the stoop with a round tin in her hands. "Hi, can I help you?"

"Oh, it's Krysta!" Donna jumped up from the table and crossed the living room to welcome the newcomer. "She said she might drop by. Gil, you never met her, she used to live down the block. Come on in, honey. . . . Mark, I know *you* remember Krysta."

He was staring in confusion at the guest who had just stepped into the living room, strikingly attractive in her red three-quarter-length coat and striped knit hat. "Oh, he probably doesn't." She grinned. "He hasn't seen me in, what, twelve years?"

"Krysta *Dolinsky*? Wow, that's amazing." His eyes bugged, or so it seemed to me. "I mean, I heard you got married and moved to Boston."

"I did, for four years. But that didn't work out . . . so now I'm back!" She handed Donna the round tin, printed with a pattern of autumn leaves. "I'm sure you already have something planned for dessert, but just for old times' sake, I made you some kolacky. From my mother's recipe."

"Aren't you a doll!" Donna cracked open the tin, and I glimpsed jam-filled, sugar-sprinkled cookies. "You made them yourself? I've missed your mother so much since she passed—she was a wonderful friend. These will be a nice reminder of her."

"We're just having coffee now," Ben told her, from the dining area. "Come on and join us."

"I don't want to impose. I just meant to drop by and say hello." But she shucked her coat and scarf to reveal a model-worthy figure in a ribbed coral sweater, skinny jeans, and boots a smidge too high-heeled for the treacherous weather. Maybe she lived within easy walking distance.

Belatedly, Mark introduced us, though he didn't specify that I was his girlfriend. "Krysta and I practically grew up together, so I'm embarrassed that I didn't recognize her when she came in the door."

She giggled with a toss of her caramel-hued mane. "Well, that was a long time ago. I was kind of chubby then, with braces and glasses."

"You always were cute, though," Donna protested. "Didn't you and Mark go to one of the school dances together?"

"Sophomore year. Pity date, I think!"

The three of them laughed, and, with a blush, Mark denied the accusation.

Krysta let herself be lured to the table. At first I thought Ben was going to usher her into my seat, but he thought better of it and pulled up an extra chair.

I reclaimed my place, which at least put me between Krysta and Mark. As the coffee was served, I asked her, "You said you're back in town. For a holiday visit?"

"No, actually, I'm moving back. My brother and his family were living in the old row house, but they needed something bigger, so he offered it to me." As she gestured with her left hand, I noticed the absence of a ring. Guess a reconciliation with her ex-husband, and a move back to Boston, might be too much to hope for.

Donna announced the coffee was ready, and Krysta accepted the offer with a shiver. "It's cold out there, and the snow's really piling up."

For the first time since her arrival, Mark turned to me, and so did the others.

"I know," I said. "I ought to be going."

Tricia explained to their neighbor about the situation with my widowed mother. Krysta expressed sympathy for that, but not for my having to leave so early.

I apologized to Donna for having to leave early and thanked her for a great dinner and for inviting me.

Mark got up from the table and accompanied me to the front door. "Want me to walk back to the garage with you?"

I was tempted to say yes, although I felt confident that my snow boots could handle the sidewalks. And at four p.m., in bad weather, I didn't worry that anyone would try to mug me over the two long blocks. "That's okay, I don't want to take you away from your family. I'll call you when I get to Mom's."

"Yeah, please do. And thanks for coming, Cassie." He kissed me goodbye. "Love you."

"Love you, too."

His send-off reassured me a bit, though before the door closed, I heard his mother say to Krysta, "What's this 'Mrs. Coccia' stuff? Call me Donna!"

Slogging my way back to redeem my car, I felt put-upon with no one to blame. I'd been only too happy for an excuse to leave the city early, and as it turned out, I'd outsmarted myself. The snowfall wasn't really bad enough for me to call Mom and beg off our evening together. Just bad enough to make the drive back to Morristown a royal pain in the butt.

Of course, the icing on the cake had been Krysta's arrival and Mark's reaction. Now he'd have until Sunday to renew old acquaintances and reminisce about his high school days with her, while I'd be miles away. Was I just too independent for my own good? I remembered Donna's comment that her son Ben and his wife might be waiting too long to start a family. She had a point, though when I watched Tricia and Gil trying to rein in Frankie, I wondered if I'd ever be ready to take that plunge. Sometimes even a shop full of feline boarders felt like more than I could handle.

Back in my car, I set the GPS for Mom's address and eased onto the slippery roadway. Meanwhile, I was haunted by the memory of Sabrina, who lost the love of her life when she'd been just a little older than I was now.

She had forged on and given her life meaning by crusading for one cause after another. Still, she had died alone at night in a snowy woods. With no one to watch over her passing except a scruffy black tomcat.

But that wasn't necessarily true, was it? Someone else might have been with Sabrina that evening and might have witnessed her death.

Her killer?

Chapter 12

In spite of my white-knuckled, slo-mo drive home—the standard two hours stretched to almost three—I revived when I got to my mother's apartment. For one thing, she seemed so appreciative that I had made the effort, and so sorry that I'd had to leave the celebration at the Coccias', that I could hardly grumble. For another, her kitchen smelled amazing. I'd warned her I might be late, so she had finished cooking everything and had kept it all warm in the oven for my arrival. If I'd tried to pull off such a feat, things probably would have come out either mushy or burnt to a crisp.

"I tried cornbread stuffing this year," she told me. "First time, but I tasted a spoonful, and I think it turned out all right. And I made sweet potatoes instead of regular mashed—hope that's okay."

"Great, Mom. I've always liked sweet potatoes." One good thing about my long drive, I thought—all that time on the road at least had given my appetite some chance to revive. She offered me a glass of wine, and I was able to indulge this time without worrying that it would dull my reflexes behind the wheel.

For the occasion, Mom wore tailored camel-colored pants, probably from her work wardrobe, and a cream sweater with beaded trim at the neckline. I felt sorry to think that she probably had few places to wear dressy outfits these days, except the occasional office party at McCabe, Preston, and Rueda. She was shorter than me, with wavier auburn hair that required only a little touching up to maintain its color, and had kept a girlish look even into her fifties. I wondered if she ever thought about getting back into the dating scene or felt that would be an insult to Dad's memory. Heck, even I had hated going to singles' events or answering online ads when I was still on the market. Supposedly, decent men got even harder to find in Mom's age bracket.

She had set our places with the pearl set of Lenox china she'd had since her wedding, which always brought back fond memories for me. The mahogany table and chairs from our old house fit nicely into the dining area of her apartment, as long as she didn't use the extension leaf.

I noticed a watercolor hanging over the sideboard that hadn't been there before, and asked, "Gee, is that one of Dad's?"

"Yes, I had it framed. They did a nice job, don't you think?"

"Beautiful. That's definitely one of his best." Light, deft strokes of green and purple captured the spring splendor of an iris garden in the park across the street from our old house. Dad had taken up painting to help him unwind after work and on weekends, and after a year or so, he'd gotten pretty darn good at it. The way he'd nurtured my fondness for jazz, I liked to think he'd picked up on my interest in art.

Shortly after his death, Mom had sold our two-story Craftsman home in the suburbs and moved into this older apartment building in more urban Morristown. At least the rooms had a similar, traditional look, with deep moldings around the doors and windows and well-preserved oak floors. Still, downsizing had been an ordeal for Mom, and though I'd tried to help, we'd usually ended up arguing over what to pitch and what to keep. In the end, she had done a pretty good job of paring down and ended up with just enough furniture to fill her modest living-dining space and two bedrooms. Of course, she'd once confided to me that quite a few boxes of memorabilia remained unopened in her storage locker in the basement.

Mom brought out the turkey breast, and I helped with the side dishes—mercifully, fewer than Donna Coccia had provided. I ate moderately, but even so had visions of the needle on my scale at home jumping ten pounds higher the next time I dared to step on. Everything was delicious in spite of having been put on hold for at least half an hour.

During our meal, I kept the conversation light and upbeat, skirting over anything worrisome, as I often did with her. She asked me if I had heard about the woman at The Reserve who had died while feeding some "stray" cats, so I had to explain that Sabrina had been a good friend of Dawn's. "She's very upset about that, of course, and now she's kind of stepping in to help with the program." I explained why it was the best way to keep the cats from annoying the community residents. That much seemed to satisfy Mom. She was not much of a cat enthusiast herself—in fact once, when she'd tried to help me out at the shop, I realized she had a full-blown fear of felines. I was able to move onto other topics without mentioning that I'd attended the contentious board meeting, that I'd also been helping out with the ferals, or that Dawn was convinced Sabrina had been murdered.

Naturally, Mom wanted to know all about Mark's family, and I could tell her honestly that they seemed like nice people. I skipped the detail about Donna's ex-husband not showing up, and made no mention of Krysta except to say, "Some of their friends from the neighborhood dropped by, too." Whether it was the wine of the sense of maternal comfort, I convinced myself for the time being that I'd just been obsessing over nothing.

Mom filled me in on what was new at work down at MP&R. During our pauses, though, she studied me quietly, and I sensed she also was holding back. But in her case, the things unsaid were probably questions.

So, Mark asked you to meet his family. Does this mean things are getting serious? She was right on the verge of it, I felt sure, but at the moment I was way too tired to broach that subject. It was only about eight when we finished dinner, but between the long drive, the wine, and the turkey—that sneaky trypto-phan!—I felt ready to hit the sack.

While Mom was pouring coffee, which I hoped would wake me up a bit, I phoned Dawn to make sure all was well in Chadwick.

"Just fine," she told me. "Keith managed to get here, and we're catching up. It seems like months since we've been able to spend some real time together, and he doesn't have to be back in New York until Monday, thank God. How did things go in Philly?"

"All went well." Conscious that Mom could hear me from the kitchen, I told Dawn, "I'll tell you about it when I see you. Were you able to check the cats tonight?"

"Checked and fed them all, though I think they knew I was a substitute caretaker and weren't thrilled about it. Especially your three—Mango kept looking past me for you, even while I was pouring his food."

I laughed. "They'll be seeing me soon enough. I arranged with Sarah to open as usual tomorrow, unless the weather's really bad."

"The snow here is tapering off now, but they're still plowing the roads. You were smart not to make the rest of the drive tonight, but you shouldn't have any trouble by morning." She paused. "I should warn you, though, that you have a rather unpleasant message waiting for you on your phone."

"Oh?"

"From Bock. I overheard him leaving it when I stopped in earlier today. He found out that you and Dr. Coccia are an item, so now he thinks you're pulling a fast one on him."

I groaned. "That man is absolutely paranoid. I don't care how painful his divorce was, he can't go around thinking everyone's out to shaft him!"

"Well, this way you'll have time to prepare your rebuttal. Meanwhile, get some rest tonight."

"Thanks, Dawn, for everything. I'm sorry you had to give up some of your time with Keith to take care of my business."

"That's okay, I'm counting on you to help me sleuth around at The Reserve on Saturday. We still on for that?"

"Sure thing." At the moment, I had trouble mustering enthusiasm for the adventure, but I definitely owed Dawn the favor. "I'll call you when I get back to work."

As I hung up, Mom set the coffee in front of me. "Everything okay at the shop?"

"Oh . . . yeah. Just one customer who's acting like a real jerk." I told her about Bock, his afflicted cat, his anxiety over having to pull her out of a major show, and his refusal to trust anything I or even a veterinarian told him.

"He's even threatened to sue me!" I finished.

"Ridiculous, he can't do that. At least, not without proof that you caused the problem, and the first vet doesn't seem to think you did." Mom frowned in thought. "Harry Bock? That name sounds familiar. I think someone at our firm might have handled his divorce."

"You're kidding! Was he a pain in the butt about that, too?"

She smiled slightly. "I think he may have been. I do remember hearing some kind of story about how messy the whole business was. I'll ask around."

Mom, the savvy paralegal, said no more on the subject. But if I hadn't been so downcast and so sleepy, I might have sensed the wheels turning behind her mild hazel eyes.

Soon after, I dragged myself off to her comfy guest bedroom and set my phone alarm for seven. Before I could open my shop the next day, I'd probably have to shovel my way to the door.

Cole, Mango, and Matisse gave me a rousing welcome when I returned home in the morning. Unlike dogs, they did not express their adoration directly but instead rubbed against my legs while complaining at full volume. They still had dry food in their dishes, so starvation wasn't the issue. It was simply outrage that I had left them in the hands of Dawn, a surrogate mother at best. With them, every feeding was a cause for celebration, anyway. I especially enjoyed Cole's reaction when he saw a dish of canned food coming his way; his satisfied mutterings clearly said, in Felinese, *Awright, awright, now you're talkin'!*

From what I've seen, cats are far more like human children than dogs are. Dogs generally do what they're told and even seem ashamed when they screw up and you scold them. Cats, at best, will behave while you're watching them, but may try to make an end run around you while your back is turned. And boy, can cats sass you, with a vocabulary that I'm sure includes curse words. Well, maybe dogs are like small children and cats are more like teenagers. At any rate, having had so much practice dealing with felines, maybe I'm better prepared than I think for becoming a parent.

While he ate, I stroked Cole's satiny black coat and told him affectionately, "You're so spoiled. There are feral cats starving on the other side of town, y'know." I remembered the day I'd gotten him, at just over a year old, from a shelter during its black cat adoption day. Rescue groups often held those drives, because black animals tend to be less popular among adopters, and black cats in particular sometimes end up with superstitious people who treat them cruelly. I pictured Omen, the tough survivor—his fur dull and bristling from the cold—and told myself that, if not for the rescue group and me, Cole could have ended up the same way.

After I'd dealt with my own pets, I tended to the quartet of boarders downstairs. Sarah, always a trouper, showed up exactly at nine, cheerfully stamping snow off her boots. She'd spent a happy holiday with her two grown children—daughter Marla, son Jay, his wife, Esme, and their four-year-old, Christopher. Being Sarah, she'd also spent part of Thursday helping out at a soup kitchen for the homeless, run by her church. She says that's the best way to stop feeling sorry for yourself and remember all the things you have to be thankful for.

To keep the holiday feeling going, I made cocoa for both of us before we tackled the grungiest job of the day—cleaning out the cat condos after the boarders had had all night to mess them up.

Once again, I felt more comfortable talking with Sarah than with my own mother about my visit to Philadelphia. "At first I did feel like a fish out of water, because it's a big, kind of noisy family. I'm an only child, y'know, used to quiet."

My assistant chuckled. "That can be an adjustment, all right."

"And Mark's mother is different from mine, too. Donna is

warm but very 'out there,' says what she thinks. I knew if she didn't like me, she wouldn't pull any punches. But after a while, I was settling in . . . until who should show up but Mark's ex-girlfriend."

Sarah's eyes widened. "Not the one who cheated on him while they were engaged?"

"No, thank goodness, not her! This was somebody he knew in high school, when she was plain and dumpy, but she sure ain't anymore."

I explained my ambivalent feelings about leaving the family gathering, but also about making any deeper commitment that might help to keep Mark in my life. "Am I crazy?"

"Naw, though you might make yourself that way by worrying too much." She looked me in the eyes. "But you know who you should be talking to about this."

"A therapist? Too pricey."

"I mean Mark. Find out where he's at. Whether he's ready to take it to the next level or likes things the way they are, too. After—what did you say, eight months?—you both should figure out where you stand. At least it doesn't sound like he's proposed to you yet!"

I laughed in awkward relief. "No, not yet."

"Some people go for years being exclusive but not getting married or having kids," Sarah added. "No disgrace in that, as long as it works for both of you."

I squeezed her arm in gratitude. "I'll never need a therapist as long as I have you. Sorry I can't pay you like one."

"I don't have those credentials. Just my teaching certification and experience raising two kids."

It promised to be a quiet day, since the few remaining boarders were staying at least until Saturday morning. The postman dropped off the mail, and in it, I found an envelope from YourWay Van Conversions. Their written estimate was a bit more reasonable than any others I'd gotten so far, but still left me wondering if it was worth the investment.

Since opening my business, I'd dealt with some temperamental cats who might have stayed calmer if I'd been able to groom them closer to home, with their owners nearby. And a few busy, working customers had told me it was hard for them to drive their longhaired pets to downtown Chadwick for a biweekly brushing that could take an hour or two. But if I could travel to their homes, their child or housekeeper could bring the cat out to my van in a carrier. I could work my magic with less time and trauma involved.

While Sarah and I had our hands full grooming a knotty fifteen-pound Himalayan—appropriately named Everest—I missed a call from Mark. He left a message saying he hoped I'd gotten home without too much hassle and spent a nice evening with my mother. The clinic was closed today, and his partner, Dr. Reed, was covering for him tomorrow morning, so he wouldn't be home until Sunday, but he hoped to see me then.

By the time I finished with the cat and returned Mark's call, I was the one who got voice mail. I let him know that I'd gotten home fine, and tried to make him feel guilty by adding that *I* was putting in a full day of work today and my usual half-day tomorrow. I said nothing about my plan to sleuth around with Dawn tomorrow afternoon at The Reserve. Plenty of time for him to be all alarmed about that if we got together on Sunday.

Sarah and I were taking a lunch break when we got an unexpected visitor—Becky, the petite, blond FFF volunteer.

"Hi!" she said, with a sunny grin. "I'm surprised you're open today."

"Matted fur never takes a holiday," I deadpanned. "Good to see you again. Say, you've never been past the sales counter of this place, have you? Want a tour?"

While Sarah staffed the front counter, I showed Becky around the playroom and boarding areas. I told her that the shop had been a beauty parlor but had stood empty for almost a year before I bought it, and I explained how, with the help of an excellent handyman, I had renovated and repurposed the various spaces. She reacted with such enthusiasm that I felt recharged.

On our way back out front, I asked her, "How are you folks coping without Sabrina?"

The young woman's smile faded. "Not so well. She was so inspiring. She'd become our driving force, y'know? We used to meet at her condo to brainstorm; now, of course, that's off-limits. Dawn has offered to let us meet at her mother's place. Who knows if Mrs. Tischler will let us continue after she gets back, but at least she'll be gone for another week and a half."

Sounded to me like Dawn was becoming more and more invested in the ferals' care. Still, against my better judgment, I heard myself asking, "Can I do anything to help?"

"Maybe. That's why I stopped by." From her canvas cross-body bag, Becky pulled a handful of trifold brochures. "Would you have room to display these on your front counter? Your customers are probably the kind of people who'd support our cause, and we need all the friends we can get right now."

I glanced at a brochure, full-color and well designed, even though it probably had been run off on someone's home printer. "Sure, I'd be glad to."

"Thanks so much. I'm really worried that, with Sabrina gone, there will be no conscience left at The Reserve to make the board stick to the TNR program. If they refuse to let us into the community anymore, we'll have no control over what happens there."

"And the cats could be doomed," I finished for her. "Well,

Dawn can be very persistent, and I intend to give her all the help I can."

"Wonderful!" About to leave, Becky remembered something. "Hey, you were trying to rehab an old van, weren't you? We put you in touch with a local guy who does conversions. How did that work out?"

I told her I was still weighing the cost of the project versus the possible benefits. We walked out to my rear parking lot, where the partially cleared snow was starting to melt, and she looked over the hulking black vehicle. I explained the upgrades YourWay had recommended and questioned whether I really needed them all.

"Sounds like you might be able to do it a little more frugally," Becky said. "Having wheels could give you more flexibility and more customers. I'm asking for a selfish reason, though. . . . Well, selfish for us in FOCA. We work with a few shelters in the area, and they've told us that well-groomed animals are more likely to be adopted. Dogs usually are easy enough to groom, but they have a harder time with cats."

I'd heard that often before—it's one of the factors that keeps me in business. "You do need a much different technique. I took courses specifically in cat grooming."

Becky's blue eyes brightened as she made her pitch. "It would be great if you could visit the shelters once in a while and tidy up the cats, especially the longhairs. One place has cat adoption days twice a year. Maybe we could combine it with a groom-a-thon, so people could watch you groom some shelter cats and learn what to do, themselves. The shelter staff might pick up some helpful tips, too."

I mulled this. Sure, I'd be working for free and spending time away from my shop. But Sarah could take care of business for an afternoon. An event like that probably would draw at-

tention from the local papers and even TV stations. The chance
to help homeless animals and get some publicity at the same
time sounded like a win-win.

Was it worth spending thousands on the van conversion?
Possibly.

I slapped the side of the sinister-looking vehicle. "Becky,
you've given me one more good reason to think about resus-
citating this ugly old beast. Thanks for the idea."

By the time she left my shop, the brochures lay fanned out
prominently on my front counter, and I felt more invested
than ever in working for the area's homeless cats. In the back
of my mind, I also wondered if, while solving that problem, I
might come across more information on whether Sabrina
Ward really had died a natural death.

And, if not, who could have murdered her.

Chapter 13

Saturday, around two p.m., Dawn nosed her bright green Jeep into the driveway of her mother's condo, a haven from which no one had the right to banish her. As she shifted into park, I said, "Okay, you're the general on this mission. What's our strategy?"

She smiled and played along. "We need to start with the common areas, where we should encounter the greatest number of targets. Unfortunately, since it's late November, we probably won't find many at the outdoor pool or tennis court. Might be a few sturdy souls on the jogging trail, though, trying to work off those Thanksgiving calories."

We'd both dressed warmly for this adventure, but I still didn't relish the idea of chasing residents through the woods in the cold. "Guess our main activity will be in the clubhouse, then."

Dawn nodded. "There, we've got the game room, the library, the fitness center, and a few common areas where people hang out with other residents and visitors. If all the folks we want to talk to are holed up in their condos, this could be a waste of time. I'm just hoping we'll get lucky. Here's the list."

She unfolded a long sheet of generic notepaper branded at the top, *Things to Do*.

That was lucky. After all, a list titled *Suspects to Question about Sabrina's Murder* might have blown our cover, especially if it fell into the wrong hands.

We stepped out of the Jeep and started walking toward the clubhouse, while I scanned the list.

"Would you know all of those people to see?" Dawn asked me.

"I think so, since they were all at that board meeting." I double-checked with her about some residents who hadn't made that strong an impression. "I know the cops already questioned Mike Lawler because of the remark he made at the meeting, that someone should 'euthanize' Sabrina. But Bonelli said he has an alibi for that evening. I also told her that Edie Seibert thought she heard a scream that night, so the cops probably have interviewed her, too."

With a sly expression, Dawn pointed into the air. "Yes, but did they talk to her neighbors? That's why I've got Alma Gunner and Dan Greenburg on the list—they live on either side of Edie. No spouses . . . she's single, and he's divorced."

"Okay, I can use the work I've been doing with Edie as an excuse to chat with them. And I'll take Bert Chamberlain, since his dog is being treated at Mark's clinic. I'll ask how Jojo is coming along and go from there."

Today I spotted a few more youthful residents out and about at The Reserve, such as a female jogger who looked just a bit older than us and a man of about forty unloading grocery bags from the hatch of his car. Probably these folks worked during the week, with long commutes, and were more visible on weekends. Approaching the plaza, we also passed a small playground outfitted with a token slide, a jungle gym, and a set of swings. On this chilly afternoon, no children played there, but an androgynous teenager in UGG boots, ski jacket, and a knit beanie slumped on a nearby bench, totally absorbed in her/his smartphone.

As we walked on, Dawn guided my attention back to discussing our strategy. "So, that leaves just the other board members to question, plus a couple of obnoxious characters, Ted Remy and Heidi Sweet. Because Mom is a resident, I can approach the board members and they pretty much have to give me a few minutes of their time. On the other hand, Heidi and Ted know me on sight and could be hostile."

I well remembered those two model citizens from the meeting. "Ted was upset about the cats doing nasty things outside his condo that might scandalize his visiting grandkids, right? And Heidi was the nutcase who thought Sabrina was an actual witch."

Dawn paused. "Well, she is . . . sort of."

"Huh?"

"Sabrina used to consider herself a practicing Wiccan, at least for a while. I didn't see any altar or charms around her condo, so maybe she got away from it. Or maybe after she moved here, she decided it was better not to put them out where her neighbors might see them."

Maybe Heidi had gotten wind of that and had blown it out of proportion. "But Wicca is a positive religion, right? Aren't they actually forbidden to cast evil spells?"

" 'An it harm none, do what ye will,' that's their creed," Dawn said. "Might sound like there are no rules, but think about it—if you're forbidden to harm anyone, including yourself, that still keeps you pretty much on the straight and narrow."

I nodded, having read a little about Wicca myself. "That's what I thought—it's just nature-based spirituality. But of course, someone like Heidi wouldn't know that. She'd hear the word *witch* and think of all the bad horror movies she's ever seen."

"Unfortunately." Dawn folded her list in two, tore it neatly along the crease, and handed me half. "So . . . you get Ted and Heidi. Think of it as a chance to use all those courses you took in abnormal psychology."

I pocketed my list with an air of bravado. "I get scratched or bitten on the job at least once a week. Those old cranks don't scare me."

"Even so, keep your cell phone handy. Just in case you suddenly realize the nice, elderly person you're talking to is, y'know . . ."

"A stone-cold killer? Good idea."

I started with the closest and easiest assignment, approaching Edie's neighbors. Searching for the right row house, I noticed the minimal holiday decorations. The working-class homes near my shop in Chadwick tended to sprout gaudy decorations for every holiday; recently they'd segued from ghosts and skeletons to turkeys and pilgrims, and no doubt they'd soon go completely overboard with the Christmas lights and maybe even lawn inflatables. I doubted those would even be allowed here, though Alma's door did wear a tasteful wreath of artificial autumn leaves and miniature pumpkins suspended from the knocker. I pressed the doorbell. She didn't answer, but I did spy a car through the window of her garage.

Dan Greenburg, who lived on the other side of Edie, had not bothered to decorate his door for the season. He did open it, though, and blinked at me through round, thick-lensed glasses, like a tortoise roused from hibernation. Seeing him closer-up now than at the board meeting, I judged him to be no more than fifty, though his rather stooped posture made him appear older. He seemed confused and a bit suspicious to find a strange young woman on his stoop.

I introduced myself and reminded him of my input at the last meeting. Making that connection, he nodded and waited for further explanation. I told him I'd been working with his next-door neighbor to solve her problem with the feral cats and wondered if he'd had any similar issues.

"Not me," he said. "Probably because I don't feed them. And I don't have any pets."

"That's why they've spared you, I'm sure." I sensed he might close the door in my face at any minute. It was chilly outside, and I doubted that I'd ever get him to relax and tell me more while I was standing on the stoop. "Are you very busy, or do you have a few minutes to talk?"

He wavered a bit but finally eased the door open wider. "I don't know what more I can tell you. As I said, it hasn't been a problem for me."

I stepped inside while I had the chance. "But I'd be interested to know how you feel about the trap-neuter-return approach. At the meeting, you sounded more positive about it than some of the other board members. You pointed out that FFF has done all of this work for the community for free."

"That's true."

He led me into his living room, and I got a chance to see how yet another Reserve resident had personalized the generic, contemporary space. Unfortunately, Dan had decorated in a haphazard style that I suspected was Post-Divorce Minimalism. His mashup of furniture included a couple of ornate but shabby seating pieces that I'll bet his ex-wife, or maybe his mother, no longer wanted. The rest was so Spartan that he might have bought it from an office supply store and knocked it together himself. What would ordinarily have been the dining room was set up as a home office, with lateral file cabinets and a matching L-shaped desk. File folders and manila envelopes were splayed out on the desktop, suggesting he was organized but busy, and the screen of his computer displayed a financial program with columns of numbers. He took the time to close that file and shuffle a few papers into a neat stack before he returned to me in the living room.

"I keep the books for some local businesses," he told me. "It gets pretty intense toward the end of the year, so I'm trying to get an early start on things. Please, sit down."

Dan didn't offer me anything to drink or eat, though, and I got the clear message that he hoped I wouldn't stay too long. His still-brown hair was scraped back from his high forehead, and a faded gray Rutgers sweatshirt hung loosely on his hunched shoulders. He wore scuffed, fleece-lined leather bedroom slippers, as if he didn't plan on going outside anytime soon.

I settled in one of the living room's two Victorian-style chairs, which had begun to leak stuffing along the seams, and smiled at him. "Did you have a nice Thanksgiving?"

He sat on the sofa, while his sour face made it plain that this innocuous question had gotten me off on the wrong foot. "They had a buffet at the clubhouse, I went to that. Took a day off from my work on Thursday, but I'm always pretty busy. I also help some of the residents here with their personal budgets."

"They must be glad to have someone like you in the community." I thought it best to return to more pressing topics. "This seems like such a quiet place, with good security. Must have been a shock to hear about what happened to Sabrina Ward."

Again, he blinked in surprise. "That was sad, of course, but

I don't see what it has to do with security. The police said she died of a heart attack."

"Did they question you?" I asked.

"No. Why would they?"

"Edie told me that, the night Sabrina died, she thought she heard a scuffle and a scream from the direction of the woods. She told the police, so I thought they might ask if her neighbors heard anything similar."

Dan shook his head. "They didn't ask me, but even if they had, I don't remember hearing anything. What time would this have been?"

"About ten o'clock. Edie said she was watching the news."

"I go to bed around that time. And even if there had been a noise outside, I probably wouldn't have heard it." He removed a small, almost invisible hearing aid from one ear. "I'm half-deaf on the left. I take this out when I go to bed, and I sleep on my right side. I hear my alarm clock because it's loud, and I'd hear a siren or a smoke alarm. But anything less than that . . ." He shrugged his narrow shoulders.

Since he seemed impatient to get back to his accounting, I stood to leave. "Do you ever talk to Mrs. Gunner, who lives on the other side of Edie? I guess she never mentioned to you whether or not she heard anything that night."

"Alma and I don't have much personal conversation. I just know, from the board meetings, that she's upset about the cats killing so many birds. Guess she and her trail-walking friends are real bird lovers."

I thanked Dan for his time. Leaving him to crunch his numbers in peace, I headed down the curving sidewalk in the direction of the clubhouse. This took me past a different street of condos, and by sheer, dumb luck I spotted Bert Chamberlain walking a frail-looking Jojo. The medium-sized, tricolored collie mix still sported a shaved area along his neck ruff, where Dr. Reed probably had taken blood or inserted an IV.

"Mr. Chamberlain, so glad I ran into you." I introduced myself. "You may not remember me, but I was at the last board meeting, when you talked about what happened to Jojo. It's great to see him up and about again."

Bert's ruddy complexion looked even more so today with the effect of the cold breeze, which also lifted the orangey strands of his comb-over for an odd effect. He thanked me for my concern, then sniffed, "Only took two weeks and a hefty vet bill to save his life. Perfectly healthy four-year-old dog, and now I'll always have to monitor him for kidney problems and other bad stuff. But at least he's still with me."

"It's terrible that someone would stoop to poisoning any animal." I decided to take a risk and lowered my voice. "In fact, after what happened to your dog, some people are wondering if Sabrina's death was really an accident."

Bert looked down at his boots and scuffed at the dirty remains of the snow, while Jojo relieved himself against a leafless bush. "Can't say I haven't wondered the same thing. Before all this, I thought of The Reserve as a nice, safe neighborhood, where people were friendly and looked out for each other. But this feral cat business sure stirred something up. I'm not a cat guy myself, but like you said, it takes a real SOB to poison a plate of food and leave it out in the open."

"You don't have any idea who might have done it?"

"The cops asked me the same thing. I sure don't, or I probably would have knocked out his teeth by now. The vet said whoever did it could have used an OTC drug that anybody could buy. At first I'd been thinking, 'What if a little kid ate that food, instead?' But if it was a human medicine, maybe it wouldn't have hurt a child, or at least not as much. It's just really bad for animals."

I nodded. "That would mean whoever doctored the food had some idea what he, or she, was doing."

The gloom in Bert's eyes lifted a bit, as if he was grateful that someone else took the attack on his pet seriously. "But like you said, could the same person maybe have gone after that lady who died out in the woods? Yeah, I can believe it. If he did, I just hope they find the jerk, get him out of our community, and put him away for a long time."

"You and me both," I assured him, mentally crossing Bert Chamberlain off our list of suspects.

Arriving at the clubhouse, I first stopped by the Activities Room, which had bold blue walls and jazzy herringbone carpeting. Deep windows looked out on the pool, currently locked down with a mesh cover for the winter. I was following up a hunch that paid off—Heidi Sweet sat alone at one of the round card tables, absently watching some men play billiards.

"Who's winning?" I asked her.

"*Pfft*, who cares? These guys all cheat." She gestured toward the blue felt tabletop in front of her. "I was hoping for a canasta game and thought some of the other girls might be here, but I guess they're still hangin' out with their families."

Though Heidi had an elfin build and the silver cap of hair to go with it, she made one peevish pixie. When I asked about her Thanksgiving, she complained that her son, an investment banker, took her to dinner for the holiday but already had gone home and back to work.

Sensing the ice broken, I introduced myself. "I said a few words at the board meeting about the feral cats. As I remember, you had some strong opinions, too."

My mention of the controversy made Heidi close up a bit. "Well," she said tightly, "at least that situation should be over soon."

"What do you mean?"

"That witch Sabrina was behind the whole thing. Now that she's gone, the board will probably get sensible. Round up all those filthy strays and take 'em away. Don't know why they even listened to that woman in the first place."

Overcoming my repugnance, I took the seat next to Heidi and tried to draw her out further. I was not going to try to explain the benign concept of Wicca to this lady—I was more interested in why she felt such hatred for Sabrina. "You called her a witch at the meeting, too. Why?"

"Because she is, I'm sure of it." Lowering her voice, Heidi confided, "She only got that condo in the first place because the last owner had a stroke. Healthy-lookin' man, only about fifty, jogged every day . . . but he went into the hospital and then right to assisted living. Before you know it, Ms. Ward's moving into his town house."

"Things like that do happen," I said mildly. "I'm sure many people who've moved here within the past few years bought their homes after the last owner got too sick to go on living here, or even passed away."

The little woman's angry head toss told me what she thought of this mundane explanation. "Ever since the great Ms. Ward moved in, bad things kept happening here. Her next-door neighbor argued with her over the cats and then came down with a terrible case of shingles, almost went blind. I heard that another guy Sabrina had problems with—not here, at least—lost his whole business. Well, she helped *put* him out of business with one of her silly protests." Heidi wagged an arthritic finger at me. "She hurt a lot of people over the years, that one. They could tell you stories."

"Is that so? Who in particular—"

"And Sabrina may be gone," she rambled on, "but that damned cat of hers still is around. That black one. I won't really feel safe until they catch him and cart him away."

"Why? Has he attacked people, or—"

"I don't know about that, but he still comes up here and watches us. Sits on the retaining wall, mostly, out here by the clubhouse steps. But one day I pulled back the blinds on the sliders in my family room, and he was right on my patio! Just sat there and *stared* at me until I closed the blinds again." She shivered her thin shoulder blades. "Gave me the willies."

From a guilty conscience?

At that point Heidi grew impatient, grumbling because none of her friends had shown for their canasta game. (I couldn't help but wonder if they might be avoiding her charming company on purpose.) Without so much as a goodbye, she slung the strap of her purse over her shoulder, jerked to her feet, and shuffled off.

And older folks say my generation is rude!

I moved on to the clubhouse Fitness Center. There, Ted Remy struggled to free himself from a looming medieval torture device designed to crush the life out of him . . . or at least that's how it looked to my untrained eye. He succeeded in forcing the padded, vertical bars apart, only to pull them back toward his chest again. Though he huffed and puffed from the effort, and perspiration shone on his bald head, he kept putting himself through this ordeal . . . on purpose! Looked like pure masochism to me.

Dawn had lent me her guest ID so I could enter the gym, though in jeans and a turtleneck, I didn't look much like I had come to work out. But this didn't seem like the best time to interrupt Remy and start questioning him, so I found myself a vacant treadmill. At least I'd worn running shoes that day. After a few minutes of experimenting, I powered up the machine and began to walk at an easy pace. Enough other people of both sexes and various ages were working out so that I was not conspicuous, and my machine put me behind Remy so I could observe him but not vice versa. Most of the treadmill walkers were watching a talk show, closed-captioned, on a TV suspended from the ceiling at the front of the room. I pretended to do the same.

I'd never enjoyed playing team sports, and exercising for its own sake—as opposed to taking a long, brisk walk to a destination—has always bored me. You can imagine that I never was crazy about phys ed classes, either, and now the clunk and whirr of the machines and faint smell of sweat revived unpleasant memories of those days. Still, an unofficial sleuth has to make some sacrifices for her craft. I marched on the treadmill and worked up a sweat of my own for about ten minutes, before the intrepid Ted finally took a break in his own self-torture. Then I struggled for a second to turn off and dismount from my treadmill without turning an ankle.

While doing some cool-down stretches, I pretended to accidentally drift into Ted's space. I smiled and glanced toward the towering weight trainer he'd been using. "You really seem to know what you're doing with that thing," I said. "I'd be scared to even go near it!"

As I'd hoped, this flattered him, and he spent a couple of minutes explaining that the machine wasn't all that complicated and how it worked. At the board meeting, he'd worn a bulky winter sweater like most of the other residents, but today his damp, clinging T-shirt revealed that some of that bulk also had been muscle. His loose-fitting gym shorts reached just below his knees, and his left shin bore what must have been a nasty-looking bruise that had begun to heal; maybe one of the fitness machines had gotten the better of him, after all. Taking a break, he grabbed a towel from the weight bench and used it to dry off his square-jawed face and thick neck.

"Do you do physical work at your job, too?" I asked him.

"Semi-retired now, but I worked in construction and as a

security guard. You can lose that muscle tone fast, though, if you don't keep working at it." He chuckled and gave me a quick overall glance. "Well, you're too young to know about that."

I didn't want to veer into a flirtation with this guy, but I needed to keep him talking. I introduced myself, then mentioned attending the board meeting and hearing him voice his objections against the feral cats.

Ted squinted at me. "You do know, don't you, that the clubhouse facilities are just for residents?"

Taking no offense, I whipped out my borrowed ID. "I'm here as a guest of Dawn Tischler."

"Who's here as her mother's guest," he quibbled. I guess old security guard habits die hard.

"Give me a break. It's not like there's that much competition for the treadmills."

"You got a business card?"

I never go anywhere without some, and I pulled one from my jeans. He scrutinized it as if it were an international passport, potentially forged, then stuck it in the pocket of his gym shorts.

"Have to admit," he said, "I don't like cats much. Nervous, sneaky things. 'Course, if people keep them in their own houses, that's not my problem. These strays, though, are a pain in the butt. The lady next to me fed them for a while, so now they hang around my condo, too. They yowl at night, they poop behind the bushes and pee on my front stoop. Before people visit me, I have to clean up the mess so they won't be disgusted. One time my little granddaughter was here and a couple of the cats started goin' at it right on my doorstep, screamin' their heads off. How am I supposed to explain that to a three-year-old?"

"I'm sure it was awkward." I sympathized. "Of course, if

most or all of the cats were fixed, you wouldn't have to deal with that kind of thing. It sounded to me as if Sabrina Ward was trying to solve the problem with the trap-neuter-return program."

He grunted. "Not to speak ill of the dead, but Sabrina should've minded her own business. Just like my ex-wife, always tryin' to run other people's lives for them. I heard plenty about Ms. Ward before she even came here. She's caused trouble for a lot of good people, butting into places where she has no authority."

"She did seem to be making enemies of some of the residents. Makes you wonder, doesn't it, if what happened to her was really an accident?"

Ted's expression turned flinty again. "If you're looking for someone to blame, I was home when it happened. The cops already questioned me, and Joan Pennisi will back me up. We happened to roll our garbage cans out to the curb at the same time and said hi to each other. After that, I went back into my condo and didn't come out again all night."

"Joan is the board secretary, isn't she?"

"That's right. She's a very smart and observant lady, and she'll tell you I stayed in that evening." He sniffed. "Anyway, none of this is going to be my problem much longer. I'm gonna find a buyer for my place, soon as I can, and get the heck out of here."

I would have asked more about that, but he shut down our conversation by walking off in the direction of the showers.

Back in the lobby of the clubhouse, I sat on a comfy upholstered bench and took a moment to make notes on what Heidi and Ted had told me.

The prickly pixie not only believed Sabrina had been an actual, spell-casting, black-magic witch, but that her malignant influence lived on in Omen because he lurked around the public areas watching the residents. To me, that simply showed he was curious about them, braver than the typical feral . . . and probably hoping for a handout.

As for Ted, he resented my asking questions or even using the gym as an outsider. He swore that, aside from a quick trip to take out his garbage, he'd never left his town house on the evening Sabrina was killed, and that his neighbor Joan could swear to it.

Of course, that was a crock. If the guy kept quiet, he could easily have left again, through his front door or his patio slider, without Joan seeing him. The only way she could guarantee that he'd never gone back out would be if they'd spent the night together.

Which would give her a motive to cover for him, wouldn't it?

Chapter 14

Five o'clock that day found me and Dawn comparing notes and nibbling on vegetarian burritos at her rustic store, Nature's Way.

Her building, as old as mine, had started out as a different kind of feed store—for livestock. Dawn had intentionally kept that earthy atmosphere by lightly sanding the weathered oak floors and painting the rough plank walls a soft, almost transparent green. Salvaged shelves and cabinets on all sides held boxed and bagged grocery items, and the back wall featured a large, glass-front refrigerator for frozen foods, such as our microwaved burritos. An original cast-iron, wood-burning stove anchored the middle of the sales floor; around it, Dawn had created a small seating area with an overturned barrel and two old armchairs draped with paisley throws. We sat there now, our plates resting on the barrel and bottles of water on the floor, as we took stock of what we'd learned that day at The Reserve.

"We got to everyone on our list," she noted, "because the only one you missed was Alma Gunner, and I ran into her and Joan Pennisi coming back from the walking trail. They both

bitched about the ferals killing so many wild birds, though
Joan admitted they'd been finding fewer dead ones since FFF
set up the feeding station. Did you know that she's Heidi Sweet's
niece and lives with her? Apparently, Heidi needs a bit of looking after."

That figured, though the relationship between the two
women was news to me. "Joan must have a lot of patience. I'd
hire a full-time nurse for Heidi before I'd move in with her."

"Well, Joan supposedly has some nursing experience. Anyhow, about Alma . . . She claimed not to have heard anything
suspicious the night Sabrina died, but she also was watching
television, and for part of that time was on the phone with her
brother in California."

I noted this additional info on the back of my own list.
"You said Lauren also talked some trash about Sabrina?"

"She was subtle about it. I think she takes her image as
board president very seriously—you know the type. But she
said she felt sorry for Victor Ward. She told me that he 'assumed responsibility' for Sabrina after his brother died, but
she's always been 'a trial' to him. Don't know if those were his
words or Lauren's."

"Did she mean because of Sabrina's activism? Ted and
Heidi went on about that, too, saying she made trouble for a
lot of people. I still think that's an angle worth investigating. . . .
Oh, no, you don't!"

Tigger, Dawn's brown tabby kitten, had crept up alongside
the upended barrel where we'd parked our burritos and now
attempted to steal the last bite of mine. I grabbed it just in
time. I was too hungry to share, and black beans and cheese
probably wouldn't be that good for him, anyway.

"Ted Remy said cats are sneaky things," I scolded the kitten, "and he's absolutely right."

With a patient smile, Dawn tore a sheet of paper from her small notepad, crumpled it up, and threw it toward the back of the store. Tigger exploded with delight and skittered madly over the old, distressed-oak floor in pursuit. Probably close to a year old by now, he'd developed a long-legged, adolescent body, but his white belly, chin, and paws still gave him the look of a stuffed toy. Watching him play manic hockey by himself for a few minutes provided us both with a much-needed laugh.

"That should keep him occupied, at least until we finish eating," Dawn said. "I don't think he's really hungry, just bored. Gotta say, though, after raising him from babyhood, I may never want actual children."

I grinned. Tigger had simply taken up residence in her storage room last spring. By the time she'd made a good-faith effort to find his previous owner—if he'd ever had one—the mischievous tabby had stolen her heart. "And yet he's single-handedly turned you into such a cat person that now you're crusading for ferals."

"Tigger was only partly responsible for that. At this point, I also want justice for Sabrina." Dawn checked her notes again. "Anyway . . . Lauren also complained that the feral issue is driving down the community's property values. People who sold their homes recently got quite a bit less than they expected to, and they thought it was because buyers read about the cats in the papers or saw them prowling around. That's a serious problem, Lauren said, because with this kind of community, you'd expect the value to go up over time."

"Probably true." I did some more scribbling on the back of my list, then helped myself to a second burrito.

"Sam Nolan griped that they spend a lot on landscape maintenance, and it's frustrating to have the feeding station and winter shelters where they can be seen from the walking trails, 'junking the place up.' He told me if there was an end in sight, he wouldn't mind so much, but FFF says for the TNR program to work, it has to be ongoing."

"Did you run into anybody who supported the program?" I asked Dawn.

"Joan seemed the most willing to support it. She sounds like an animal lover and has owned cats in the past. She said she felt awful about Bert's dog and the idea that someone would put out poison near the trail. After Alma had stepped away, Joan told me privately that she thinks almost half the residents feel the way she does, but the controversy has gotten so nasty that they're afraid to get involved."

"Hmm." I considered this. "Wonder if there's any way to rally those folks?"

"They might be outraged enough if we can prove Sabrina was murdered. Especially if it was over this issue."

Dawn had been brewing organic coffee in her French press, and she poured some into earthenware mugs for us. She had just started using the new coffee maker, and I had to admit the richer flavor was worth the extra effort. While we savored the results, she asked me, "I'm not keeping you away from a romantic evening with Mark again, am I?"

"No, I don't think he's driving back from Philly until later tonight, or maybe even tomorrow morning. He said he'd see me Sunday. Of course, by that time, he could be engaged to Krysta Dolinsky."

Dawn made a face and slapped my arm. "Stop torturing yourself. I'm sure he's been missing you the whole time and can't wait to come back to you."

"I dunno. You should have seen his blue eyes pop when he realized his dowdy high school pal had morphed into a honey-blond, long-legged swan. She even brought a better hostess gift than I did—Christmas cookies she baked from her late mother's recipe."

My friend winced. "She bakes? Crap, maybe you do have something to worry about."

It was my turn to swat at her. "The trouble is, this whole business of visiting his family for Thanksgiving made me wonder where our relationship is going and how quickly. Sarah, bless her, reassured me that it isn't so strange these days for a person my age not to want to settle down and give up her independence. And you and Keith have been a couple for years, even though you never married and don't even live together. But Mark has an older brother and a younger sister who are both married. When his mother talked about how Ben and his wife shouldn't wait too long to have kids, and how his younger brother, Artie, needed to find a girl and settle down . . . I knew Mark must be feeling that kind of pressure, too."

Dawn shrugged. "You won't really know whether he is, or how he feels about it, until you ask him."

"Yeah, that's what Sarah told me, too. When I see him tomorrow, I guess we'll have to have the talk. But it's scary, y'know? What if Mark *is* ready to take the next step? If we did, I don't think he would have to make all that many changes in his lifestyle. On the other hand, I might have to turn mine completely upside down."

"Good point," my friend admitted. "As you said before, Keith and I have our separate lives, and we're still going strong as a couple. I don't worry about him spending his nights with other women—just with demanding clients! He and I talked all of that out years ago, though, and you guys should, too."

Dawn was right, of course. But for me, it would be a scary conversation. If Mark found out that he and I wanted different things, I could lose him.

Even interviewing people who might have murdered Sabrina Ward hadn't felt this daunting.

Almost as if he'd heard us mention him—which he couldn't have—Dawn's significant other, Keith Garrett, came trotting down the iron spiral staircase at the back of the shop, which led to her apartment. "Just returning a work call," he told us. "These New York guys sure don't understand the meaning of *off the clock*. I'm billing them for every change in the design, plus every minute I spend on the phone."

"You need to," I agreed.

Lanky and bearded, Keith stooped to peck me on the cheek. "Hi, Cassie. Hope you had a good Thanksgiving. Dawn tells me it was a busy one."

"Yes, my presence was in such demand that I had to cross state lines and actually partake of two turkeys. A gobble-gobble here and a gobble-gobble there."

Both he and Dawn groaned at my kindergarten humor. "Well, you're welcome to stay and have leftovers tonight with us," she said. "But I'm afraid it would be more of the same."

"What, no Tofurky?"

"I know, I really should have. I've actually got a couple of those in the shop's freezer, for my vegan customers."

"We had a real bird, but it was pasture-raised and Certified Humane," Keith added in his best politically correct voice. When Tigger leaped onto a display cabinet, and from there onto his shoulder, he grabbed the kitten in his arms and pretended crush it against his chest. "We would have eaten this guy, but he's too tough!"

In response, Tigger tried to bite Keith's fingertip. A light tap on the nose discouraged him.

"He's a scrapper, all right," I said with a laugh, and started to gather up my things. "Which reminds me, I've really got to get back to my place. My own three cats haven't seen much of me lately and they're liable to rebel, which could result in property damage. So, tempted as I am by yet another turkey dinner . . ."

"We won't take it personally." Dawn showed me to the front door. "Really, Cassie, thanks for all of your help. We'll keep in touch."

From her secretive tone, I found myself wondering how much she had told Keith about our unofficial investigation of Sabrina Ward's death.

Back at the shop, I did a quick check on the four boarders, and all seemed well. The message button was lit on the store phone on the front counter. I doubted that would be Mark—he almost always called me on my cell. On closer inspection, the ID window showed Angela Bonelli's number at the police station. I pressed play.

"Cassie, how do you know an Edie Seibert who lives at The Reserve? Call me as soon as you can."

If Chadwick's resident police detective was asking me that question, it didn't bode well, and I got right back to her. Figuring Bonelli might not approve of Dawn and me questioning the condo community's residents, I gave her only the information she had requested. "Edie asked me for help because the ferals were hanging around her patio and stirring up her own cat. I got her a couple of motion-sensitive gizmos that fire bursts of air when anything comes onto the back patio. Last time I checked with her, they seemed to be doing the trick."

I heard a dark chuckle. "So *that's* what it was. Scared the crap out of one of my guys tonight."

"Cops were over at Edie's tonight? Why, what happened?"

Bonelli's voice turned grim. "Sorry to tell you, but Edie Siebert is deceased. Looks like an accident, but we're covering all the bases, talking to anyone who saw her today. And she had your business card lying in plain sight on her coffee table."

★ ★ ★

I spent the next hour at the police station talking to Bo-nelli. Of course I had to tell her that Dawn and I had visited The Reserve in the afternoon, though I made it sound as if Dawn was just taking care of her mother's condo and I was just checking the cat feeding station. I said I'd talked to one of Edie's neighbors but had not seen Edie herself, and that Dawn and I had left around four.

"I hope she wasn't alone, in some kind of distress, while I was over there," I added. "If only I'd dropped by to say hello, maybe I could have helped her."

"The ME thinks she had her accident a bit later than that," Bonelli said.

"Accident?"

"She fell down the stairs inside her home and probably died of head trauma."

The detective started to say something else but was drowned out temporarily by a commotion in the hallway. Through the glass wall, we could see two of Chadwick's finest marching a belligerent suspect toward one of the interrogation rooms. Most of the crime in Chadwick ran to domestic disturbances in the residential neighborhoods, car thefts, petty burglaries by teen druggies, and fights at the biker bar out toward Rat-tlesnake Ridge. In other words, typical small-town stuff. Once in a while, though, we got a doozy that stood out from the rest and made headlines. I'd actually had the misfortune to get mixed up in a couple of those—helping out the cops, of course, not the criminals.

After the rowdy guy had passed, I turned my attention back to Bonelli. "Hot Saturday night, huh?"

"And this is quieter than usual," she told me. "So, Cassie . . . when you were over at Mrs. Seibert's town house, was she using a walker?"

"Yes. In fact, I asked her how she managed the stairs, and she showed me that she could use the walker on those, too."

"Strange. The walker was found near the foot of the stairs, folded up. She must have gone up without it. And her bed was made, but there was a depression in the covers as if she had been lying down on it."

"She told me she had dizzy spells. Maybe she felt well enough to go upstairs on her own, then got dizzy and was trying to get back down to her walker."

"That's what we're thinking. Edie's cell phone was downstairs, too, on a small table in her entryway. If she had only reached that, she could have called for help. But she did suffer a head trauma. Maybe when she fell she was knocked unconscious, or even killed instantly."

I felt tears welling in my eyes. I hadn't known Edie well, but I'd liked her. "That's so sad. She seemed like a sweet person. She had problems with the feral cats, but instead of just complaining and saying they all should be carted away, she hired me to help her find a solution."

"If that blast of air scared the cats as badly as it did Officer Waller, I'm sure they hightailed it for the woods and never came back."

I had met the young, redheaded cop during an incident the previous summer, and the picture Bonelli painted now made me smile. "Maybe I should have put up a sign, 'Warning—Motion-Sensing Cat Deterrent System in Use.' Say, what about Edie's pet, Sonny? A big, yellow tabby. Did your guys see him around?"

"I don't think so, but the ME mentioned that there was food and water for a pet in the kitchen. I think he was wondering if she might have tripped over the animal."

I sincerely hoped not. Edie had loved her cat, so I'd hate to think he'd played any role in her demise. From what I'd seen, she'd been very careful maneuvering around him and he gave her a wide berth when she was on the move. But, of course, that had been when she was using the walker.

"Will somebody check on him?"

"I knew that would be your next question. We've still got an officer at her condo, so I'll call over and tell him to make sure the cat is taken care of."

"If there's any issue and Sonny needs to be removed from the house, you know I'll gladly board him until you find someone to take him."

The detective gave me an indulgent smile. By now, she knew I was a sap for any cat suddenly orphaned by the death of its owner; my boarding facility had sheltered such emergency cases a couple of times in the past. "I'll keep that in mind, Cassie. Thanks for coming in. How was your Thanksgiving?"

I gave her the capsule version. "I had two dinners. One with Mark's family in Philadelphia—after which I drove home in the snowstorm—and a second that night with my mother in Morristown. By the way, is it an Italian tradition to serve lasagna before the turkey on Thanksgiving?"

My explanation of Donna Coccia's first course drew a rare, hearty laugh from Bonelli. "I've heard of serving mini lasagna bites as appetizers, but not a whole pan!"

"That makes more sense. Anyway, Dawn and Keith invited me to have leftovers with them tonight, but right now I never want to see turkey again in my lifetime."

"Well, count yourself lucky. My husband and one of my sons were sick with the flu, so we're not having our celebration until tomorrow."

"Yikes! Well, as long as they're feeling better now, enjoy it."

An officer knocked on Bonelli's door, no doubt needing

her input on another case, and she told him she'd be right with him. "Thanks for your help, Cassie," she dismissed me. "From now on, try to stay clear of The Reserve, okay?"

Back at the shop, I gave the boarders one feeding for the night, fed my own cats, and had a slice of leftover pizza—no trace of turkey—before hitting the sack early. Coming so soon after all of the holiday tensions, the news of Edie's death had depressed me, and I figured I'd try to just sleep it off.

My plan backfired, though. My subconscious kept working through my dreams, and I woke around three a.m. with my heart pounding.

Bonelli hadn't even mentioned the possibility of foul play, so it didn't sound as if she was pursuing it. But could Edie have been killed because of what she'd heard on the night of Sabrina's death?

Chapter 15

The question still troubled me the next morning, Sunday, as I turned Spooky out in the playroom, checked my supplies for the upcoming week, and generally caught up on anything I'd neglected over the holiday weekend.

Should I suggest to Bonelli that the most recent death at The Reserve also might not have been an accident? I'd already told her what Edie confided to me about hearing a scream, so she had all the pieces to put together. Well, maybe not all. I hadn't admitted to her that Dawn and I were at the community yesterday asking people questions.

Damn, I told Greenburg that Edie heard something. Was he Sabrina's killer? Or did he, accidentally or otherwise, tip off the killer?

If Bonelli knew we'd been stirring the pot among the community's residents, she'd be ticked, for sure. Better not to confess that unless it becomes absolutely necessary . . . wait until she gets the tox results. Edie could have popped a strong sleeping pill on her own, gotten disoriented, and taken a tumble. A sad way to go, but with no outside villainy involved.

I was making a list for a grocery run—figuring the store

shouldn't be too crowded on the Sunday after Thanksgiving—when Mark called.

"Just got back this morning," he said. "At least I missed the heavy traffic and bad weather. How did you do? I gather from your text that you made it to your mom's okay."

"It was a bit of a slog on Thursday, but no serious problems. I'm really sorry I had to leave so early. Gotta say that eating turkey twice in one day was a challenge. I ended up more stuffed than the bird."

He chuckled. "I'm sure. Mom does like to put out a spread. Every year we rag her about the two kinds of cranberry sauce. And lasagna as an appetizer? Crazy!"

"Well, everything was delicious, though. At least you have a big enough family to consume that much. And I suppose later on you had more people dropping in."

"Not too many. But boy, was it a surprise to see Krysta! She moved to Boston for college, then we heard she got married. . . . I haven't seen her for maybe fifteen years."

"A lot can change in that time," I said.

"That's for sure." He seemed to catch himself before he started enthusing too much about the charms of the new and improved Krysta Dolinsky. "Anyway, before we both get caught up in the rat race again, dinner tonight at Chad's? They've probably got turkey on the menu, but also enough other stuff that we both can avoid it."

"Sounds great. We have a lot to talk about, more than I want to go into over the phone."

"Uh-oh. I hope you're not getting into trouble again," he teased. "See you around six."

Ironic, that he mentioned getting into trouble just before I hung up . . . and Dawn burst through the door of my shop. "Edie Siebert's dead?"

I nodded. "Bonelli had me down at the station for half an

hour last night, asking about my dealings with Edie. I mentioned that you and I had dropped by The Reserve to tend to the feeding station and cat shelters. I deliberately neglected to mention that we were sounding out some of the residents as to their feelings about Sabrina."

"Probably smart, because Bonelli would have a problem with that, no doubt. But really, Cassie, two fatal falls in just a couple of weeks?"

"They were both elderly women with health problems," I pointed out.

Luckily, the sign on my glass front door was turned to CLOSED, so even if passersby saw the two of us in the front of the shop, we probably wouldn't be interrupted. I poured coffee into two colorful Laurel Burch cat mugs—a thoughtful shop-warming gift from Mom—and brought them up front to the sales counter.

Dawn perched on one of the high stools there, tucking her long, knitted-wool skirt around her booted legs. After a sip of the hot brew, she returned to arguing her case. "But Edie seems to have been the only one who heard anything unusual the night Sabrina died. If she did scream, that points to murder."

I took the opposite stool and tried playing devil's advocate. "Sabrina could have felt herself falling and called for help."

"While she was having a heart attack? Or being strangled with her own scarf?" Dawn shook her head. "You scream when someone's assaulting you. That's what Sabrina taught us in the self-defense class. She demonstrated, and she had a set of lungs, believe me. If she could still scream anything like that at seventy, it's no wonder Edie heard her all the way from the woods. The real surprise is that no one else heard anything."

"I only talked to Dan. Like I told you, he wears a hearing aid that he takes out at night."

"Well, I asked Alma, and she had her excuses, too. At least

one of them could be lying, or . . ." Dawn blanched. "Oh, God, Cassie, what did we do?"

"What do you mean?"

"I can't blame you, 'cause I put you up to it. But between us, we told two people that Edie heard a scream. Who knows whether she ever mentioned it to anyone before, but if not, we let the cat out of the bag . . . so to speak."

"You don't think Dan or Alma killed Sabrina? Neither of them is very brawny—in a grappling match, she might've been able to hold her own."

"I'm not saying either one of *them* did it, but they could have spread the word to other people on the condo board."

"So you think someone on the board is involved?"

"I think they've been too quick to accept the idea that her death was nothing more than an accident. I don't see them warning the other residents that there could be a killer on the loose."

"Would you? I'm sure the management doesn't want people moving out en masse." I reflected on this for a minute and came up with a new, disturbing possibility. "Crap, maybe I was too quick to confide in Dan. He came across as such a dull guy that I started to think he couldn't possibly be involved. But he balances personal budgets and does tax returns for some of his neighbors, so he could know their secrets. I still can't see him murdering anyone. . . ."

"But he could be covering up for the killer," Dawn suggested. "Out of loyalty, or fear."

"Edie, though . . . Why would anyone find it necessary to get rid of her? She thought she heard one scream, nothing incriminating."

My friend gripped her mug fiercely, and her amber eyes burned into mine. "Cassie, think like the murderer. What if someone mentioned to you that Edie was out in her family room that night, watching TV, and thought she heard a commotion in the woods and a woman's scream?"

To my surprise—shock?—I could follow the killer's line of reasoning pretty easily. "I'd wonder if she heard or saw something more, something she might remember if the police questioned her. *Sabrina also screamed my name—did Edie hear that, too? Did she see me later, when I ran out of the woods?*"

"Exactly. The killer knows more details than we do about what happened, and he could be afraid that Edie does, too. So why take a chance?"

Though the winter sunlight through the display window warmed the front of the shop, I shivered. "They do say when a person has killed once, they find it easier to kill again. And in some ways, Edie would have been even easier to deal with than Sabrina." I reminded Dawn that the woman suffered from dizzy spells and used a walker. Privately, I reflected that Edie also was a gentle soul and probably would not have known how to put up much of a fight.

On the other hand, the crime had been committed in her home, with no sign of a break-in. By someone she knew and trusted?

"You're right, I admit," I said. "But what more can you or I do? The cops investigated Sabrina's death and found no hard evidence. Technically she died of natural causes, a heart attack. So she screamed. Bonelli might say, she could have seen a wildcat or a coyote that frightened her to death." When Dawn made a dubious face, I added, "Yes, you and I know it would take more than some wild animal to scare Sabrina that much, but the cops still could draw that conclusion."

My friend pondered the situation again. "They found no drugs in Sabrina's system. But what about Edie's?"

"Bonelli's guys went through her condo and, I guess, confiscated her medications. Of course, they're doing a tox screen on her, too. I do think you're on the right track there, Dawn. Whether or not there was foul play, Edie could have taken something that made her extra dizzy. We'll probably just have to wait for the test results."

My friend clenched her fists on the counter. "Damn. I just can't stand the idea that someone could have murdered those two women. One who was such a champion of the underdog all her life, such a force for good and for change."

"And the other, a sweet lady who never bothered anyone," I added. "Who went to the trouble and expense of letting me install that cat deterrent system, just so she and Sonny could coexist with the ferals. Neither of them deserved to die by violence, that's for sure."

Dawn raised sad, helpless eyes to me. "So, what can we do?"

I offered the only answer I could think of. "Figure out who had the strongest motive. I don't think we should question people at The Reserve anymore, but there's always the Internet. We'll investigate the backgrounds of our suspects—starting with the board members."

Chapter 16

Toward evening it started snowing again, but that didn't keep me from meeting Mark at Chad's, the town's retro diner known for its chrome and turquoise décor and its large and varied menu. It sat on the tracks of a defunct railroad spur and had been renovated, a couple of years before I came to town, to attract the growing number of weekend tourists. Its name paid a wry tribute to our town's founder, General Grayson Chadwick, who did something-or-other not terribly important during the Revolutionary War. No relation, I'm pretty sure, to Chad Everett, the heartthrob actor whose slicked-down, early-1960s head shot hung near the diner's cash register.

Mark and I shared a quick hello kiss in the parking lot. When we'd first started dating and I'd been new to the area, I'd been too self-conscious for public displays of affection. I'd already gotten the sense that this was a pretty small town in terms of gossip, and it made me squirm to imagine strangers talking about the pet groomer dating the local veterinarian. But these days anyone who cared knew we were a couple, and I no longer worried about such trivia.

Tonight I was glad, though, that I probably didn't have to

worry about running into anyone from The Reserve. The community was far enough out of town, and close enough to the highway, that its residents had a lot of other restaurants to choose from without traveling all the way to Chad's.

Inside, we were shown to a booth by a forty-something waitress whose uniform cap—basically, a white ruffle attached to a hair band—struggled to restrain her abundant black curls. I wondered if she was related to the owners; despite its all-American name, Chad's, like most New Jersey diners, was operated by a Greek family.

As Mark and I had vowed over the phone, neither of us ordered anything featuring turkey. He got the meat loaf special and I went for a vegetarian stew that seemed perfect to counteract the chill in my bones—physical and psychological.

After the waitress had taken our orders, collected our menus, and left, Mark leaned back on his turquoise vinyl bench seat with a contented sigh. "A few more hours to relax, then tomorrow it's back to the clinic. Any time I take off more than a weekend, the first day back is always rocky. Dr. Reed sent me an e-mail bringing me up to speed about some cases that came in over the holiday, so at least I'll be prepared."

"Nothing too ghastly, I hope," I said.

"No, fortunately. Oh, they finally got the tox results back on Chamberlain's dog. Just what I figured—he ingested some NSAID drug. Doesn't tell you much, though, about who could have doctored the cat food. Anyone could have something like that in their medicine cabinet, and a simple Internet search could have told them it's potentially lethal to animals."

Mark was right—that didn't narrow the list of suspects much. "At least Jojo has pretty well recovered. I was over at The Reserve yesterday and saw Bert walking him."

Fortunately for his patients, but unfortunately sometimes

for me, Mark doesn't miss a thing. "You went over there again? How come?"

This wording alarmed me for just a second. My last boyfriend had turned out to be possessive, controlling, and finally abusive. That experience had left me hypersensitive to being grilled about where I went and with whom. I reassured myself that Mark wasn't like that and had a perfect right to ask the question.

"Dawn had to deal with stuff at her mother's place and check on the feral cats, and I tagged along to help." Before he even had a chance to warn me again about investigating Sabrina's death, I added, "You remember that woman I told you about, whose cat was acting up because of the ferals? I installed motion-sensor devices outside her door to scare the cats away? She was found dead in her condo last night."

"Gee, that's too bad. You weren't the one who—"

"No, it happened after we'd left. But I had to go to the police station, because the cops found my business card on her coffee table."

"Do they think it was suspicious? Her death, I mean."

"She had a chronic balance problem and she fell down her stairs, so right now it looks like just a tragic accident. But after what happened to Sabrina Ward, I guess they're leaving no stone unturned." I would not tell him, yet, that Dawn and I also intended to leave no stone unturned. That would certainly inspire a lecture on how I should leave the investigation to the police, who carried firearms to protect themselves.

"Well, that's a sad turn of events. I know you said she was a nice lady."

"I will miss her," I told him. "And as usual, I'm concerned about who'll take her cat. Bonelli said she'd keep me posted on that."

"The orphans always have a home with you, right?" Mark snapped his fingers. "I almost forgot one piece of good news that Maggie told me. Apparently our cantankerous Mr. Bock has had a change of heart. He called to say he's going to try my elimination diet to see if Looli has an allergy."

"No kidding! Is it a Thanksgiving miracle? Or did he finally see a therapist for his paranoia?"

"Not quite. But he said he got 'some very level-headed legal advice from a nice lady' over the weekend. Apparently she made him realize that it wasn't fair for him to accuse you and me of conning him when he hadn't even tried what I'd prescribed. She probably also told him he wouldn't have a leg to stand on if the case went to court."

I smiled at the image. " 'Nice lady,' eh? I suspected that some of his bad temper was related to his divorce. Maybe if this new woman keeps talking sense to him, it will make him more pleasant to deal with, all around."

"Bock doesn't have any other family? Kids?"

"He didn't mention any to me. Maybe that was another reason he was depressed, because he expected to be spending the holiday alone."

Our meals arrived then, and since the fare at Chad's is always excellent—as well as reasonable—for a few minutes, enjoying our food took precedence over conversation. By the time Mark spoke again, I could see that my last comment had reminded him of our Thanksgiving trip to Philadelphia.

"Speaking of divorced guys, my dad finally did show up late on Friday. Said he'd had an emergency. He was sorry he missed you."

"I'm sorry I missed him, too. What does he look like? Do any of you resemble him?"

"Physically, he looks the most like Ben. Has that same reserved, straitlaced personality, too."

"I get the feeling you're not so sure he had to work at the hospital."

Mark pulled a cynical face. "Well, we know he's seeing someone else these days. Calls her his fiancée. You can imagine how that makes Mom feel."

Having met Donna, I doubted she would take it well. "Does sound like rubbing salt in the wound."

"He gives the 'emergency' excuse a lot, too. Even before the divorce, when he and Mom had an argument, he'd tell her he got an emergency call and had to go in to work. We never knew if it was completely true. And since they split, he especially tends to avoid coming over on the holidays. Too many memories, I guess, good and bad. Too much tension."

Although my mother had lost Dad through death, not divorce, the syndrome of mourning sounded familiar. I decided that now would be as good a time as any to broach my own uncomfortable subject. "I admit, I was a little tense, too, about the whole family holiday thing."

"I thought you seemed quieter than usual. Hope my mom didn't say anything to upset you. She can be . . . outspoken."

"No, she was very nice to me. But some of the comments she made about the rest of you—that Ben and Nancy had better get started if they're going to give her grandchildren, and Artie needs to get a decent job and find a steady girl—made me realize how important it is to her to see her kids settled."

The corners of Mark's mouth quirked slightly. "We call that Mom's 'iron fist in the velvet glove' approach. Don't let her manipulate you!"

"I wouldn't, but it also made me wonder how important those things are to *you*. You're a little older than I am, and you've dated more. Maybe you're ready to settle down. I'm not talking about just being exclusive—I think we're there already.

But moving in together, marriage, kids? Do you feel ready for any of that?"

He pondered the depths of his water glass for a few seconds. "Let's just say, I'm not compulsive about it. Especially on the last subject. . . . Right now, my clinic keeps me so busy that I can't imagine raising a kid, too. And I don't want to be just a drop-in kind of father, like my dad got to be toward the end. Maybe in a couple of years, Margaret and I can take on another partner, even part-time, and we'll each have a little more space to breathe. But just as important, Cassie, are you ready? I get the feeling you're not."

"It has nothing to do with our relationship," I hurried to assure him. "I love you, Mark, and can't imagine being with anyone but you. It's just that . . . as you know, my last boyfriend was so domineering that I didn't feel free to make my own decisions. Starting my business and being on my own has been so exciting for me . . . all right, sometimes a little too exciting. . . ."

He laughed. "Yeah, we both could have done without the close scrapes you've gotten into over the last few months."

"But right now I can't see giving up all of that freedom. I don't see us going on and on like Dawn and Keith, either, never even moving in together. And I'm sure your mother, and maybe mine, too, would tell me at my age I should be married and popping out kids. . . ."

Mark covered my hand with his. "They're from a different generation. Look, it sounds to me like you and I are on the same page. We're busy with our jobs, satisfied with our living situations, and happy getting together as often as we can. Maybe in the near future, something will happen to change that and we'll take the next step. Until then, let's not worry about what anyone else says, okay?"

I nodded and exhaled deeply, for what felt like the first time in a week.

The waitress cleared our plates, then returned with her dessert pitch. "If you think it's too cold for ice cream, we have all kinds of pie, cheesecake, baklava. . . ."

Mark raised an eyebrow at me, but I shook my head. "Just coffee for me."

"For me, too," he told the waitress. "I think we're both still in recovery mode from Thanksgiving."

When we had our privacy again, I confessed to Mark that I was glad we'd talked things out.

"So am I," he said. "I'm sorry that you felt concerned about all that while you were around my family."

"Well, frankly, what really kicked it into high gear was when Krysta dropped by. You seemed so impressed by her changed appearance that I was almost afraid to drive back to New Jersey."

He laughed. "Seriously? Did it come across that way? I was surprised, yeah, but nothing more than that. Anyway, I think she's already got a new boyfriend—that's one reason she moved back to Philly." With a teasing gleam in his eye, he added, "Besides, from the way she avoided poor old Daisy, I don't think she even likes animals."

"Not even Daisy? Who wouldn't love her?"

Mark turned up his palms. "There you go. How could I ever trust a woman like that?"

"So I don't need to teach myself to make kolacky?" I asked.

"Too sugary for me. You make a great cup of coffee—that's a more useful skill. Speaking of which . . ." He nodded toward the waitress returning with two turquoise mugs, branded CHAD'S, and our check.

★ ★ ★

Mark and I spent Sunday night at my place, and that also helped put to rest any worries I might have had about the status of our relationship . . . at least, for the time being. Of course, the next day he had to leave early for work, and I had to get the shop ready for Sarah's arrival at nine.

As she and I took care of the morning chores, I filled her in on the ups and downs of my visit to Philadelphia, and how I'd finally resolved things with Mark.

Sarah didn't seem surprised by his response. "Men aren't usually in as big a hurry to marry and start as family as women. I've known a few exceptions, but more often they get caught up in their careers and figure they still have plenty of time for all that. 'Course, in their case, they do have a lot more time than we have!"

"You sound like Mrs. Coccia," I told her, with a smile. "Bad enough to have my own mom tell me I'm not getting any younger—I don't need to hear it from my boyfriend's mother! Though, to her credit, she didn't exactly say it about me. Anyway, how was your holiday?"

"Less stressful than yours, at least from the sound of it." Sarah opened Spooky's condo and shook dry food into his dish. "We all went to Jay's house, and his wife cooked the bird. Their little guy, Chris, is about the same age as Mark's nephew you were telling me about, and about as lively. My daughter, Marla, is more like you, only her talent is with numbers. She just got a good job with an accounting firm, and that's all she cares about right now. And, like Mark's family, we had some friends and other relatives stop by." On her way to rinse out the Persian's water dish and refill it, she stopped short. "Oh, I almost forgot—my cousin Yolanda called to wish us all a happy Thanksgiving."

"The one who was harassed at her hotel job?"

Sarah nodded. "She's in Maryland now. Like I told you before, she's a reservations manager these days at another hotel, with no more problems along that line. But I told her what happened to Sabrina Ward, and she was very sorry to hear about it. She said if not for Sabrina, she and the other women would never have had the courage, or the money, to take their case to court, much less win."

I paused in scooping out Jeckle's litter box. "Sarah, I have something else to tell you, too." I explained what little I knew about Edie Seibert's death. "Of course, it could have been just an accident, but Dawn and I are wondering whether the poor woman might have been killed because of what she heard the night Sabrina died. Do you think we're crazy?"

Sarah pondered this. One of many things I like about her, she thinks a question through before she answers. "Depends on how you look at the situation, I guess. On the face of it, they both look like accidents. Two older ladies, living by themselves, whose luck ran out."

"Aha! Sabrina did take chances, with her health and otherwise. But Edie seemed to be very sensible, even cautious, to me. And there's the timing of her 'accident'—right after Dawn and I told some other residents that Edie had heard a woman scream."

My assistant nodded slowly. "Still, two murders sound like a lot of trouble for somebody to go through just to get rid of a feral cat colony."

"What if it's about more than just the colony? We're thinking somebody might have a grudge against Sabrina from years back. A couple of the residents I talked to said that the protests she organized 'hurt a lot of good people.' I'd question the 'good' part, of course, but it just goes to show that she left some hard feelings in her wake."

Sarah nodded. "She was almost a saint to Yolanda and her

friends, but that hotel chain did take a major hit. Not only did they have to pay damages, but it's taken them years, I think, to recover from the bad publicity."

"Sarah, do you think I could give your cousin a call and ask her about those days? Dawn and I may have worn out our welcome at The Reserve, at least for now, and I don't want Bonelli to get on my back about doing my own investigating. So we're trying to work through other channels to find out who might have had grudges against Sabrina."

She shrugged. "Sure, I'll ask Yolanda. Can't imagine why she'd have a problem with it. If it was murder, she'd probably be glad to help you get to the bottom of it."

During our lunch break, Sarah phoned her cousin and left a message. Meanwhile, I started my research. Dawn and I had agreed to work from our original list of Reserve residents, but to swap suspects. So this time I would be investigating the board members.

I was lucky enough to find Lauren Kamper's full profile on one of those sites where executives post to connect with other professionals. She held a BA in business with a minor in science, and had parlayed that into a career as a pharmaceutical rep. Apparently she'd worked for three different companies, all in different states. At her present firm, in New Jersey, she'd risen to pharmaceutical sales manager. That didn't surprise me—the way she ran a board meeting, I figured her for some type of boss.

From another site, I found out the typical salary for that position. Not bad. At least it was no mystery how Lauren could afford to live at The Reserve.

Idly, I checked out a Connecticut firm where she'd worked in the past. Interesting. They'd been cited about two and a half years ago for unethical practices, such as offering kickbacks and favors to doctors who prescribed their products. There had even been a couple of incidents of drugs gone missing, possibly to be resold on the black market. Not much could be proven, though. In the end, the company had gotten off with a slap on the wrist, but that must have created a rather tense climate for the employees. Possibly that was what had spurred Lauren to move to Jersey, escape the shadow of scandal, and get a fresh start.

The same executive search site offered a section for freelancers, and there I came across a head shot of Dan Greenburg. It showed him smiling, something I'd never seen him do, so far, in person. Apparently he had worked for only two accounting firms, one in New York and one in New Jersey, before striking out on his own last year. The profile mentioned golf as one of his hobbies, and a wider search turned up a picture of Dan as part of the winning team in a local charity tournament. He was smiling there, too; maybe I just kept encountering him in low moments.

Too bad I didn't do this research before I talked to him. Golf might have made a good icebreaker, not that I know anything about it. At least it was good to know Dan had some interest in life besides crunching numbers and grumbling about his ex-wife.

Sam Nolan was employed at The Reserve through MAR Property Management; I found that out from a recent news article about the feral cat issue, in which the reporter had asked him for a comment. Nolan echoed the same sentiments Dawn and I had heard from him already: He was concerned about the negative effects on The Reserve's landscaping and general quality of life, as well as the property values for homes on the market. He was willing to give the TNR program a try, but warned that some residents might run out of patience while waiting for it to take effect.

MAR's website stated that, earlier in his career, Nolan had worked in public housing, where he had demonstrated an expertise in "resolving tenant disputes, handling repairs, keeping up the property, and dealing with emergencies." I'm sure moving to The Reserve had boosted his salary, and he'd probably also expected less stress than he'd faced overseeing low-income properties. I wondered if he was having second thoughts these days.

Joan Pennisi showed up on a similar site peddling her services as an executive secretary with a medical background. The last job her résumé listed was as a certified nurse with the Morris Regional School System, which jibed with what she'd told Dawn. For her head shot, Joan had dressed in much the same ultrasensible mode favored by Angela Bonelli—crisply ironed powder-blue shirt, navy blazer, pearl earrings, dark hair pulled up in some kind of a twist. She'd worn a ruffled blouse and her hair down at the meeting, so maybe she'd loosened up a bit in retirement; her face also looked a little slimmer in this old photo than it did lately.

Joan must have kept a low profile in recent years, because no more personal information about her came to the surface. It was funny that so many people seemed to leave these old career sites up long after they'd stopped using them to find employment. But it sure made things easier for anyone who wanted to check up on their professional backgrounds, like me.

With Ted Remy, I struck a potential vein of gold in terms of my actual murder investigation. A career website had interviewed him a while back for advice on how to make a living as a security guard. Remy said he'd started out volunteering as a bouncer at a friend's rock club; he'd worked his way up to providing security at outdoor concerts and taking night jobs that no one else wanted. After he passed a security officer training course, he moved up to guarding office buildings and hotels. At the end of the interview, he mentioned that he'd just signed on with one of the hotels in the Merrywood chain, which he described as offering "good money and a great bunch of people to work for."

That article had appeared only a few months before the sexual harassment suit went to trial, bringing scandal upon the company and forcing it to downsize its properties and staff. Could Ted have gotten laid off in that purge? He'd made a point of telling me that Sabrina "made trouble for a lot of good people, butting into places where she has no authority." He might well see things that way if the lawsuit she'd instigated had cost him a lucrative job.

Sarah called for my help, then, to answer questions for a potential customer who'd stopped by. After that, I figured it was time to shut down the laptop and get back to my real job. Sarah and I then worked on Moe, a semi-longhair mixed breed who used to be able to groom himself, but now was sixteen years old with arthritis. His owner was afraid of hurting him, so she let us do the job to be on the safe side. Moe whined a little when he found a position uncomfortable, and we learned to avoid doing anything that seemed to hurt him. He never tried to scratch or bite us, though, and when we'd finished, he looked every inch the distinguished older gentleman that he was.

I had just returned him to temporary quarters in one of the condos when Chris Eberhardt from FFF came through the door of the shop. A good-looking young guy with shaggy black hair and a boyish build, he might or might not have had a thing going with Becky; at least they had become dedicated partners through their work with FOCA.

"Hi, Chris!" I greeted him, slightly surprised by the visit. "How have things been going up at The Reserve?"

He sighed. "Not so great, as you can probably imagine.

They haven't kicked me and Becky out yet, but it's probably only a matter of time. Now that Sabrina's gone, we haven't got too many defenders."

"Dawn is gung ho for the cause now," I reassured him, "and I'm willing to help in any way I can."

He perked up at this promise. "That's why I'm here, actually. Becky told me you have an old van that you want to have outfitted to use for grooming."

"True. I haven't had time yet to do much with it, though, and I'm still trying to decide how much I can afford to spend."

"Doesn't matter right now. The main thing is, we need a vehicle that can transport a good number of cats. We got permission to do one more trap-neuter-return at The Reserve on Thursday night. We're hoping to deal with all of the ferals who escaped us the first time around. Nolan, the resident manager, made it sound like this is our last chance. If it doesn't bring the colony under control . . ." Chris shrugged his narrow shoulders and didn't finish the sentence.

"You want to borrow my van?"

"If you'd lend it to us. We use wire mesh traps that are almost three feet long, so even empty they take up a lot of room. I figure we've got about a dozen cats still to deal with. It might take us more than one night, but I don't think the residents will stand for us being up there more than two."

"Is Dawn in on this?"

He smiled. "I stopped off to talk to her before I came here. Yeah, she's in. Becky and I really appreciate her help, because we need all the hands we can get."

"I'm sure you do. So, how about I lend you my hands along with my van?"

I could see relief wash over him. "I didn't even want to ask, but that would be fantastic. It really helps if everyone involved is used to handling cats, even difficult ones."

Sarah joined us at the counter in time to hear the last part of my exchange with Chris, and widened her eyes at me.

"Don't worry," I told her, "I'm not volunteering you."

"Not that I don't support the cause," she said, "but I think I'm a little old to be stumbling around the woods at night and wrestling with wild cats. Some of our boarders are challenging enough!"

Chris gave me the details of the foray, which he and Becky had planned for Thursday night. We would show up at The Reserve around seven, and the security guard at the gate would have instructions to let us in.

"You'd better give Nolan a description of my van," I advised.

Chris chuckled. "Becky told me it's pretty rough-looking."

"Like a cosmic black hole on wheels. If Lee isn't warned, he's going to think The Reserve is being infiltrated by terrorists."

"It sounds perfect, though, for helping us keep a low profile in the dark." With a grin, Chris zipped up his down jacket and started for the door. "Now I just have to make one more stop, at the clinic. Gotta ask Dr. Coccia and Dr. Reed if they can help with the neutering and vaccinations."

I imagined how delighted they would be to deal with a dozen charity cases on Thursday night, but they'd probably still agree to do it. "Feel free to drop my name."

Sarah waited until our visitor had left to needle me. "Drop your name? Think that'll help, or hurt?"

Chapter 17

Trouble was, I had never driven the van more than a few blocks across town before. The former owner had it restored by the local garage to full operating condition before he sold it to me, and at least it came with automatic transmission. As Dawn and I headed out on the highway, though, I remembered the aged vehicle took more effort to steer than my trusty Honda CR-V, and also rode a little roughly. I hoped the feral cats—if we caught any tonight—wouldn't object too much. Becky and Chris had given me six of their empty traps to haul to The Reserve; they'd bring six more cages in their vehicle, a large, older-model SUV.

Dawn, as my only passenger at the moment, took the bumps in stride. She was dressed for action tonight, in jeans, low boots, and a tan suede jacket with sheepskin lining (both faux, I was sure); she'd managed to gather all of her hair into one fat, messy braid to keep it out of the way. She was totally psyched about our rescue mission and also excited to swap information with me about what we blithely referred to as our "suspects." I'd already given her the rundown on what I'd learned from the Internet about Dan, Lauren, Sam, Joan, and Ted, and she was able to flesh some of it out further.

"Last night I tapped into a priceless background source—Mom!" she told me. "She finally called from her hotel in Casablanca. Apparently, cell phone reception is pretty unpredictable in some of the places where they've been touring. Besides, Morocco is six hours ahead of us, and she was thoughtful enough not to want to wake me in the middle of the night."

I stuffed down a pang of jealousy. Would the day ever come when I could take such an exotic, extended vacation? Right now, I couldn't foresee ever being able to spend the money or take the time off. Of course, Gwen Tischler was a successful fiber artist who juggled various jobs, such as teaching, mounting gallery exhibits, and writing catalog copy. I guessed when she did get some free time, she made the most of it.

"How's her trip going so far?" I asked.

"Great, I guess. She said Casablanca is fascinating, and they've also gone out to small towns to meet Berber rug weavers, leather dyers, and felt makers. This week they're heading to Marrakech, where they'll see more artisans at work in the marketplace."

"Sounds fantastic," I said. "Do you wish you'd gone with her?"

"A little, but she's with her own friends. She's not tied down to running a business, like I am—in fact, this will *help* her business. I could never afford to shut down Nature's Way for more than a week or so."

She sounded a bit jealous, too, that fifty-four-year-old Gwen could have such an adventure halfway around the world while Dawn and I were tethered to our shops and responsibilities. Youth wasn't necessarily wild and carefree!

"Anyway," Dawn went on, "Mom had a little downtime

between excursions, and a reliable phone connection, so she was happy to share what gossip she knows about her neighbors at The Reserve."

"Do tell!" I goaded my friend.

She pulled a little spiral notepad from her deep purse and flipped it open. "Dan Greenburg does accounting for a few of his neighbors as well as some small businesses in the area. There have been rumors that he hides sources of income for some of them at tax time. Could be he's worried about someone finding that out."

I shrugged. "Even if he were, I don't know how that would involve Sabrina or Edie. They might have found out that he was cooking some books, but neither of them seems the type to blow the whistle on him for no good reason."

"You never know. But you're right—even though it's an interesting tidbit, it doesn't seem to point directly to our victims." She flipped to the next page. "Here's something more promising. Remember those documents in Sabrina's file about Graversen, New Jersey? The neighborhood that was so polluted?"

I searched my memory. "Was that the town where they built houses, in the sixties, on the site of an old paint factory? It was back before there were strict regulations about such things. The site was never cleaned up properly, and a few years ago, the toxins leaked into the water and people started getting sick."

"Exactly. It was a poor neighborhood, and the mayor kept making excuses, saying it would cost too much to tear down the homes and relocate the families. But when Sabrina organized them, they went to court and finally got some compensation."

"Good for her. How did she end up getting involved?"

Dawn smiled slyly. "Probably not too many people know

this, but Sabrina's maiden name was Rodriguez, and she had a rough childhood. She grew up in a suburb of Paterson, not dirt poor but working-class. I think her father knocked her mother around a bit, too. Sabrina was smart enough that her teachers helped her get a scholarship to college, and of course, that's how she met Phil Ward. But when she heard about the situation in Graversen, knowing Sabrina, I imagine she saw a chance to help her own kind of people."

I turned off the highway and slowed the van a bit. The semirural road that led to The Reserve had minimal lighting after dark, and in the fall months, I always stayed alert for buck that might dart across the road. In this vehicle I probably ran less risk of damage than in the CR-V, but I'd probably still crash trying to avoid hitting the deer.

Meanwhile, I had time to absorb Dawn's fresh insight into Sabrina's background. Her upbringing probably also explained why she'd gone to bat for the harassed minority women of the Merrywood Suites chain. "Could anyone from the Graversen lawsuit still be holding a grudge against her?"

"Well, Mom reminded me that the town's mayor, who balked at the cleanup, ended up looking like scum and didn't even bother to run for reelection. That made me check back through the documents I photographed from Sabrina's files and a news article from the time. I came across a familiar name— the mayor's secretary back in those days was Alma Gunner!"

I almost asked Dawn if she could be sure it was the *same* Alma Gunner, but really, how many people with that name could there be in North Jersey? A lot of folks at The Reserve sure seemed to have shady pasts of one kind or another. "So Alma could've had a beef with Sabrina even before the two of them both ended up living in the same community."

"And long before the cats started leaving dead birds along her favorite walking path."

By now, I'd visited The Reserve often enough to be able to spot the small, tasteful sign for the turnoff, even in the dark. I shifted into first gear to climb the slight hill to the entrance. At least this route was well-lit, with antique-style streetlights.

From the corner of my eye, I saw Dawn check her notepad again. "One more hot tip from Mom: Mike Lawler, our 'euthanize her' loudmouth, used to work for a pet shop of some kind in South Jersey. I'm wondering if it could've been Wags 'n' Hugs, the puppy mill where Sabrina led a demonstration. That was one business she and her group actually managed to shut down completely, even before New Jersey put stricter laws in place for breeders."

I smiled. "Your mom could turn out to be one of our most valuable spies in this case, and she's thousands of miles away."

"Makes sense, though. She's lived next to these people for five years and knows them better than either of us do."

I reached the community's tidy security shed, neatly trimmed in white with a little cupola on the roof. It was flanked by tall, wrought-iron gates—one in, one out. I rolled down my window and showed Dawn's guest pass to the guard, Lee, who'd seen us before. He smiled and let us right through in spite of our unfamiliar mode of transportation. Maybe Nolan had warned him that we'd be arriving in a matte-black van, the ideal conveyance for a serial killer.

Luckily, by now I'd also learned my way around the winding roads lined with almost identical beige town houses. Not able to distinguish many landmarks, I'd memorized the number and direction of the turns on the way to the guest parking lot. The fact that the community's layout revolved around the central, oval plaza made things a bit easier.

I asked Dawn, "So, I guess Mark and Maggie agreed to do all the spaying and neutering?"

"They did. Chris said they sighed a little about trying to fit it into their busy schedules, but in the end they do support our cause. They have to charge something, but they're still giving FFF a big discount."

In the main parking lot, close to the woods, we met up with Becky and Chris to coordinate our efforts.

"We haven't stocked the feeders since yesterday morning," Becky told us. "And we blocked the entrances to the shelters this afternoon, so the cats won't be able to hide in those. We really need them to go into the traps tonight and nowhere else."

Chris added, "The tricky thing will be that about half of the ferals are notched—their ears have been nicked, meaning they're already neutered and vaccinated. So if we catch any of those, we'll want to release them. If those cats start to eat all the bait and spring the traps, though, it'll be a problem. It could scare the others off, so the ones we want might just run away."

Sounded like a challenge, all right. "Any way to avoid that?"

"Not really," Becky said. "On the other hand, the cats who've already been captured could be more wary. That would leave the less suspicious ones to go for the bait. We won't know until we get started."

Trying to move slowly and quietly, we trekked fairly deep into the woods, each carrying a cage that was already baited with strong-smelling food—canned tuna, sardines, or mackerel in oil. Chris told me that those usually brought the ferals running, but Becky promised mysteriously that she had something special in reserve to lure even the most stubborn cats.

Of course, the animals were used to being fed at night by now, and a few showed up to watch us from a distance. We put the traps down, spaced a few yards apart; imitating Becky and Chris, Dawn and I covered each of our cages with a small tarp and a layer of soggy, fallen leaves. Once those traps were set, we brought out four more and placed them in a wide arc a little nearer to the parking lot. Depending on how things went, we might or might not need all twelve.

"Now we wait for a while," Becky told us. "Want some coffee? I brought a box from Mickey D's."

"You guys do think of everything!" Dawn told them, with a smile.

Since the night wasn't too cold, we sat together on the stone retaining wall of the parking lot and sipped our hot brew from paper hot/cold cups. Dawn and I felt we could trust the FFF kids almost as coconspirators, so we told them we were quietly looking into the deaths of both Sabrina and Edie. I wasn't surprised to hear that Becky and Chris had their suspicions about the first case, but it was news to them that someone claimed to have heard a scream the night Sabrina died. Becky pounded a fist on her knee, and Chris muttered a curse under his breath.

"I have to say, much as saving the ferals is important, I suspect it goes much further than that," I told them. "Sabrina rocked a lot of boats over her lifetime. I don't think we need to look back too far, though. I doubt that someone has held a lethal grudge against her for decades. It probably was someone she ticked off over the last ten years or so."

Dawn gave a grim chuckle. "That still spreads a pretty wide net."

Becky's normally soft, pretty face turned set and angry. "I'm not sure you have to look that far to find a suspect."

"Oh?" I asked.

"There's her damned brother-in-law," Chris explained. "Not much family feeling there, or mourning, that I can see."

"He's been in a huge hurry to clean out Sabrina's condo and get it back on the market, as if it were worth all that much," Becky said. "We wanted to get some cat food she had stored in her kitchen, and he acted like we were trying to loot her valuables . . . such as they are. Have you been in Sabrina's place?"

"We were," Dawn told them. "We went through her files, and I photographed as much material as I could find about protests and issues she was involved in recently."

The two of them looked surprised and pleased to hear this.

"Anyway," said Becky, "she used to have us over for coffee and strategy sessions, so we know our way around. But what's in there to steal? It's all related to her projects, or else it's personal clutter."

"No offense, but she didn't clean too often, either," Chris put in. "Victor will have to hire someone to get it in shape before he even gets a fair price for it."

"But Sabrina could have money put away," I suggested. "The Wards were wealthy, so she must have gotten something when her husband died. Maybe she invested it and her next of kin will inherit a pile."

Becky laughed out loud in satisfaction. "Don't think so! She told me once that when she died it was all going to various causes. I think FOCA even gets a little."

"Not enough worth killing for, though!" Chris hurried to add, tongue in cheek.

Privately, I wondered if Victor knew that for sure, yet. Or even Bonelli, though she'd said she suspected it.

We'd been chatting for over half an hour and suddenly heard a startled yowl from the woods. It was soon followed by another, of a different pitch.

We all exchanged smiles. "Should we check?" Dawn asked.

Still trying to be quiet, we made our way back through the woods to the traps. Even under their blankets of tarps and leaves, it wasn't hard to tell which three contained cats—they rocked from the animals' thrashings, pierced by the occasional wail. I felt sorry for the creatures, who had no idea we were trying to help them. Some hissed or spit when we peeked in. Using small flashlights, we tried to check their ear tips.

"This one's good," Chris called out. "No notch."

"Good here, too," I reported.

"Me, too," said Dawn. "Nailed it!"

Two of the cats were only kittens, maybe a year old, which might have explained why they were naïve enough to get caught. Keeping the canvas covers over the traps to stress them as little as possible, we carried them back to my van. The cats wouldn't be any colder there than in the woods, and they had enough food to hold them for a while. We brought out more traps, baited them, and set them in slightly different locations.

On our way out the second time, my flashlight picked out a pair of glowing golden-green eyes watching us through the trees. They looked so eerie, almost disembodied, that I knew the cat's face must be jet black. I could imagine superstitious Heidi taking this as proof that Omen was some kind of demon. I knew that, in reality, the same feature that helps cats see well at night also makes their eyes reflect light and seem to glow in the dark.

Was Omen upset that we were catching and removing his mates and kittens? I pointed him out to Becky, and she smiled sadly.

"I don't hold out much hope of trapping that guy," she said. "He's so wily, he's escaped every time so far. But at least if we finish spaying the females, it won't matter—Omen won't be making any more babies. The colony already has stabilized quite a bit since we fixed the younger males a month ago."

We had returned to the parking lot to wait some more when a stocky male figure in a hooded jacket strutted toward us. Even before he came near enough to recognize, I knew it was Mike Lawler by his distinctive, angry bark.

"Whadda you guys think you're doing, hanging around here all night? I been watching you from my deck—you been out here for an hour."

Dawn gracefully ran interference for the rest of us. "Oh, didn't Sam tell you? We're repeating the TNR tonight. We've caught three cats already, and we've got eight more traps set in the woods. If we're lucky, we'll catch all the ones we missed last time."

That took just a little of the belligerence out of Mike. "Well . . . good. An' you're gonna take 'em away?"

"To be vaccinated and neutered. Then we'll bring them back."

His pug-nosed face twisted in disgust. "Aw, no, not that routine again. What the hell good does that do?"

I had to chime in. "Mr. Lawler, we went through all of this at the board meeting. As long as this colony stays here, controlled, you won't have to worry about other cats moving in."

Chris helped me. "If we remove them, it'll create a vacuum. You could get a whole new bunch that aren't fixed, and then you'll be overrun again. Wouldn't you rather have twenty or so cats that stay in the woods, near the feeder, but don't breed or hang around the condos?"

"I'd rather have no cats, and most of the people who live here agree with me!"

A stern baritone interrupted us. "Is there a problem?"

I was relieved to see Sam Nolan striding toward us from the direction of the town houses. I knew he lived on the property, and our public argument probably had disturbed his restful evening. Still, in his beat-up leather bomber jacket and faded jeans, he appeared ready to kick butt, if necessary.

"No problem on our end," I assured him.

Mike tried out his complaint on the resident manager but got shut down quickly.

"These people have my permission to carry out this job tonight, for as long as it takes," Sam informed him. "Everyone's been complaining that they didn't totally solve the problem the first time—well, they're trying to finish it. If you don't want hungry, lovesick cats hanging around your stoop, I'd suggest you go home and let these folks do their job."

"They'd better the hell solve this problem," Mike fired back at Sam, "or I'll be calling your bosses at the management company."

This threat did not seem to faze Sam, who told him dryly, "Hey, you do what you have to do."

Mike wisely decided to back down, maybe since Sam stood almost a head taller. He turned on his heel and hiked back up the rise to the town houses.

"Guy's a notorious pain in the ass," Sam said to us. "Always whining that he's had a tough life. Who hasn't?"

"Has he got any family?" I asked.

"A son in Delaware, I think, who he rarely sees. No real hobbies, except an old Chevy Vega he tinkers with in his garage and drives around the community sometimes. I heard a rumor that he got in trouble with the law once. Nothing too serious, I guess, but he felt unfairly accused and it soured him on life."

"Where did he work, do you know?" Dawn asked.

"Believe it or not, I think it was at a kennel." Sam sniffed at the irony. "Pretty crazy, because now he seems to hate animals. Or maybe it's just cats."

"Do you think Mike could have put out the poisoned food that made Bert Chamberlain's dog sick?" I asked.

"Who knows? If he did, there's probably no way to prove

it. Now I try to keep an eye on the woods at night. Not really part of my job description, but I've never had the luxury of working nine to five."

"Can Mike get you in trouble if he complains to the management company?"

"Ha, they all say that. MRA trusts me to do my job. They won't care about complaints unless people actually start moving out. 'Course, Ted Remy could be doing that soon, he told me yesterday."

I remembered Ted saying that, too, when we'd talked at the fitness center. At the time, I'd figured it was just wishful thinking on his part.

Sam squared his broad shoulders and assessed our group. "So, any chance you folks might be able to finish up this project tonight?"

Becky shrugged. "Depends on the cats. If we don't get them all by this round, can we leave a few traps overnight and come back to check them in the morning?"

He tilted his head. "Don't see why not. I'll let the front gate know."

"Terrific," she said. "Thanks for all your help."

This time, Dawn and I took our coffee and retreated to my van to warm up.

"Maybe I'm too trusting," I said, "but I think we can scratch Sam Nolan off our list of suspects."

"I agree." Dawn turned thoughtful. "So, Ted's moving out. Lauren told me no one in the community could afford to sell their homes—that property values had plunged because of the feral cats."

"Maybe she was exaggerating. Or maybe Ted's so fed up that he's willing to take the loss. Whatever, it'll be good riddance, won't it?" I took a long swallow of the rapidly cooling coffee, hoping it would keep me alert for the short drive home.

"Becky sounds convinced that Victor Ward is involved in some way. But would he murder his own sister-in-law?"

"She did have a heart attack," Dawn reminded me. "If it wasn't cold-blooded murder, that opens up a wider range of suspects. And don't forget, Victor's got a professional stake in The Reserve, too. I checked the website for his marketing firm, and Gladstone Development is one of their biggest clients. Mom also told me this place is a flagship community for Gladstone—one they point to when they pitch projects for other parts of the state."

"So if it gets bad publicity for any reason, or seems to be going down in value . . ."

"Gladstone's other projects may fall through. Which could make Victor's job of marketing them even tougher."

I shook my head, impressed. "Sounds like your mom has been a font of inside information. Did she have any other useful gossip?"

Dawn smirked. "I don't know about useful, but she said that Joan Pennisi and Ted were an item for a while. Can you believe that?"

"Get out! Ladylike Joan and that macho beast?"

"They do say opposites attract, though that's never worked for me. Maybe they broke up because she's a bird-watcher. I'm sure the bluebirds of happiness all scatter when Ted storms down the walking trail."

Chris startled us then by knocking on the van's window. With a gloved hand, he gestured for us to come out and check the traps again.

This time we found five more cats. One didn't count because it was notched, but another probably counted double—or quadruple—because she was obviously pregnant. Mark or Maggie would have the added "fun" of delivering kittens.

Now it was close to midnight, and we'd rounded up eight cats out of the twelve we'd hoped for. But Becky was not discouraged yet.

"Time to use my secret weapon." She pulled out a paper bag of fried chicken tenders, from the fast-food place.

"You've had them this whole time?" Chris accused her. "And here we're all starving!"

"They're not for us, they're for the last holdouts." She demonstrated how to tie string around a piece of chicken and hang it from the very back of the cage. "Never known a cat to resist these. We'll leave behind about six baited traps, in case we get a few more notched cats. They should be okay in the covered cages overnight, especially now that they've had the food. Chris and I can come back around dawn to pick them up."

We spaced the last of the traps widely. As we were leaving the woods, I noticed an unfamiliar light-colored tabby already watching us with interest, sniffing the air at the smell of the chicken.

"This could work," I told Becky. "Who knows, this time you might even catch Omen."

Chris scoffed at this, though. "No way. That dude is totally rogue."

His partner agreed. "I doubt he'll ever be caught, and maybe that's okay. Omen always watched out for Sabrina." Becky turned her gaze to the starry sky. "Maybe she's up there watching out for him."

Chapter 18

En route home, we stopped at the Chadwick Veterinary Clinic with our charges and helped the tech who worked the night shift settle them all in cages. We alerted him that Becky and Chris would probably be by in the morning with a few more cats. Then, bleary-eyed, Dawn and I went our separate ways to grab a few hours of sleep. Each of us still had to rise early so our respective shops would open for business on time.

When Sarah arrived at nine, I briefed her on my adventure of the previous evening, and she listened with interest. "I always wondered how those programs worked," she said. "You do have to know what you're doing, don't you?"

I nodded. "And the FFF guys really seem to. I wouldn't be surprised if they've caught all, or most, of the cats by this morning."

"If they do, think that will be the end of the controversy at the condo community?"

"Who knows? I'm sure there are some residents who won't be happy as long as there are any wild cats at all roaming around the property." I thought again of Ted and hoped he would make good on his threat to move out.

Sarah and I released a pair of Siamese cats from the same home into the playroom together. Then, for the next two hours, we risked our limbs to groom a high-strung Siberian who especially objected to having her nails clipped. In spite of our best efforts—and the aid of latex gloves and a grooming harness—when it was all over, we both were left doctoring ourselves with antiseptic and Band-Aids. At least the cat came through unscathed, and if she ever returned, next time we'd know what we were getting into.

At my lunch break, I called Mark on his cell phone. I knew he wouldn't pick up if he was busy with a patient, but to my surprise, he answered right away.

"Thought I might hear from you," he said.

"Are you cursing us out by now?" I asked. "Are you totally inundated?"

"These critters are a little tough to handle, for sure, but we were prepared for that. Gotta wrap a towel around 'em and be quick with the first injection."

"Did the brown tabby have her litter yet?"

"No, so we'll have to keep her here until she does. Really, though, things are going pretty well. We've got all hands on deck, and we're snipping away. There'll be no more kittens from this bunch."

"The FFF kids brought in more this morning?"

"Another three. Becky said there was just one who got away, who always gets away. A male."

I smiled to myself. "Omen, a scrappy black tom. He was Sabrina's favorite."

"Hmm . . . guess that's why there are so many black kittens. Well, he can't do any more breeding now, with his whole harem neutered."

"That's really good news," I told Mark. "Thanks so much for helping with this."

"I probably would have done it anyway, but you and Dawn did a very effective job of twisting my arm. Listen, I don't have much time to talk, as you can imagine, but I got some more good news today."

"About what?"

"You won't believe it, but our Mr. Bock called to say he's been following the elimination diet with Looli and thinks her skin is clearing up."

"Aha!" I said.

"He made an appointment for next week to come back, go over what he's fed her, and see whether anything caused a reaction, so we can figure out what the allergen might be."

"Sounds like the guy is finally listening to reason."

"Amazing, right? He even sounded more cheerful and easygoing than when he was in my office. Whatever's gotten into him, I hope it lasts."

Mark needed to get back to his surgeries then, leaving me to wonder some more about the "nice lady" who had talked legal sense to Bock. If she had such a positive effect on him, I wished them a long and happy future together.

I'd just released two more of our boarders into the play-room—black-and-white brothers Heckle and Jeckle, who'd been here before—when the front door opened and the fuzz walked in. No, I never would have called Angela Bonelli "the fuzz" to her face. But although she'd become a friend, her quietly authoritative body language and serious demeanor always made me hope that I had no unpaid parking tickets. Though her status as a detective did not require her to wear a uniform, her navy blue wool, three-quarter-length trench coat might as well have had POLICE stenciled across the back.

Always the optimists, Sarah and I greeted her cheerfully.

"Cassie, you were up at The Reserve again last night." It

wasn't a question. Bonelli had no psychic powers, just her own ways of finding things out.

"Dawn and I helped out the FFF people with their trap-neuter-return program. We pretty much hit our goal, too—caught eleven of the cats that still needed to be vaccinated and neutered. They're over at the clinic now, being processed."

A hint of a smile. "That's what we call it when we jail suspects. But I gather these cats are going to be released again."

"That's the deal. Even if some of the residents up there might not be happy about it."

Bonelli folded her arms, still in the bulky coat, and leaned back against the sales counter. "Find out anything useful?"

"We've been hearing things." I knew better than to tell her that Dawn and I had been aggressively digging for information. I filled her in on the most pertinent background we had found out about the board members and other residents. "Mike Lawler actively hassled us last night, but Sam Nolan got him under control," I added. "Becky says Victor Ward has been giving FFF a hard time. I guess you've looked into Sabrina's will. Does he stand to inherit anything?"

The detective frowned. "Ordinarily I wouldn't answer that question, especially if there was any chance of foul play. But in this case, I think you and Dawn already had predicted the contents of the will. It's very unlikely that anyone killed Sabrina for her money. It's all earmarked for various charities and causes, most of them national organizations."

"Becky thought that was the case. She and Chris said that FOCA might be getting some, but certainly not enough for them to bump off one of their strongest allies!"

"Having seen the will, I'd agree with that. So, despite the controversy over Sabrina's activism, there's still a good chance she died of completely natural causes," Bonelli said. "However, we did get a sort of confession, secondhand, from one of the Reserve residents."

"What?" I asked, startled. "And you didn't lead with that?"

"Not about either of the human deaths. Apparently Heidi Sweet was the one who put out the poisoned food for the cats and ended up making Bert Chamberlain's dog sick. She got the idea from a TV report warning that NSAID drugs, while safe for most humans, could be poisonous to pets."

I remembered my last conversation with that nasty elf of a woman, when she again accused Sabrina of being a witch who had cursed their community. "That's awful, but I'm not too surprised. She's really got a screw loose."

"Actually, that's her defense. Joan Pennisi, her niece, told me that Heidi admitted everything to her. Said her aunt was sorry about Bert's dog, but desperately wanted to get rid of the black cat that she thought was spying on her. Why Heidi thought *that* cat in particular would eat the food, who knows?"

"She still ended up injuring the dog and costing Bert a lot in vet bills. Can't anything be done about that?"

"Joan says her aunt's got a mild dementia that's getting worse. She's working with some of their other relatives to have Heidi moved to an assisted-living community with an Alzheimer's unit. Joan has explained the whole thing to Bert and offered to pay his vet bills, but wants to keep the matter quiet otherwise. She hopes to go on living in the community and serving on the board, so she'd rather not have everyone remembering her aunt as the crazy lady who almost killed her neighbor's dog."

I sighed. There was no sense in punishing Heidi for her irrational behavior, I supposed, and at least she ought to be moving out before she could do any more harm. "How about Edie Seibert? Any more news there?"

Before Bonelli could answer me, a customer came in to ask

about the cat trees and scratching posts that we offered for sale. Sarah waited on him, and the detective suggested that she and I find a place to talk more privately.

We slipped beyond the screened door into the playroom and found a couple of relatively fur-free hassocks to use as seats. Bonelli even shrugged out of her winter coat and hung it out of harm's way. Heckle and Jeckle—black longhairs with white bellies, paws, and faces—hopped down from their wall shelves to say hello. I popped Jeckle onto my lap while Heckle rubbed his face assertively against Bonelli's pants leg. More of a dog person, she unbent enough to half-heartedly stroke his back.

"Seibert's death is still under investigation," she told me. "Some puzzling things there. Edie was found at the bottom of her main staircase and apparently had been in bed. But, like I told you before, her walker was folded up and leaning against the newel post at the foot of the stairs."

"That is weird. Guess there's a chance she tried climbing the stairs without the walker this time." *And didn't live to regret it,* I added silently.

"But the tox tests showed that she'd also taken a strong OTC sleeping pill," Bonelli went on. "Combined with her usual antivertigo medication, that would make her much woozier than normal."

"I'm surprised she'd do that. I didn't know Edie well, but she seemed to be the careful type and pretty good at managing her disability." Jeckle purred and kneaded my lap; I reminded myself to give his nails another clipping before we sent him home.

Meanwhile, Heckle had gotten bored with Bonelli's luke-warm company and hopped onto a nearby cat tree. The detective seemed just as well pleased, as she continued. "There was a cup of tea in Edie's sink that had been rinsed, but it still held traces of sediment. Forensics matched the drug to a new bottle of pills in her medicine cabinet. But here's the thing. If you were going to take a fairly small pill—a tablet—would you crush it and mix it into your tea?"

I saw where she was headed. "Not unless maybe I had a problem with swallowing . . . or a phobia about it."

"Which, as far as we know, Edie didn't. The pill bottle had her prints, but very faint and just her fingertips. Not as if she'd actually gripped it hard to twist off that child-proof cap. And two pills were missing, while one is the normal dosage. Now, she might have taken one previously, or—"

"Or someone made her a cup of tea, mashed up two sleeping pills in it, put her to bed, and brought her walker downstairs. But if they wanted to kill her, that's pretty chancy. How did they know she wouldn't just stay in bed until she slept it off?"

Bonelli shrugged. "I don't have an answer for that. If it was deliberate, it was carefully staged to look like an accident. Otherwise, Edie took a couple of sleeping pills that combined badly with her usual medicine, wandered around dizzy under the influence, and took a header down the stairs. But it's fishy enough that we're looking into it further."

"One angle that I'm sure you've already thought of," I said. "If she let somebody into her house to make her tea and even put her to bed . . ."

The detective nodded. "It had to be someone she knew pretty damned well. Someone she trusted."

Only after Bonelli had left did I remember that, according to her online résumé, Joan Pennisi had worked as a school nurse. Were she and Edie friends? Might she have known what medication the older woman was taking and how it would interact with the sleeping pills? Edie probably would have trusted her.

But Joan was ethical enough to go to Bonelli and admit that Heidi poisoned the cat food. If she felt guilt-stricken about that, it doesn't seem likely that she would turn around and drug Edie, causing her to fall to her death.

Too bad those motion-sensing devices I put in back of Edie's condo didn't include security cameras! They might have caught whoever was poking around her place that night.

A joke, of course, because Edie never would have gone to that much trouble and expense just to monitor some feral cats.

I remembered Bonelli's story about one of the Chadwick cops being startled by the blast of air when he'd stepped onto Edie's patio. Anyone putting her town house back on the market would probably dispose of the devices now, because they might discourage buyers.

I installed them, so maybe I should remove them. I can ask around and see if anyone else at The Reserve, with a similar cat issue, could use them.

Half-consciously, I heard the front counter phone ring and Sarah answer it. Now she called to me, "Cassie, it's my cousin Yolanda. I told her you wanted to talk to her."

I definitely did and hurried to take the phone. Yolanda Carter introduced herself in a soft, ladylike voice. "I was so sorry to hear about what happened to Sabrina. Sarah said you're looking into the possibility that it might not have been an accident?"

"The police are looking into it, officially, but so far they haven't found any real evidence of foul play," I explained. "My friend Dawn Tischler is more suspicious because she knew Sabrina well, as you probably did. She thinks someone Sabrina crossed in the past might have wanted to silence her."

"That would be awful," Yolanda said, "but I suppose that might have been the case. She always was very outspoken and ruffled a lot of feathers."

"I'm hoping you can tell me about your experiences working for Merrywood Suites. Anything leading up to the lawsuit, anything at all that might be relevant."

I heard the other woman draw a deep breath, as if going back to those days, even in her head, took an emotional toll. "I worked at the Morristown hotel for about five years. Started as a waitress, but after a while the manager took a liking to me and promoted me to hostess. It meant more pay and better conditions, so I thought it was great at first. Then he started acting like he expected favors from me that, shall we say, weren't in the job description. I'd put up with a little harassment as a waitress, but mostly from customers, and I never had to be alone with them. But this manager would find ways to corner me in a hallway or an office, until I was really afraid of him. At the same time, I needed the job!"

I thought of similar situations I'd faced, mostly at school and in short-term gigs afterward, though luckily none had gone far enough to really frighten me. "What did you do?"

"I was ready to just quit, and take my chances, when I heard that the maids had it even worse. One guy on the maintenance staff was notorious for saying and doing sexual things to them, and there also had been a couple of assaults by hotel guests. The women made complaints, but nothing ever happened . . . except sometimes they got disciplined themselves, or even fired."

I had read a short summary of this in the news story about the lawsuit, and from the tension in Yolanda's voice, I could tell how much the memory disturbed her, even today. "How did Sabrina get involved?"

"I think one of the maids had grown up with her, in the same neighborhood, and knew she was an activist. When Sabrina heard our story, she jumped in with both feet. She said all the women who'd had problems should file a class action suit. When we told her we couldn't afford that, she just smiled and said not to worry—she'd foot the bill and show us what to do." I heard a happy lift in Yolanda's tone. "You know the rest. We went to court and won!"

"That's so great," I said. "But I also heard that Merrywood ended up with a blackened reputation, and went from a thriving chain to a struggling one. The Morristown hotel completely shut down, didn't it?"

"It did. Frankly, I had trouble finding work for a while, too, because I was 'one of those troublemakers.' Eventually, I did end up in a place where they appreciate me for my actual work skills."

"Dawn and I are just trying to figure out if anyone named in that scandal could have been keeping track of Sabrina's moves and waiting for a chance to bring her down. I'm working right now, and you probably are, too. But maybe I could e-mail you a list of names, with a little background about each person. And if you can think of any people who should be added to the list, could you send me those names, too? I promise, no one will see this or know about it except me, Dawn . . . and of course, Sarah."

Yolanda chuckled dryly. "I'm not really worried about that. If there's any chance that one of those lowlifes killed Sabrina, I'll be glad to help you bring him down. Or her, I suppose. After all, some female employees lost their jobs, too, when Merrywood went bust."

We exchanged e-mail addresses, and I thanked her sincerely for her help. Then I got off the phone and went back to helping Sarah at the front counter.

My assistant wore a hint of a smile. "Yolanda was helpful?"

"Well, she had quite a story to tell, and the lawsuit was only six years ago. Certainly there could be people involved with that hotel chain who could still be in this area now . . . and who might still have wanted to strangle Sabrina Ward."

Later that afternoon, when Sarah and I had finished with our boarders and weren't expecting any more customers for the day, I e-mailed the list of suspects to Yolanda.

My assistant had left for the evening when Dawn called, to tell me that all of the ferals had been successfully neutered. "Becky and Chris want to bring the three males back up there tomorrow night," she said. "The rest of the females should be able to go back the end of the week. Mark said they're holding the tabby with the new kittens a couple of days longer."

"Sounds like the project was a total success," I said.

"Yeah, we did good. I've love to help return the cats, but there's something wrong with my darned car. When I started it up this morning, it was actually smoking from under the hood. So it's down at Gillis's Garage for tonight—let's hope he can figure out what's wrong."

"I was planning to go back to The Reserve one day soon to shut off those motion sensors on Edie's patio. If the place is put on the market, they could scare off buyers and just call more attention to the feral problem. So maybe when I go I can take along some cats . . . and you, too, of course."

Dawn laughed. "I'm an afterthought, eh? That would be great, if we can coordinate it. Maybe Saturday, after we close? You should talk to Sam first, so nobody questions why you're hanging around Edie's place."

"Good thinking, I will." I brought Dawn up to speed on my phone conversation with Yolanda.

"Wow," she said. "I heard a little about that harassment suit at the time, and like you, I skimmed some of the documents in Sabrina's files. But it's a lot different to get the inside scoop from someone who went through it."

"That's the way I felt. I could hear in Yolanda's tone how much it bothered her to even relive and talk about what happened. Well, at least the hotel chain suffered for it. I don't feel much sympathy for them, after management ignored the problem for years."

I was about to hang up when my phone alerted me to a new message. "Hold on a sec. Looks like Yolanda is getting back to me."

I read the e-mail, and my scalp prickled. She was asking if I had a photo of Mike Lawler.

"Would there be any pictures of him around?" I asked Dawn. "He isn't even on the board."

"Yeah, that could be tough. Try online, though. I think he was one of the first people to buy into the community, so maybe he was interviewed."

Not by a newspaper, but I found him mentioned in a press release about The Reserve put out by Victor's promotional firm, To Market. It included a shot of pudgy Mike from the waist up, smiling and chest puffed out, standing in front of his new town house.

"Score!" I copied the link and sent it to Yolanda.

Dawn reminded me, "Bonelli said her guys questioned Mike, and he has an alibi for the night Sabrina died."

"He was supposed to have been out of state, visiting his son, who backs him up. But at this point we're investigating *two* possible murders, aren't we?"

Over the phone, I could hear Tigger complaining loudly to Dawn because his dinner was late.

"I have to deal with this demanding child," she said. "Let me know if Yolanda has any more information. But tomorrow. Tonight, I need to get some real sleep!"

"I hear you on that."

I closed up the shop for the night, then trudged upstairs to feed my own cats and have my own dinner. Like Dawn, I was still dragging from the TNR marathon of the night before and looking forward to hitting the hay early. Luckily, I had some leftovers I could nuke for a decent meal, accompanied by a glass of white wine, since I didn't expect to be driving. After dinner I settled in on my slipcovered sofa, Mango on my lap and Cole and Matisse sprawled nearby. I tried to read some more of an older Sue Grafton novel that I'd gotten from the library, but even though she's my favorite author, my eyes kept closing from sheer fatigue.

I dozed off on the sofa for about ten minutes until my cell phone's version of "Stray Cat Strut" woke me. It was Yolanda.

"Hi, Cassie? Yes, it's the same Mike Lawler. He was actually named in the Merrywood suit for harassing one of the maids. He was staying at the hotel for some kind of event—a family wedding, or maybe it was a bachelor party. The maid said when she went in to clean his room, even though it was the afternoon, he was kind of drunk. He told her to come in anyway, closed the door, and tried to keep her there until she threatened to scream. I don't know if his name got into the papers at the time, or if he was fined or punished in any way. But even if he wasn't, word probably got around."

Wow, I thought. The general public might not know about Mike's misbehavior, but he surely would have known that Sabrina had backed the lawsuit. "Supposedly he has an alibi for the night Sabrina died, but that doesn't necessarily mean he wasn't involved in some way. He may be the first person we've come across who has a strong motive."

"Glad if I could help," Yolanda said. "His picture went out with this press release? That's funny. If Victor Ward does marketing for The Reserve, I'm surprised he wasn't aware of Mike's connection to the Merrywood scandal."

"How come?"

"Didn't you know? Gladstone Development, which created the whole Reserve chain, was also behind Merrywood Suites. In fact, they started developing condo communities after the hotels went into a slump. Probably figured selling private homes meant less chance of another harassment scandal."

What I'd seen at first as an easy solution was turning out to be just another strand in a very tangled web. Skilled as I might be at untangling knots, this could prove beyond my abilities. "Thanks so much, Yolanda. I'm sure all of this will turn out to be helpful to me and Dawn . . . and maybe to Sabrina, also."

"That's what I'm hoping. You're very welcome."

I clicked off, then stared at the open book in front of me for a few minutes without absorbing anything I read. Glass of wine or not, I probably was in for another restless night.

Chapter 19

When I stopped by Dawn's shop Saturday to pick her up, she was already in a mood.

"I still haven't got my car back," she groused. "Bob Gillis checked a whole bunch of things yesterday and finally found diesel fuel in my gas tank! I was low on gas before our last trip to The Reserve and never got a chance to refuel. So that means somebody deliberately added diesel to my Jeep. And it wasn't parked at a gas station or even at The Reserve!"

I shared her alarm. "That's creepy, all right. Where did you drive it yesterday?"

"Only for local errands. When it started smoking, I took it right to the garage and walked home. Before that, it was parked either on the street or in my private lot. But hell, all of our friends at The Reserve probably know about my shop by now, and know my car."

It certainly could have been done deliberately. Even if Dawn had parked on the street or at a strip mall, her gecko-green Jeep could be spotted from a mile away. Beyond that, anyone who wanted to make sure it was her car only had to memorize her license plate. "Did the wrong fuel do any serious damage?"

"No, but Bob has to clean the engine before he can give the car back to me. So you're my transportation for today, Cassie, if you don't mind too much."

"If you don't mind the jouncy van, it's my pleasure. Since we're bringing cats *back* to the community, which isn't such a popular thing to do, you may want me along for support, anyway."

First we swung by the clinic, where I said a quick hello to Mark and promised to call him later. His forty-something but tall and athletic partner, Maggie, helped us load four of the spayed females into the van. Becky and Chris already had taken some back to The Reserve and would return in a couple of days to pick up the new mama and her four kittens. Dawn and I hit the highway to a chorus of plaintive mews from the rear of the vehicle. Though the cats all seemed calmer and more resigned now than when they'd first been trapped in the cages, I knew they'd never make suitable pets and was glad we'd be releasing them soon.

On our way out of town, I told Dawn what I'd found out about Mike's connection with the Merrywood Suites lawsuit.

She gaped at me from the passenger seat. "My God, that's just the kind of link we've been looking for, isn't it? What kind of alibi is he supposed to have?"

"He told Bonelli he was visiting his son out of state and stayed overnight. Of course, she checked the story out with the son."

"And of course, the son wouldn't *ever* lie to protect his father," Dawn scoffed.

"I hear you. Still, I can't see going back to Bonelli and suggesting that maybe her department didn't check Mike out thoroughly enough. At least, not without some real evidence against him."

My friend fell into a disgruntled silence, as if she understood that I could only push the detective so far, but she still wasn't happy about it.

Alerted that we were coming, Lee, the Asian-American guard at the community's front gate, let our van pass without question. We parked at the curb near the walking trail so we could return the cats quickly and with a minimum of fuss. All of them soon sprinted to freedom, a couple hesitating for a few seconds until they grasped where they were. I glanced around to see if Omen would greet any of them, but he never showed.

"I'm just going to check the shelters and refill the feeder," Dawn said. "Do you want to run up to Edie's and pick up those canisters?"

Her condo was so near that I could almost see it from where we stood. "Okay . . . if you're sure you'll be all right here alone."

"*Pfft!*" Dawn dismissed my concerns. "It's broad daylight. I'll be just a few yards from the walking trail. And anybody who messes with me will find out I'm bigger, younger, and stronger than poor Sabrina. Go!"

I hiked up the rise to Edie's town house, reassuring myself that if Dawn yelled for help from the wooded area, I should be able to hear her . . . if Edie had been able to hear Sabrina.

The motion-sensitive canister that I'd set up outside the patio door had been knocked over, which didn't surprise me much. Probably landscapers often went around clearing the walks and patios, or maybe Officer Waller had kicked it over when it had hissed at him. The second canister, secured to a bush with a bungee cord, had stayed in place. The cord had gotten tangled in the small lower branches, though, so I had to work it free and pull it out far enough to reach the off switch.

Meanwhile, I noticed bits of stray trash that had collected under the patio's bushes. Again, I figured landscapers with snow or leaf blowers, or even just the wind, had pushed this stuff around until it finally caught somewhere. I picked up a chewing gum wrapper and a faded and crumpled store receipt. I also tried to grab what looked like a fragment of a pale plastic bag, but the breeze scudded it just out of my reach. Oh, well, I wasn't about to chase it—I wasn't on the maintenance crew.

A furry black bullet shot out from behind the bushes and pounced on the plastic fragment. I instantly recognized Omen by his lean, tough appearance and his bushy tomcat jowls. "Hi there, pal!" I squatted to greet him. "I was wondering where you were. We brought a bunch of your girlfriends back today! You should go say hello to them."

This suggestion didn't tempt Omen. For the moment, he amused himself by tossing the limp plastic fragment, about six inches long, and then catching it again. Strangely, he worked his way closer and closer to me. Finally he dropped the ragged thing just a couple of feet in front of me and retreated, as if it were a freshly killed mouse.

"Oh, thank you," I told him graciously, "but I really don't think—"

I stopped, took a closer look at the scrap, and picked it up. It wasn't a piece of bag after all—it was a pale latex glove, the same kind Sarah and I used when we were grooming. Pretty shredded from being blown into the bushes, though, and Omen's claws and teeth hadn't helped. Well, probably home health aides or even nurses came to visit the community's older residents. Any one of them could have lost it.

I glanced up at the feral tomcat again. He had retreated to the edge of the patio but sat staring at me. I remembered Heidi complaining that Sabrina's "familiar" gave people the evil eye, made them ill, and brought them other kinds of bad luck. I certainly didn't feel any evil vibe from this black cat. But, just as weird, I did feel as if he were sending me a message.

I held up the glove between us. "This?"

Satisfied that the dense human finally understood, Omen scampered away down the rise.

Back at the van, I showed Dawn my small collection of debris and told her about the cat's strange behavior with the glove. "Maybe I'm getting as superstitious as Heidi. Just because it was all outside Edie's patio doesn't mean it has any significance."

Dawn smoothed out and scanned the weather-bleached receipt. "Or maybe it does. This is from the CVS out on the highway, and one of the items listed sounds like a bottle of sleeping pills."

I left a message with Bonelli about my latest discoveries, and she asked me to bring them by on Monday morning. With her permission, I invited Dawn along. Though my friend played it cool, I could tell she was intrigued to see the inner sanctum of the Chadwick police station.

Behind the desk in her office, Bonelli studied the receipt and the tattered glove for a couple of minutes in silence. Finally she said, "If these were outside Edie Seibert's condo, I can't believe we missed them."

Maybe because I didn't want her to think Dawn and I were

trying to one-up the cops, I made excuses. "They might have been under the snow when your guys checked the grounds, or in a trash bin waiting for the next collection. Heck, they could even have blown over from somebody else's property."

Dawn chimed in. "But you have to admit, it's pretty coincidental. You said it looked like Edie had barely touched the bottle of sleeping pills, but there were no other fingerprints on it, either. And no others on the walker, though it was parked downstairs while she was upstairs."

Picking up on Bonelli's grim expression, I sighed. "I guess it still doesn't get us much further. You probably can't even get fingerprints off gloves like that."

The detective surprised me with a faint smile. "You're wrong. It will be harder if they've been exposed to the rain and snow . . . but people's hands perspire when they wear latex gloves, and the inside surfaces often pick up the wearer's prints. I'll have this one checked out."

The detective had begun to take the questions about Edie's death more seriously after I'd told her about the connections between Mike Lawler, Victor Ward, and the Merrywood Suites lawsuit. I'd convinced her that there at least might be a link between the latest "accident" and Sabrina's death in the woods. Now Bonelli agreed that the apparent sabotage of Dawn's Jeep also seemed to suggest that she and I were getting too close to the truth.

My friend leaned forward in her seat at this sign of hope, but I worried that it still might be too early. "Even if they do find prints inside the glove, if the person who wore them has never been fingerprinted . . ."

"Ted Remy has worked as a security guard, so his prints should be in a database from those days," Bonelli pointed out.

"You said Joan Pennisi was a school nurse? Anyone who works with children gets fingerprinted these days, so hers also may be on record somewhere." The detective dropped the two pieces of trash that we'd brought her into a clear plastic evidence bag. "If we do get something traceable, we may have to fingerprint Edie's nearest neighbors and anyone else who's been raising a stink about the feral cat business."

Dawn sat up straight, as if shot through with fresh energy. "You'd really do that? That would be terrific!"

Bonelli's smile took on a sardonic twist. "Anything to keep you two ladies out of more trouble. Can't you *please* stay away from The Reserve from now on, before one of you gets hurt?"

I sensed she was dismissing us. As we both started to get up, I remembered one more detail. "Did you hear anything about Edie's cat? Do I need to—"

"Alma Gunner has taken him in. Officer Waller said she seemed pretty happy to do it, and collected all the food dishes, litter pans and what have you. So that's one job off your plate, Cassie."

"I'm still helping FFF monitor the feral cats at the community," Dawn reminded the detective. "But as far as the human residents go, I'll be happy to avoid them. Oh, except for my mother—she's due home next weekend."

Bonelli shook her head. "When she hears what's been going on in her absence, she'll probably turn right around and book herself another vacation."

"She went to Morocco on an 'adventure' tour," I told the detective.

"Seems ironic, huh?" Dawn smiled.

"Yeah," Bonelli said. "If she'd wanted to risk her neck, she could have stayed home at The Reserve!"

★ ★ ★

Walking back from the police station, Dawn and I quietly discussed our theories. This new evidence seemed to expand our field of suspects.

"That glove didn't look too large," I recalled. "Might suggest the person who bought it was a woman. They do say poisoning is usually a woman's crime, and overdosing someone by tampering with her medicines is a type of poisoning."

"Heidi tried to poison the cats. Maybe she also got to Edie."

"Possibly . . . except Joan said she'd been keeping a closer eye on her aunt since the dog poisoning incident. Also, with dementia, I'm not sure Heidi would be able to find out what medicine Edie was taking, drive to the CVS on the highway, and pick out just the right—or wrong—kind of sleeping pills. Or remember to put Edie's walker where she couldn't easily get to it *and* to wear gloves to commit the crime. All of that took a lot more knowledge and planning than just doctoring a can of cat food."

Though it was only around noon, the overcast sky threatened more snow and made it feel much later in the day. As we walked back from the station, Dawn turned her gaze toward the storefronts that we passed, though I doubted she really saw any of the displays. "Like Bonelli said, Joan supposedly was a nurse," she recalled. "Heidi could have made the suggestion and Joan could have carried it out. Edie probably knew her well enough to trust her."

"True. But when I talked to Joan, she sounded genuinely upset that her aunt had tried to poison the cats and had accidentally sickened Bert's dog. I can't imagine she'd go along with any plan to hurt a human being, especially a harmless neighbor who already had a disability."

Bundled once again in her long, Peruvian-patterned wool

coat, my friend shrugged. "We don't really know any of these
people well, do we? Remember how surprised you were to
find out that Joan used to be romantically involved with Ted?
She told me both of them took their big, rolling garbage cans
out to the curb around nine o'clock. Then she saw him go
back into his town house, and as far as she knows he never came
out again that night."

"Key phrase—'as far as she knows,' " I said. "I'm sure Ted
could have left quietly, on foot, without Joan seeing him. Or, if
she's still got a thing for him, maybe he persuaded her to tell
the cops that story so they'd stop hassling him." The sharpen-
ing breeze stung my face, and I was glad when we turned off
of Center Street and headed down the slight incline toward
my shop. "And then there's the latest issue, the business with
your Jeep."

Dawn threw me a crooked smile. "I know it's sexist, but if
poisoning is a woman's crime, sabotaging a car would be more
of a man's. How many people even know that if you add diesel
fuel to regular gasoline, the car will still run a little while and
then die? It's as if someone wanted to keep me from getting
back to the community for a few days."

"They didn't count on me coming to the rescue with my
terrorist van!" I laughed.

"No, but that's also very recognizable. Maybe from now on
you should—"

Dawn choked off her words. From the street, we could see
and hear someone sprint away from the rear parking lot of my
shop. The frozen ground crunched beneath running feet.

"Hey!" I yelled, but the black-clad figure already had disappeared into a neighborhood fringe of trees. A second later,
some unseen vehicle on the next block started up and sped
away.

"What the hell?" Dawn said. With caution, she and I followed my gravel driveway back to the parking lot. Maybe because of today's gloom, the safety light over my rear door already had kicked on. Had that helped to scare away the prowler?

Not soon enough, unfortunately. When we reached the van, I saw that the two left tires had gone flat, from deep slashes.

Chapter 20

Dawn and I must have interrupted the trespasser before he'd gotten to the van's other side. Those two tires still were intact.

"I should have kept my mouth shut," she joked darkly. "Guess I jinxed you."

I moaned. "Damn, this is too much. First your Jeep, now this?"

Dawn then helped me look over the CR-V, parked closer to the rear of the building and farther under the light. "At least these tires look okay," she said. "Hope he didn't tamper with anything else on this one. Have it checked in the morning before you take it anywhere."

"I will. Right now, though, my biggest concern is that I had a prowler roaming around here today with a knife."

Dawn straightened up and planted her hands on her hips. "That bothers me, too."

I hugged myself, shivering even in my wool pea jacket and fleece-lined boots. "Sometimes I think living over my store isn't the greatest idea. But the fact that I do helps to keep my boarders safe—in theory—and that's reassuring to my customers."

Dawn glanced up toward the second-floor apartment of the building next door. "I don't suppose Mrs. Kryznansky saw anything, either."

In the past, when there had been someone suspicious lurking around the shop, my middle-aged neighbor had been able to give some description of the intruder. But she had a part-time job at a dental office, so she might be at work now. I didn't see the car in her driveway, and when I rang her back doorbell, I got no answer.

I unlocked my back door, noting that the alarm system had not gone off or been disabled. At least he hadn't tried to get inside.

Dawn also pointed at the small electronic panel. "Thank God you have this, anyway."

Yes, a couple of attempted break-ins over the past year had taught me that lesson. After the first time someone had pried a rear window partway open, I'd gotten the alarm, and it had worked well enough to foil a similar attempt a few months later. You wouldn't think so many people would be brazen enough to walk right into a store's private parking lot and cause trouble, even by daylight, but I guess they felt secure that they couldn't be seen from the street.

Dawn and I checked on the feline boarders, but none seemed disturbed. Meanwhile, I said to her, "We both saw someone running away, all in black. Medium height, maybe five-eight or nine. Do we agree that it was a man?"

"Definitely, and not just because of my theory that men tamper with cars." She chuckled grimly. "He also *ran* like a man—heavily."

"I thought so, too. Anyway, I'm going to call it in. The Chadwick PD must be getting real tired of hearing from me by now."

"Trespasser with a knife, Cassie. You can't let that go."

After I'd made the call and the desk sergeant said he'd send a patrol car, Dawn asked, "Want me to spend the night here? Or want to come to my place?"

"Thanks, but . . . like I said before, I hate to leave the boarders unguarded, not to mention my own cats. And you've already been through your share of hassles. First, I'll try playing the damsel in distress and call Mark."

She laughed. "Good idea. I'm sure he'll be even better at offering you TLC. And better at scaring off your vandal, if he dares to come back."

The cops checked out the damage and made a report. They even dusted the driver's side of the van for fingerprints, but didn't hold out much hope of finding any. It was glove-wearing weather, after all, and the intruder could have made the cuts without ever touching the vehicle. No footprints showed, either, because of my gravel parking lot.

By the time all of that had taken place, it was after three p.m. I hated to call Mark and tell him I was concerned about being alone that night, but he responded like a true Prince Valiant. Well, he didn't hunt down the vandal and skewer him with a lance, but when he got out at five, he came straight from his clinic to my place. He kept a change of clothes in his locker at work in case of emergencies, and normally wore scrubs on the job, anyway. And unlike me, Mark had no pets waiting at home in his 1980s-vintage condo across town.

He shook his head over the violent-looking slashes in the tires, so clean that I wondered what kind of blade could have made them. *A hunting knife? Box cutter?*

"I don't like this, Cassie," he said, in a tight voice. "It's risky enough for you to be questioning people up at The Reserve, knowing that one or more of them might be dangerous. But if some bad guy has figured out where you live and work, he could decide he needs to shut you up, too. Today it's just your van, but tomorrow . . ."

I held up one hand in a plea for mercy. "You're not telling me anything I haven't thought of myself, Mark. The cops have promised to check my parking lot a couple of times on their rounds, which ought to keep the guy from doing any more damage. Honestly, I can't think or talk about it anymore tonight, okay? Let's just drop the subject, go inside, and have some dinner."

Not that my culinary talents are enough to make you forget all your troubles, but I did pull together a decent meal for the two of us from some leftover chicken, rice, and vegetables, and we finished off the rest of my bottle of wine. Later, Mark did an excellent job of taking my mind off my worries, as only he could. Afterward I dropped into such a sound sleep that in the morning it took my alarm clock, three whining cats, and Mark shaking me by the shoulder to bring me back to consciousness.

Over a cold cereal and coffee breakfast, his tone grew serious again. "I didn't want to give you grief last night, because you already were upset enough. But y'know, it's really tough on me, Cassie, the way you keep getting into these dangerous situations. Sometimes I don't even find out about them until the damage is done, so I can't help you. That drives me slightly crazy."

The anguish in his tone startled me; I hadn't considered the worry I caused him by not always letting him know what I was up to. On the other hand, I also didn't want Mark telling me what I should or should not do—too many overtones, again, of my last boyfriend. Heck, I didn't always let Bonelli tell me what to do, and she was the fuzz!

"I never *meant* to get so involved in this mess at The Reserve, and I didn't expect it to be dangerous," I insisted. "Almost everyone accepted, at first, that Sabrina's death was an accident. Only Dawn thought otherwise, so I promised to help her find out the truth. Unfortunately, the deeper we dug, the more it did look like murder . . . and then, suddenly, there was a second possible victim."

"I get that, Cassie. At this point, though, both of you need to realize that you're in over your heads. From now on, leave it to the cops."

"Nothing against Bonelli and her guys, but *we* had to persuade them to take these cases seriously. They questioned some of the Reserve residents, but I doubt that Angela spent much of her time combing the Internet for background on those people. And between Dawn and me, we've been able to pump most of those folks for gossip that they were too cagey to tell the police."

Mark had been subjected before to my stubborn arguments, and held up his hands to ward off any more artillery fire. "All I'm saying is, since you've given all of that to Bonelli now, and she's pursuing it, back off. She has a badge and a gun, you don't." He set his empty coffee mug aside. "Going to call Gillis to come tow the van?"

I sighed, imagining what two new all-weather tires would cost me. "Yeah, as soon as Sarah shows up to watch the shop. How about you—anything exciting scheduled for today?"

He smiled. "I don't know about exciting, but Bock is bringing Looli back in, supposedly much improved. We're hoping to finally figure out what caused her skin condition."

After Mark left, it occurred to me that we might soon be facing another decision regarding the Christmas holiday. Did he plan to go to Philly again, and would he want me to come with him? I decided that, with everything else going on, I couldn't worry about that at the moment.

I called Bob Gillis about tires for the terrorist van. Since it had been at his garage for repairs before, he knew what to order and said he'd have them soon. After that, Sarah and I tended to the usual morning chores around the shop: cleaning litter pans, feeding boarders, and turning the first cat of the day out into the playroom.

Meanwhile, I tried to focus on a more cheerful subject—what to give Mark for Christmas. Not a tin of homemade ko-lacky; Krysta could beat me at that game too easily.

I was considering predictable items like a nice, woolly muffler or leather winter gloves while, during a short break, I skimmed the day's headlines on my laptop. An ad along the margin of the screen heralded a jazz concert in mid-January at the Morristown Arts Center.

Russell Jordan . . . wasn't he one of Mark's favorite gui-tarists?

I asked Sarah's opinion, and she grinned. "Sounds like a sure thing to me. Go for it!"

There were two shows, and the one on Saturday night was nearly sold out. On Sunday afternoon we could have better seats, and workwise, that would be a safer bet for Mark, any-way. With just a few clicks, I'd bought us tickets.

"Christmas present—purchased," I announced.

Sarah commended me. "You are an efficient modern woman."

We'd just sent Everest home with his surprisingly petite fe-male owner when Harry Bock strolled in the front door. I hardly recognized him with a smile stretched across his face. It improved his demeanor so much that I decided, in spite of his receding hairline and washed-out coloring, that he wasn't bad-looking for an older guy. Bock greeted both me and Sarah in a pleasant tone and set his gray, soft-sided cat carrier on the sales counter.

"Just thought you might be interested to see how Looli is doing," he said.

I could have taken this for sarcasm if Mark had not already told me that the cat was better. "I am, very!"

Bock unzipped the carrier, and his pet stepped out. She still wore her onesie, because it was darned cold outside, but I could see instantly that her head and legs looked more normal. Her owner undressed her and, although a few pink spots still speckled Looli's ivory skin, it looked worlds better than when he'd brought her in the last time.

"Fantastic!" I stroked the peach fuzz of the cat's head and back, which I'd hesitated to do while she had inflamed sores. She rubbed her big-eared, Yoda-like head against my hand, livelier and more affectionate now that she felt better. "So, it was a food allergy?"

"Apparently, the premium fare that I'd been feeding her was too high-protein. She doesn't seem to do well on beef, generally—she started to break out again as soon as I added that back into her diet. Dr. Coccia says I can probably keep her healthy, and save a little money, too, by giving her a more mainstream brand of canned food."

"Good idea. Canned also is less likely to have additives than the dry stuff." I let Sarah have a turn petting the wrinkly but sweet Sphynx. "I'm really glad you stopped by. It's so good to see her on the road to recovery. Guess before long you'll have her back in the show ring, too."

Bock shrugged with an uncommon air of nonchalance. "We'll see. After all Looli's gone through lately, I'll be careful about stressing her out again."

"That's smart," commented Sarah. She passed the cat back again, and Bock dressed Looli once more in her traveling outfit.

In a sincere tone, he said, "I really want to apologize to you ladies about the way I acted over this whole thing. I was too quick to blame you for the problem, and I wouldn't accept any other explanation, even when the rash got worse at home. I guess having the first vet recommend those expensive tests only made me angrier. On the other hand, Dr. Coccia's advice sounded almost too simple."

"Sometimes the simplest answer is the best," I said, waxing philosophical. "What made you change your mind?"

Humor sparked in Bock's blue-gray eyes. "Not what, who! I'm sorry to say, I actually considered filing a suit and went to the law firm that handled my divorce. The representative I met with convinced me that legal action would be very foolish. She pointed out that unless I at least tried the vets' suggestions, I'd never be able to prove your shop had caused the problem. She talked sense to me—perhaps with a certain amount of charm—and I finally listened."

I got the same vibe as Mark, that Bock and his legal advisor had hit it off. "Well, I hope from now on everything goes smoothly for both Looli and you. Keep in touch, okay?"

"Oh, I expect I will." With another mysterious smile, he thanked me and Sarah and departed with his pet.

My assistant marveled, "What a personality change! Did Mark slip him an animal tranquilizer on the side?"

"I doubt it, but someone sure mellowed him out. Which is probably a good thing for his poor cat, too."

I rotated boarders in the playroom, putting away a Siamese and turning loose an Abyssinian whose owner was visiting family in California. On my way back to the front of the shop, I accidentally kicked one of the air canisters that I'd carelessly left on the floor the previous night, when I'd been exhausted by all of the day's drama. That made me think suddenly of

Edie—how sweet she'd been, and how hard she had been try-ing to stay independent—and I blinked away a tear. I won-dered how Alma was getting along with Sonny, the big yellow tabby, and vice versa.

I sure hope Sonny isn't spraying in Alma's family room. Just be-cause the ferals are neutered doesn't necessarily mean they won't still come around looking for food. And if Sonny starts stinking up Alma's condo, she could lose her patience, figure he wasn't really her cat any-way, and drop him at the nearest shelter. After he's just lost his owner, that would be too sad!

Maybe I should offer to give Alma the canisters. . . .

I found her number on Dawn's list of suspects and gave her a call. Luckily, though it was the middle of the day, I caught her at home.

"Thanks so much for thinking of that, Cassie," she said. "Edie told me about the problem and how you set up those motion-sensor gizmos for her. But so far"—I heard her knock on a wooden-sounding surface—"Sonny has been behaving just fine. The first few days at my place he hid a lot, just com-ing out for meals, but now we're finally getting to be buddies."

"I'm really glad," I said. "Well, it's a standing offer. If you find later on that the ferals are hanging around and agitating him again, I'll be happy to set up the canisters near your patio. They seem to have worked for Edie."

Alma sniffed. "Funny that she was open to that idea, but not to wearing one of those Life Alert gadgets around her neck. I tried to persuade her time and again. Lauren even of-fered to get her one at a discount, because she's in pharmaceu-tical sales. But Alma said she'd feel like an invalid wearing something like that all the time, and that anyway, she always kept her walker nearby."

"She didn't have it nearby when she fell." Cautious about

revealing too much that Bonelli had confided in me, I thought it was okay to explain that Edie's walker had been found neatly folded downstairs.

"That's very odd. Maybe she was getting absentminded, poor thing. Happens to us all, sooner or later." Alma sighed. "A few of us tried to look in on Edie fairly regularly. Ran errands for her, things like that. I dropped over once or twice a week to visit, and sometimes Lauren filled prescriptions for her. Joan also used to give her rides to the store, before she got involved with Ted."

"I heard they broke up." I tried to sound like an insider.

"Who knows? They're like oil and water, those two, on and off. Maybe too different to ever really get along. Now, the matchup that didn't surprise me at all was Lauren and that guy Victor . . . the one handling Sabrina Ward's estate."

My antennae twitched. "Really? They're dating?"

"Seem to be. I guess he met with the board earlier this year, trying to work things out over the cat issue, and of course she's board president. But a month ago I was out to dinner with my sister and her husband at Dolce's, that fancy place on the highway. I saw Lauren and Victor at a booth across the room, having dinner. And from the way they were smiling at each other, I don't think they were talking condo business." Alma laughed sharply at herself. "Don't I sound like an old gossip! Heck, nothing wrong with it. They're younger than most of us. Make a nice couple—attractive, professional. And they're both single, as far as I know, so I guess they're not hurting anybody."

"I'm sure you're right," I told her, though I wasn't sure at all. "Anyway, it's been nice talking to you, and I'm very glad you and Sonny are getting along okay. If you do start to have any problems with him, please let me know."

"Thanks, Cassie. And for everything you did for Edie."

I hung up and stared into space for a minute, until even the Abyssinian, crouched on one of the playroom's high shelves, eyed me curiously. Then I dialed Bonelli's number.

No answer, but I left her a message. "If you do find prints on that glove, and start checking people at The Reserve for a match, top of your list should be Lauren Kamper."

Chapter 21

Bob Gillis, a heavyset, genial guy in his fifties with a raspy, smoker's voice, stopped by the next day to replace the tires on my van. Since I had no garage, I silently hoped the new tires wouldn't suffer the same fate as the old ones. While in my parking lot, Bob also checked over my CR-V for any damage that a vandal could easily have done without taking it apart. He finally pronounced it safe to drive, as far as he could see. I told him only a little about the intrigue going on at The Reserve, and how Dawn and I might have rubbed some people's fur the wrong way. Bob very wisely advised me to steer clear of that community from now on.

I really did intend to follow that advice, especially since I also was hearing it from so many other people who had my best interests at heart. And they didn't even include my mother, who still knew only that I'd been helping a rescue group deal with feral cats at the condo community, and that the woman spearheading the project had recently died of a heart attack while feeding the cats in the woods. Like certain branches of our government, I mete out information strictly on a need-to-know basis when it comes to Mom. Otherwise she might be constantly hysterical, which wouldn't benefit either of us.

Yes, I fully intended to give The Reserve a wide berth and to let Bonelli pursue the investigation through regular police procedure. But like Michael Corleone in *The Godfather Part III*, I soon found myself pulled back into a treacherous web of intrigue.

The call came, of course, from Dawn. A snowstorm was forecast for the next day, and Becky and Chris had their hands full dealing with some other ferals across town, so Dawn would have to replenish the feeding station and make sure the shelters were still viable.

"I can't even put it off until tomorrow," she told me, "because I've got to pick up Mom at the airport. Providing her flight isn't delayed by the weather, anyway."

"And you need an extra pair of hands again tonight," I concluded.

Her tone was apologetic. "It would really help. To be honest, I'm a little reluctant to take the Jeep back up there until I find out who sabotaged it. It does kind of stand out like a neon sign."

"While my CR-V blends in with all the other midsize, silvery-toned crossovers," I agreed. "Okay, I'll take you up there. But this is it, Dawn! From now on, you and your mom can carry on the battle . . . unless she has the good sense to tell you to keep out of it."

A husky laugh on the line. "You don't know Gwen very well, do you? Okay, I'll close up the store and wait for you."

At Nature's Way, we loaded my hatch with four sacks of dry cat food and six plastic jugs of springwater. Since the nights had gotten colder, FFF had begun putting the drinking bowls inside a few white Styrofoam coolers to insulate them and help keep the water from freezing. (Of course, some com-

munity residents instantly had started to gripe that the coolers
were even more of an eyesore in the woods than the camou-
flaged black shelters.) When we got to The Reserve, Dawn
refilled the automatic feeders while I topped off the water inside the coolers.

While I worked, I heard dragging and thumping sounds
from the direction of the condos, up the rise. I took a peek
through the trees and saw a good-sized U-Haul box truck
parked in the driveway of one of the town houses. It was nose-
out, so I guessed the back was open, facing the building. As I
watched, a burly man in a thick winter jacket carried a couple
of stacked cartons out of the garage and disappeared behind
the truck, no doubt loading them into it. I recognized Ted
Remy by his broad shoulders and distinctive, strutting walk.

*Well, he did say he was moving out soon. Odd to do it after dark,
though, and loading up his own U-Haul. Maybe he took a loss on the
town house and is trying to save money?*

Now two other figures, swathed in long, probably wool
coats against the chill, strode briskly down the sidewalk in his
direction. Ted seemed to deliberately ignore them, and even
turned to go back into his house, before the taller figure grabbed
him by the arm. Ted spun so violently that I thought he was
going to punch the man, Victor Ward. At first I couldn't hear
the argument, but their angry gestures set the tone. After a
minute the third figure, Lauren Kamper, joined in.

Dawn had crept up beside me. "What's all that about?"

"I don't know, but I think it's worth trying to eavesdrop.
C'mon, we'll stay behind the bushes."

We took advantage of the landscaping, which luckily included a lot of full-bodied evergreen shrubs, to steal nearer.
We stopped about thirty feet away, because the trio of voices
had risen to a volume where we could make out most of what
was being said.

"You're not hanging this whole thing on me!" Ted warned them. "I'm in the clear, and I'm getting the hell out of here. I wish I'd never seen this damned community or met either one of you. *Or your witch of a sister-in-law.*" He aimed the last comment at Victor, then started again for the town house's front door.

The taller man stepped into his path. "You're going nowhere until we get some answers. That detective called a bunch of us down to the station to be fingerprinted today. How come? We had two deaths here that the cops decided were accidental. Now suddenly they're suspicious?"

"Yes, what kind of game are you playing, Ted?" Lauren demanded. "Trying to sell us out to make yourself look better?"

His voice wavered a bit. "W-why would I do that? Things were settling down. Why would I stir 'em up again?"

"Maybe somebody poked a hole in your alibi," Victor suggested. "I figure it had to be you who caved, because you've got the most to lose."

"Holy crap!" Dawn whispered to me.

Crouching low to hide any glow from my cell phone, I punched three numbers. When a voice responded, "Nine-one-one, what's your emergency?" I realized I didn't know what to say. No punches actually had been thrown . . . yet. Did I dare to speak at all, or would the three conspirators hear me? Finally I whispered, "Trouble at The Reserve. Send cops."

"I'm sorry, can you repeat that?"

I couldn't, and hung up. But it might still be okay. *The police are supposed to check out any emergency call that comes in. They figure if no one speaks, it could mean the caller is seriously ill or injured.*

And if necessary, they probably could track my location by my cell phone.

Meanwhile, Dawn elbowed me and pointed. Omen had

emerged from the woods, a black dot against the snow, and began trotting up the rise toward the hostile threesome. None of them even noticed.

"I'm tellin' you, I didn't say anything to anybody." Ted slipped his hand, significantly, inside the front of his down jacket. "Now, I'm leaving, and neither of you are gonna stop me."

Victor looked taken aback for a second. Then he smiled and lowered his voice, though I could still hear it. "What are you going to do, Ted? Shoot us out here in the open, where anyone could see or hear it? Some busybody could be watching us from a window right now." He gestured toward the other townhomes that faced them across the snowy plaza. With a sneer, he added, "Go back to strangling old ladies in the woods. That's more your speed."

Omen sprang onto the retaining wall of Ted's driveway. From about ten feet away, he sat quietly watching and listening to the group, who mostly had their backs to him. Only Dawn and I could see the tomcat's tail lashing irritably back and forth.

Meanwhile, Ted cocked his head at Victor, his voice dripping contempt. "You're a real piece of work, aren't you, Ward? She was family to you!"

"She was ruining the reputation of this community and of the whole Reserve chain. As for her being 'family,' she killed my kid brother. Dragged him halfway around the world to godforsaken places . . . made him take all kinds of crazy chances . . ."

Ted wheeled on Lauren. "And you're just as bad."

She scanned their surroundings nervously. "Look, we can't stand around hashing things over out here. For better or worse, we're all in this together. If we just keep our stories straight—"

"I told you, I'm gone. Get Lawler to do the rest of your dirty work." Starting back around the truck, Ted finally spotted the black, staring cat. As if this was the last straw for him, he muttered a curse, picked up a hard-packed chunk of snow, and heaved it at the animal.

Omen nimbly dodged the missile, but not before Dawn had sprung up from our hiding place with a shout. "*No!*"

All three of the others swung in our direction. Victor yelled, "Who's there?"

"Run!" I hissed to Dawn, and tried to pull her away. But I might as well have tried to budge the living Sabrina.

"You're murderers!" she screamed at them. "You're going to pay for what you did, all of you."

"Not if there are no witnesses." Ted hadn't been bluffing—he finally produced an actual gun. Bobbing it in my direction, he said, "You, too. Outta there."

I froze with indecision. I *could* try to dash for the car and go for help. Ted might not be an expert shot, and the shrubbery would give me some cover. But once I reached the open parking lot, he might still nail me. And if Victor decided to give chase, I'd still be screwed, because he had much longer legs.

But mainly, I couldn't leave Dawn alone in the hands of this nasty bunch. I stepped out from behind my bush to stand beside her.

Lauren scowled. "Might have known. These two have been poking around here, asking questions, for weeks. Honest to God, you really think saving a bunch of flea-ridden cats is worth all of this trouble?"

"How much was getting rid of them worth to you?" I asked her. "Worth killing a sweet old lady who thought of you as a friend? Who trusted you?"

She stiffened. "I have no idea what you're talking about."

"Hey, nobody was supposed to die!" Victor blurted. "A couple of bad falls, that's all. Just injuries that would have sent them to the hospital and then to an assisted-living facility. Gotten them out of our hair."

"You're talking too much," Ted snarled at him. "Now we'll *have* to shut them up." He eyed the open maw of the U-Haul. Closer up and from an angle, I now could see the inside. It was packed pretty full of boxes, but still had room for a couple of unwilling passengers.

"In there," he ordered us.

Dawn jutted her strong chin and stood her ground.

I'd read that when someone accosts you, the dumbest thing in the world is to get into a vehicle with him. So I also balked, telling Ted, "You've got to be kidding."

Meanwhile, Lauren whispered something to Victor, then dashed off down the sidewalk. I presume, to her own town house.

Ted's focus never left Dawn and me, and he pulled the sleeve of his thick jacket down as if to muffle the gunshot. "I can't shoot both of you at once. But you seem to be good friends. Which of you wants to watch the other die first?"

We both kept silent and refused to budge, still gambling that he wouldn't dare take such a chance with windows and neighbors on all sides. After all, there are only so many witnesses a guy can eliminate.

By this time, I feared that the local 911 operator on duty tonight had shrugged off my silent call as a misdial. And while someone across the way *could* be watching this drama out their window, they very well might be afraid to get involved. It was a small community, after all.

This wasn't even the first time I'd been held at gunpoint, but I guess it's not the kind of thing you ever get used to. My hands and feet had gone numb, even beyond what was normal on such a cold evening, and I willed myself not to pass out. I admired Dawn's stoicism until I realized that faint clicking sound actually came from the chattering of her teeth. She reached out for my hand, and we linked arms. That made me feel better, somehow, even though we might just die together.

"Touching," Victor sneered. He stepped forward and tried to wrestle Dawn into the truck.

She stomped hard on his instep and screamed her head off. I'd known Dawn for many years, but never imagined she possessed such lung power. It almost deafened me for a second. Then I also shrieked, with as much gusto as I could.

Porch lights came to life on a couple of the nearest town houses. I saw at least one neighbor peer out through the blinds of her front picture window.

Ted's normally healthy color blanched. "*Shut up*, or I'll start shooting. I swear!"

We did, but I hoped we'd bought ourselves some time.

Lauren, the efficient board president, came trotting back in her high-heeled boots over the snowy sidewalk. It occurred to me that, with her icy efficiency, she might have been cast as one of those treacherous Hitchcock blondes. She carried a white paper bag, from which she pulled a large wad of gauze and a small bottle.

Limping a bit from Dawn's stomp, Victor grabbed her again, this time with a strong arm around her neck. My friend still struggled furiously for a minute. Lauren poured liquid from the bottle onto the gauze pad and pressed it to Dawn's face.

Sick with horror, I started to her rescue. Ted stepped in between, gun raised, to stop me. I worried now that his shaking hand might pull the trigger at any second, even accidentally. Helplessly, I watched Dawn finally go limp in Victor's grasp.

Once she was out, he and Lauren lifted Dawn into the back of the vehicle. Then Victor caught me by the shoulders and held me still, too. I was afraid to fight him because Ted still had a bead on me. Meanwhile, Lauren crossed back to where she'd left the paper bag. She got another gauze pad and the bottle, which I figured was chloroform. She hurried over the icy cobblestone pavers of the driveway, unscrewing the bottle's cap, toward where I stood.

Halfway, she pitched forward with a screech and fell to her knees. The bottle hit the pavers a few feet away and smashed.

A black streak skimmed away over the crusted snow. I realized that Omen must have tripped her.

Her good wool slacks torn at the knees and her air of control also tattered, Lauren staggered to her feet. The stream of obscenities she fired off would have shocked her fellow board members, I'm sure. Victor also hurled some colorful words after the retreating cat, who by now had disappeared into the dark woods.

Two points for our team. Between Omen and Dawn, we've at least lamed two of the bad guys. But Ted was still in one piece and still armed. Though his smirk suggested that he found Lauren's mishap amusing, he probably knew he was in too deep now to just drive away and escape any consequences.

He turned the gun on me again. "Enough screwing around. Get in there with your friend and keep quiet. If we can't dope you, there'll be only one way to shut *you* up."

Moving slowly and keeping my eye on Ted and his weapon, I backed up to the truck's high deck. I sat on it and swung my legs up. He pushed me the rest of the way in and pulled down the heavy door with an ominous rumble, leaving us in total darkness.

The latch snapping into place sounded even more final.

This is it, I thought. *Ted's going to drive us to some remote area—easy to find one out here—shoot us, and get rid of our bodies.*

Not easy to bury us at this time of year, but he probably hasn't thought that far ahead. If he didn't mean to kill Sabrina, only to scare her into hurting herself, he obviously doesn't take the unexpected into account when he plans his crimes.

Maybe Dawn and I can use that—tell him we realize he never meant to murder anyone. Maybe once he's away from Victor and Lauren, we can bargain with him. . . .

Dawn. I hadn't heard a peep from her! She must still be out. In the dark, I groped in her direction. She'd fallen between two stacks of cartons, so I felt my way around them until I touched her sleeve.

I reached upward for her face, whispered her name, patted her cheek. She didn't wake up, though, and her breathing seemed shallow. I called her name more loudly and shook her by the shoulders. Still no response.

What the hell did Lauren give her? She's in pharmaceuticals, and at that Connecticut company some of the stuff went missing. . . . She could have gotten her hands on anything. Maybe even an anesthesia drug.

How long would it take for Dawn to wake up? *Would* she wake up? And even when she did, would she have any permanent damage?

I called Lauren Kamper a string of foul names that made her own bad language of a few minutes ago sound like a lullaby.

Again, I listened hard for my friend's breathing, and in the silence I heard a new voice outside.

"Evening, folks. Mind telling me what's going on here?"

Sam Nolan! My first instinct was to pound on the door and holler for help, but . . . could he be in on this scheme with the others? Could anyone in this community really be trusted?

My eyes had begun to adjust to the darkness inside the truck. But although a faint glow from Ted's garage light crept around the edges of the door, I could see nothing of what was happening outside, and still had to rely mainly on my ears.

I heard Ted trying to sound relaxed and normal, as he answered Sam. "Just getting a few last things out of my place. Stuff I didn't want to trust to the movers."

"And Victor and Lauren came by to help you?" I heard skepticism in Nolan's tone. "That's thoughtful."

"We're just wishing him *bon voyage*," said Victor, smoothly.

"What happened to your slacks, Lauren? Take a tumble?"

Her laugh was edgy. "Oh, one of those cats startled me, and I slipped on the ice. It's nothing."

"Someone reported a loud scream from back this way. Any of you hear that?"

They seemed to be muttering denials. Lauren added, "Maybe it was another one of the cats."

"Hmm. Or maybe it was whoever broke this bottle over here?"

Okay, Sam definitely was not in league with the three of them, and he was starting to get the picture. But if I made a racket to draw his attention, would Ted just turn the gun on him?

I heard another vehicle stop nearby. From the direction of the engine noise, toward the cab end of the truck, it must have pulled up near the foot of Ted's driveway. Sam called out, "Howya doing, Lee? Thanks for coming."

Lee . . . the security guard from the gate, the young Asian-American guy? He ought to have a gun of his own. . . .

"What's happening here, folks?" he asked.

"Well," said Sam, "I was just trying to figure that out myself."

That sounded like my cue, and I banged on the rear doors of the U-Haul with all my might. "Watch out! Ted's got a gun!"

The U-Haul rocked and the cab door slammed, as if somebody had jumped behind the wheel. I heard Lee holler, "Don't do it, Ted!" But the truck's engine roared to life and we lurched forward.

More shouts from Lee and Sam. Maybe the security vehicle had actually blocked the driveway; I felt a sharp jolt, as if Ted drove over the stone edging. Then I scrabbled for my balance as he sped down a slight incline. He must be cutting across his own lawn, I thought, desperate to make a getaway.

It's like he's totally forgotten about me and Dawn. What will he do with us, though, when he remembers?

A siren screaming down the community's main road, headed our way, finally made him slam on his brakes. Beautiful music, if I ever heard it.

Even more beautiful was the muffled sound of coughing from in back of me. I swung around, and could just about see Dawn clawing at the stacked cartons for a handhold, trying to pull herself upright.

She choked out the cliché words of every knockout victim in a B movie. "Where are we? What happened?"

Chapter 22

Once Lauren, Victor, and Ted had been hauled off to the police station—accused, for starters, of unlawfully imprisoning me and Dawn—I drove her to the nearest ER to be checked over. We brought part of the broken bottle, the label still attached, and a doctor determined that Lauren had indeed used a type of anesthesia meant to be inhaled. Luckily, Dawn only had received a small dose and would recover pretty quickly, but the doctor warned her not to drive or operate machinery until the stuff was totally out of her system.

It was morning by the time they let her go home. I put her to bed in her apartment above the shop and played nursemaid for a day. Dawn already had a sign that read CLOSED—SORRY FOR THE INCONVENIENCE, so I hung that on the shop's front door. Best to be discreet, I decided, since a sign saying CLOSED DUE TO ILLNESS might set the wrong tone for a health foods store.

Of course, I had called Keith right away. He immediately took a train back from New York so he could care for Dawn that evening, and called from the station to say he was getting a cab. I gathered that, up to now, she hadn't told him too much about our investigation of the Reserve murders. On the phone, I filled him in only as much as was necessary, figuring it would be better if Dawn and I explained things in person.

Her apartment was maybe a little smaller than mine, because she used what would have been a second bedroom to store merchandise. Like Sabrina, Dawn was a bit of a clutter-bug, but with more style and comfort. Where I had just a few easy-maintenance plants in my front window, hers was almost a rain forest—snake plants and succulents lined the sill, and ferns and ivies cascaded from hanging pots. She probably had a few cooking herbs mixed in there, too. Her walls showcased a few of her mother's abstract, earth-toned weavings.

By the time I called Keith, Dawn felt well enough to hang out in the living room on her secondhand sectional sofa, bolstered by mismatched throw pillows. She talked me through using the press to make organic coffee, and I brought the pot to her, resting it on the wicker trunk with brass fastenings that she used for a coffee table. Dawn's peach-toned chenille robe seemed to bring more healthy color back to her face, but with her unbraided hair fanned over her shoulders she still looked almost fragile, like a Victorian heroine from a Rossetti painting.

When Keith arrived, he hugged her tightly for a long, wordless moment, as if all too conscious that he'd almost lost her. He left one arm around Dawn's shoulders while the two of us summarized our adventure at The Reserve. He reacted with a troubled expression, an occasional bad word, and a lot head-shaking.

"Dawn really saved our necks," I emphasized. "She put a hurtin' on Victor with those stack-heel boots of hers, and shrieked like a banshee. . . . Is there such a thing as a Jewish banshee?"

With a wan smile, my friend explained, "I used Sabrina's

patented stomp-and-scream defense. Not foolproof when your attacker has a gun, but I guess at least it scared one of the neighbors into calling security."

"This whole damn story scares me." Keith raked one hand through his short brown curls. "I know I've been tied up with work lately, babe, but you didn't have to risk your life to get my attention."

"You know it was nothing like that," Dawn reassured him. "Cassie and I never expected to get tangled up in anything this nasty. We just spotted a few clues the cops had overlooked, thought of a few different angles, and . . . one thing led to another."

"Well, next time you start spotting clues and thinking of different angles, let somebody else follow up on them, okay?"

Pretty shaken by the whole ordeal myself, I couldn't have agreed with him more. Still, I was glad to see that old rebellious gleam pop up again in Dawn's amber eyes.

"Sorry," she told him. "Can't promise anything."

Keith's reaction somewhat prepared me for Mark's, so I waited until I'd returned to my own shop to phone him. When he answered in a cheery voice and asked what I'd been up to, I told him, "Quite a lot, actually. Now, don't be mad. . . ."

After I'd finished, I heard a long groan over the line. "Cassie, these people may be killers, but you're the one who's going to put me in an early grave! Are you really okay?"

"Absolutely fine. Dawn had it rough, but the doctors say she'll be okay. Maybe all those health foods do her some good, after all. Her mother is due back this week, though, and Gwen's probably going to freak at the idea that she's had all of these murderous neighbors living in her community."

After a pause, Mark admitted, "I can't even yell at you for

taking a dumb chance, because who'd have thought the condo board president and Sabrina's brother-in-law would be behind it all?"

"At least I dialed 911 before we approached any of them. But really, Dawn and I couldn't let Ted just drive away!"

"If he'd done anything to you, Bonelli would've had another homicide to deal with. 'Cause I'd have hunted him down and killed him."

I hate to admit it, as a feminist, but I was flattered and mildly turned on by this uncharacteristically macho declaration. "You sound like Keith—he told us he'd like to go a couple of rounds with Victor. I'm sure he'd like to deck Lauren, too, though he stopped short of saying that."

By the time Mark came over to my place later that night, he'd calmed down a bit. He brought along some Chinese takeout, lo mein for me and Szechuan chicken for him. He'd mellowed out enough, at that point, to raise his beer bottle in a toast to the successful arrest of The Reserve's murderous trio and the role I'd played in their capture.

"Makes me wonder, though," he added. "This stuff about your wanting to hang onto your independence . . . Is it really so you can concentrate on your business? Or so you can keep getting involved in these hair-raising escapades without me spoiling your fun?"

I frowned. "Believe me, Mark, being trapped in that U-Haul, with poor Dawn unconscious—and not knowing if either of us would escape with our lives—was anything but fun!"

"Okay, maybe that was a low blow. But honestly, to go questioning all of those residents, digging up dirt on them, trying to trick them into incriminating themselves. And then brainstorming with Detective Bonelli . . ."

"All right, that stuff *was* kinda fun." When he shook his

head in mock despair, I added sweetly, "That's what I love about you, Mark. You really get me!"

"It's not a joke, Cassie."

"You're right, it isn't. I scared myself pretty badly this time, and I promise I'll be more careful in the future. Okay?"

"I sure hope so." His haunted expression worried me, though. I got the feeling that if anything ever came between us, it was less likely to be another woman than my urge to play amateur detective.

That night I did my best to compensate Mark for having caused him so much stress. I was tempted to also tell him about the tickets I'd purchased to the jazz concert, but figured I'd better keep something in reserve. After all, Christmas was coming soon enough, and the question of whether or not I'd go with him to Philadelphia might arise once again.

Sarah also was aghast the next day when I told her what had gone down at the condo community. She blurted, "Get out!" more than once during my recital.

"That's insane," she concluded. "And poor Dawn is still laid up?"

"She's running her store but taking it easy. At least one more day of no driving. Her mother's due back from her trip today, so Keith is going to get her at the airport."

Sarah still looked spooked. "I used to think I'd like to retire to one of those nice gated communities, but this changes my mind. I grew up in a pretty tough neighborhood, but I think it had less crime than The Reserve!"

I counted on my fingers. "Only four crimes, really, if you include drugging Dawn and poisoning the dog. Well, maybe six, if you count off-premises stuff like our vandalized vehicles. But with a total of five perps, it does seem like even more."

★ ★ ★

Once in custody and facing some serious charges, Victor Ward lawyered up. The other conspirators, though, apparently made excuses and passed the blame around like grade-schoolers caught brawling on a playground. Bonelli helped by setting them subtly against each other, and a couple of days later she shared the highlights with me.

Victor and Lauren originally cooked up the idea that Sabrina should have an accident, after which he could pressure her to move to an assisted-living facility. They knew Ted was impatient to relocate but lacked the funds, and they figured his security background could be an asset, so Victor paid him to deal with Sabrina. Ted studied her usual time and route to visit the cats' feeding station and laid a trip wire across her path; the idea was that he would pull it, cause her to fall, and leave the scene before she even spotted him. But the wire snagged on her cane, and when Sabrina heard him rustling in the bushes, she screamed. (Remembering the prominent bruise on Ted's shin, I wondered if Sabrina had done a little damage—maybe with her cane—before he'd overpowered her.)

Anyway, Ted grabbed her by her scarf to shut her up, they struggled, and she collapsed. Thinking he'd strangled her to death, Ted wound the end of the scarf around a branch to make it look like an accident, removed the trip wire, and split. He knew he'd leave no footprints because snow already was blanketing the ground.

Bonelli told me most of this during a visit to my shop, where we had another confidential chat over coffee in the cat playroom. Her office would have provided better coffee, because of the Keurig, but I'd rather sit on top of a carpeted cat tunnel than in her torturous visitor's chair.

Bonelli's explanation of Edie's subsequent murder left me feeling guilty, because Dawn and I might have triggered it.

After we'd questioned the community's residents, Lauren asked Edie about what she'd heard the night of Sabrina's death. Edie told her and added that she was trying hard to remember if she'd heard or seen anything else that could help the police. "That worried Lauren, who decided another 'accident' would take Edie's mind off the subject," Bonelli explained. "Lauren said she didn't expect her neighbor's fall down the stairs to be fatal, either . . . but, of course, she took the chance that it might be. By the way, we did find a couple of prints inside the latex glove, and they matched the ones we took from Lauren."

Nice work, Omen! I thought.

As for Mike Lawler, he did not "euthanize" Sabrina. But, aware of his hostility toward her, the felonious team of Victor and Lauren did hire him to sabotage Dawn's Jeep and slash my tires. Working on cars had been a lifelong hobby for Mike, which probably explained how he knew about mixing diesel fuel into regular gasoline. In hindsight, I guess what Sam had told us about Mike rehabbing an old Chevy should have tipped us off.

"The others are all looking at some heavy charges," Bonelli assured me. "Aggravated manslaughter, second-degree murder, conspiracy. Victor's partners at the marketing firm will not be pleased—this will be *very* bad publicity for The Reserve chain."

"Victor knew Sabrina had caused a lot of trouble for Merrywood Suites," I pointed out. "He probably was afraid her campaign to save the cats would have the same effect on the condo communities."

"Well, he brought about the very thing that he feared," Bonelli said. "These creeps usually do, which is sometimes a real boon for those of us in law enforcement."

She almost sounded, I thought, as if she were including me in that last category. Or maybe she meant to reinforce the idea

that *she* fit that official description, and I didn't. Which was
fine with me—I really had no desire to wear a badge, carry a
gun, or risk my life on a regular basis.

"I actually feel sorry for the folks who have to go on living
at The Reserve," I told her. "All of this is going to be a major
shock for them, especially the other board members."

"On the other hand," the detective added, "you have to
wonder how much they suspected. It sounds like several of the
residents provided alibis for their neighbors that weren't a
hundred percent true. We may never know just how deep this
thing ran."

I knew the story was about to hit the papers, and there was
no way to keep my name and Dawn's completely out of it, so
I had to alert my mother. One evening, fortified with a glass of
wine, I dialed. When she answered the phone, I began, "I need
to talk to you about something. We promised a while back
that we'd be more open with each other—"

Mom cut me off with an uncharacteristic, nervous giggle.
"Oh, Cassie, I'm sorry. So you found out? I just wanted to help
you, and I actually think I did."

Okay, this was unexpected. "Help me? How?"

"Well, he changed his mind, didn't he? Gave up that silly
idea of suing you. He also started following Mark's advice, and
he says his cat is doing much better these days."

Finally the puzzle pieces fit themselves together. "You're
talking about Harry Bock. *You* were the lady lawyer who talked
sense to him?"

"I never claimed to be a lawyer. He knows I'm just a paralegal and that I'm your mother. But he came to MP&R looking for someone to take his case, and I realized he was the same
man who'd been giving you such a hard time. So I invited him
out to lunch."

I had to smile. "You persuaded him *not* to hire your firm to take me to court?"

"Oh, he had no case anyway. I convinced him of that, and also vouched for your character. The poor man wasn't thinking clearly. He went through a terrible divorce just six months ago."

"That's right," I remembered. "He told me he'd gone back to the same law firm."

"I remember the case, Amy Preston handled it. The wife was so greedy, you had to wonder if she ever cared for the guy at all, or just married him for his money. She got their nice house on Lake Hiawatha, but she also wanted most of the furniture! Amy made sure that got divided up fairly, anyway." A rare note of outrage crept into Mom's voice. "But she even tried to claim his chess set, which his father left to him! I'm surprised she didn't take his cat, too. And it wasn't even for spite, because apparently she was the one playing around, not Harry."

Now he's "Harry," is he? I remembered how fondly Bock had spoken of the "charming" woman who'd talked him out of suing me, and had even hinted that he and I might be seeing more of each other in the future. That unnerved me a bit. Not that I had any problem with my mother having a social life. Dad had been gone for three years, and I sometimes wished she had someone else to nag and worry about besides me, her only child.

But . . . Harry Bock? This could take some getting used to.

"I guess he finally told you," she went on. "I asked him not to, because I didn't want you to think I was interfering in your life. I know you like to solve your own problems. But as you say, we promised to be open with one another. And I guess it wouldn't stay a secret much longer anyway."

"You're still . . . seeing him?"

"So far we've just been out to dinner and a movie, but I

think we both had a nice time," she said. "For now, I'd say we're just good friends."

"That's great, Mom. If you like him so much, he must really have turned over a new leaf."

"I think he has, or at least he's showing a better side of himself. Stress can do awful things to a person. That poor, bald kittycat was all he had left to love, and it upset him so much to see her with that nasty, painful rash."

Mom, you don't even like cats—you actually have a cat phobia! All of this blew my mind. Then I realized it might work to my advantage. "Speaking of relationships, Christmas is just a few weeks off, and I don't know if Mark will ask me about visiting his family again. Who knows, he may not even bring it up after all we went through at Thanksgiving! Anyway, I was thinking that this time I could—"

"Oh, Cassie, don't worry too much about that. After you drove through that snowstorm to come back and have dinner with me, I felt awful about putting you through so much trouble."

"It wasn't that bad, Mom. I don't want you to be lonely, and I—"

"No, if you want to celebrate with Mark's family, go and enjoy yourself. It's probably time I stopped relying on you to keep me company. I have a few friends who'd probably be happy to get together with me on Christmas. Other people who are divorced or widowed and have no family nearby."

Like Harry? I thought. *And here I thought my relationship with Mark might be moving too fast!*

"Thanks, Mom," I told her. "I wouldn't be quite so eager, but there's this high school classmate of Mark's, a rather attractive divorcée, who's moved back into the old neighborhood. She dropped by at Thanksgiving and might come around again at Christmas. Mark claims she's already got a boyfriend, but . . ."

My mother laughed. "Then by all means, get down there and defend your turf! Now, Cassie, you called me about something, and it sounded serious. If it wasn't about Harry . . . ?"

Chapter 23

At least I was able to prepare Mom before the full story about the murders came out in the local media. Dawn and I requested that Bonelli downplay our sleuthing efforts when she talked to the media. So she made it sound as if, while tending to the feral cats, we'd just ended up in the wrong place at the wrong time. Still, the notoriety brought a few more curious customers to both of our storefront businesses.

Chris, from FFF, stopped by to thank me for "breaking the case." He also brought the welcome news that, following all the negative publicity, The Reserve was bowing to public pressure and continuing the TNR program.

"They promoted Alma Gunner to fill in as the new board president," he said, "and she's a lot more reasonable about the issue. It helps that all the cats in the original colony are neutered now. Well, except for Omen."

I grinned at the memory of the feisty black tomcat. "Never managed to snare him, huh?"

"Way too crafty. Becky hung some of that fried chicken at the back of one of those long cages? Damned if he didn't manage to grab it and run off without springing the trap. Cat's a freakin' genius."

"You don't know the half of it." I told Chris how Omen had drawn my attention—deliberately?—to the torn latex glove and crumpled drugstore receipt in back of Edie's condo. Also, how he'd startled Lauren so that she'd slipped on the driveway and smashed the bottle of Ultane before she could use it on me.

"That's just too crazy!" he marveled. "Guess he knows his friends from his enemies, all right."

"It's probably a fantasy, but I like to think he wanted justice for Sabrina, the same as we did. At least he helped us to get it."

Chris and I talked a little more about my plans to rehab the van, and he said FFF would like to help in any way they could.

"I certainly don't want to take any money from your group," I told him. "You need it for your own work."

"True, but some of us are handy with cars and could volunteer our services. We have an ulterior motive," he admitted. "There's a major cat expo in the works for next spring, at the new convention center on the highway. FOCA wants to do a promotion involving shelter cats, and we thought maybe a grooming demonstration in the parking lot would be a good angle. So if you had the van up and running by that time . . ."

I smiled. "You guys are as sneaky as Omen! But I do like that idea. I'll talk to Gary, from YourWay, and see what we can work out."

Late on Friday, I drove Dawn up to The Reserve so she could visit with her mother overnight. Gwen Tischler's condo had the same basic layout as Sabrina's and Edie's, but a whole different character. Gwen had held a variety of artistic jobs, from weaving and selling her own textile artworks to teaching at an upstate New York art colony to writing for museum catalogs. She'd transformed her home's bland interior with hand-carved and hand-painted furniture, paintings and sculptures by her friends, and her own woven pillows and throws in rich earth tones.

A little more petite than her daughter, Gwen otherwise resembled Dawn in her strong but elegant features. They had the same irrepressibly wavy hair, though Gwen's had gone mostly gray and only reached her shoulders.

I noticed, to my relief, that Dawn was looking healthier tonight and more like her old self again.

We happily let Gwen brew us some Moroccan mint tea and regale us with the highlights of her trip. She had brought back a few special textile pieces, including a blanket striped in rich red and gold that she'd already draped over the back of her sofa. She explained, in technical terms I could barely follow, the tribal weaving technique used to create it.

On her laptop, Gwen shared other moments easier for us to appreciate. The professional-quality photos included piles of colorful, exotic produce at the Marrakech market, a magenta sun sinking behind a flowing desert landscape, and Gwen grinning in a tall saddle atop a camel. With winter just getting started in New Jersey and snow falling once again outside, I enjoyed browsing through these travel shots as if it were a mini vacation.

Of course, while Gwen had been away, her daughter had told her on the phone about Sabrina's suspicious death, and had picked her brain as to whether any of The Reserve's residents might have had a hand in it. Still, Gwen was horrified to hear the full story and to learn that so many of her neighbors had conspired to dispatch both Sabrina and Edie.

"And for such superficial reasons," she marveled, in revulsion. "The community image, the property values!"

"In the end, I guess it all came down to money," I philosophized. "Although Victor talked as if he also blamed Sabrina for his brother's death. It sounded like he'd resented her for a long, long time."

Unlike everyone else we'd told, Dawn's mother praised both of us for pursuing our investigation even when the police seemed to consider it a dead end.

"Good for both of you," Gwen said. "How awful it would have been if those arrogant bastards got away with their scheme. Too many people these days are afraid to get involved."

"I kept thinking that if it were the other way around, and I'd died under suspicious circumstances, Sabrina wouldn't have given up," Dawn said quietly. "But I'm afraid I dragged Cassie into it against her better judgment. She thought she was just going with me to a board meeting to speak up for the TNR program, and she ended up risking her neck, too."

"Don't blame yourself too much," I told her. "Pretty soon, I got just as caught up as you. The more questions we asked, the surer I was that those folks were hiding something. And of course, when Edie died, that really made me see red, because I'd gotten to know and like her."

"Well, the two of you turned out to be excellent sleuths and came up with answers when no one else could," Gwen commended us.

It occurred to me that we didn't deserve all the credit. "We did get a little help from someone else—someone who'll never get his name in the paper. He'll probably never even get a pat on the head, because he won't come near enough to anyone."

Dawn smiled. "You're talking about Omen, right? Well, Heidi did swear he was Sabrina's familiar, her magical cat. Maybe there's some truth to that, after all."

"Animals understand much more than most people think they do," Gwen agreed. "I think we've all heard someone say that he doesn't trust anyone his dog doesn't like. Animals may not communicate with us verbally, but they respond to our energy. They can tell a person who is kind and respectful from an aggressive bully."

I took her theory a bit further. "Omen might have witnessed Sabrina's murder. And the FFF kids took away his lady friends, but he saw Dawn and me return them to the woods."

"Exactly. So when the bad guys started manhandling you, he might already have had a sense that you were the good guys, and he came to your defense."

"To Omen!" Dawn toasted him with what was left of her mint tea, and her mother and I did the same.

Privately, though, I thought of another possible explanation, even more mystical. Maybe Sabrina had worked through Omen to get justice for herself and Edie?

Lauren planned her crime so carefully. . . . Through what twist of fate did she somehow lose track of that one latex glove, and the incriminating receipt from the drugstore?

I didn't share these musings with Dawn or Gwen, but wondered about them later as I walked back out to my car.

The snowfall of the past hour or two was winding down, so I figured I'd have no trouble driving home. The contours of the traditionally styled condos looked less cookie-cutter and more inviting with a frosting of snow, but I'd never again judge a neighborhood by its appearance. Supposedly the most dangerous residents of this community were now in custody, and no cars even passed by on the main drive. Still, I couldn't help scanning from side to side, and listening for the faintest noise, on my way back to the parking lot.

A peaceful night, though. No movement, no sound. No sign of any other living thing . . .

Except for a line of delicate paw prints that barely broke the fresh snow. They angled straight away from Gwen's doorstep and off into the wild mystery of the woods.

Connect with Us

Visit us online at
KensingtonBooks.com
to read more from your favorite authors, see books
by series, view reading group guides, and more.

for sneak peeks, chances to win books and prize packs,
and to share your thoughts with other readers.

facebook.com/kensingtonpublishing
twitter.com/kensingtonbooks

Tell us what you think!

To share your thoughts, submit a review,
or sign up for our eNewsletters, please visit:
KensingtonBooks.com/TellUs.